THE ORCHARD

THE ORCHARD

THE ENCHANTED ORCHARD™
BOOK ONE

KELLI ROBYNS

MICHAEL ANDERLE

DON'T MISS OUR NEW RELEASES

Join the Florid Romance email list to be notified of new releases and special promotions (which happen often) by following this link:

https://floridromance.lmbpn.com/about/sign-up-for-our-newsletter/

Published by Florid Romance
an imprint of LMBPN Publishing
2375 E. Tropicana Avenue, Suite 8-305
Las Vegas, Nevada 89119 USA

Version 1.01, April 2025
eBook ISBN: 979-8-89354-687-3
Print ISBN: 979-8-89354-688-0

CHAPTER

ONE

Emma Turner pressed a palm against the bus window and watched clusters of tall pines blur by as the driver navigated the winding coastal road toward Crestwood. The last hour of the trip brought a sense of unreality, as if she were floating between two worlds.

Each bump in the road tugged her back toward the memory of the storm that took her parents. She still swore she could taste the salt in the air from that awful night, mixing now with the tang of the sea outside.

Her shoulders felt stiff from sitting too long, so she straightened, gathering herself to face a new reality with her grandmother, Sadie Turner. She had only spent a day or two each year visiting her grandmother in Crestwood since she was little. And she had always called her simply, Sadie, never grandmother or nan or any other grandparent title of affection. And until this moment, she never thought that was strange.

Emma had spent years imagining what adulthood

would feel like—late-night adventures with friends, choosing her own path, stepping into a future that felt limitless. She had graduated high school in June, turned eighteen in July, and was supposed to be starting fresh, independent and free.

Instead, she was here, sitting stiffly on a bus bound for Crestwood, her hands clenched so tightly in her lap that her nails dug into her palms. Adulthood had come, but not the way she had planned. Her first lesson hadn't been about freedom or the possibility it had been about learning how to exist in the hollow space left behind when her parents were suddenly gone.

She barely remembered the weeks after the accident, only that people had spoken softly around her, touched her arm like she might break apart if they weren't careful. She hadn't cried at the funeral. She still hadn't. The grief sat somewhere deep inside her, heavy and unreachable, like a stone lodged in her chest.

Maybe that was why she hadn't protested when Sadie offered her a place to stay.

Maybe that was why she had packed her bags without really thinking about what came next.

She wasn't making choices, not really. She was just moving forward because standing still hurt too much.

When the bus finally wheezed to a stop, Emma stood on unsteady legs. The driver, a gray-haired man who spoke in a gruff but not unkind voice, offered to lower the small step, but Emma managed her suitcases alone.

Her hands trembled, partly from fatigue but mostly from the swirling confusion that had defined her life since the accident. The door closed behind her. She found herself standing on a narrow strip of sidewalk next to a modest station sign that read *Crestwood.*

The late afternoon sun drifted low on the horizon, bathing the edges of the town in pale gold. Clouds, tinted pink around the edges, eased slowly across the sea. The scents of coffee and fried food from the nearby café mingled with diesel fumes from the bus, reminding Emma of half-remembered vacations by the shore when her parents were still alive.

She closed her eyes, inhaling the crisp air to steady herself. The moment she reopened them, her gaze roamed around the station: one or two travelers meandered away, and a couple stood with mismatched suitcases, probably waiting for the next departure.

She turned to see Sadie approaching, her expression full of understanding rather than pity. It had been more than a year since Emma had last seen her—but now here she was, standing with her arms loosely folded, wrapped in a simple coat, her gaze steady and warm.

Her face held the soft lines of someone who had weathered both time and loss. Emma gripped her luggage handles tighter, bracing for any flood of emotion that might come at their first in-person moment since the funeral.

"Emma," Sadie said, voice soft enough almost to be carried away by a gust of wind. "Welcome to Crestwood. How was the journey?"

Emma wanted to respond with a brave smile, but her lips felt tight. "Not bad. A little long." She forced the smallest curve of her mouth and searched for the barest courtesy to keep her voice steady. "Thank you for picking me up. I know it was an inconvenience."

Sadie reached for one of the suitcases, but Emma clutched it reflexively before relenting. "Oh, I can manage," Emma mumbled.

They made a delicate dance of who would carry what. In the end, Sadie carried the lighter bag. Emma's thoughts churned with childhood memories of being in Crestwood with her parents chasing waves along a shoreline, laughing.

She blinked hard to dismiss the image before grief could overwhelm her. Step by step, she followed Sadie toward a small truck parked along a patch of gravel. The quiet purr of its engine and the worn leather seats welcomed Emma with a sense of old familiarity, though the memory of riding in her father's car flickered painfully in her mind.

Sadie navigated the narrow roads of Crestwood at a leisurely pace, giving Emma moments to take in her new surroundings. The town itself appeared quaint, as though it resisted the modern rush of the world beyond. Gabled rooftops pressed close together, their paint chipped by decades of salt-laden air.

Lampposts lined the cobblestone streets, and greenish moss clung to the edges of old stone steps leading into shops. A handful of townspeople drifted along the sidewalks, pausing to give Emma's grandmother subdued nods along with curious gazes turned toward her. She told herself it was normal for strangers to notice the new girl, especially in a town this small. Her chest tightened anyway.

Soon they left the town center behind and turned onto a narrower route flanked by towering, ancient trees. Gnarled branches tangled overhead, forming a canopy that filtered the waning sunlight. Emma noticed the way leaves scattered across the truck's hood, swirling in the breeze. The sense of isolation expanded as they traveled further along the road.

The waist-high black iron gate stood nearby, its delicate scrollwork curling into elegant patterns. A faint patina clung to the metal, hinting at age, but its craftsmanship remained evident. It wasn't imposing, yet there was a quiet elegance to it.

Beyond the gate, Emma caught a glimpse of a weathered cottage. The off-white paint was peeling around the windows, revealing the wood beneath. A porch stretched across the front, where a flower box overflowed with late-summer blooms.

For a moment, her gaze flicked past it to the orchard beyond—rows of apple trees stood in a neat line. Their branches swayed gently in the breeze, but something about that simple movement sent a jolt of unease through her, though she couldn't say why.

Sadie turned off the ignition and said, "I'm glad you're here. I know it won't feel like home right away, but I'll make sure you're comfortable."

Emma forced another small smile. She had no idea how to respond except with polite gratitude that felt too stiff in her throat. "I remember this place. It's...quiet out here."

"It is. Crestwood can be both peaceful and...watchful at the same time." Sadie's tone was measured, each word chosen with care. There was a weight to the way she spoke, as if she were feeling out the edges of a truth she wasn't sure she wanted to name.

Emma frowned. She wondered if her grandmother was aware how unnerving that description sounded, like the entire town might be watching her right now. Together, they lifted the suitcases from the truck bed. Emma's arms trembled more from fatigue than weight, and she bit her lip to steady herself. She followed Sadie through the creaky gate and up the porch steps, noticing how the floorboards groaned beneath them.

The front door opened into a living room that smelled of something herbal and vaguely sweet, perhaps thyme or rosemary, alongside the honeyed scent of dry cedar wood. A small lamp cast a warm glow across the space. Emma set her larger suitcase down, letting out a slow exhale. Her gaze flicked around the living room: bookshelves lined with worn spines, a modest fireplace, and a worn armchair that faced the hearth at an angle. Everything felt cozy, if a little old-fashioned.

She noticed a crow perched on the window ledge outside. It peered in, tilting its head as if to assess her. Emma's stomach tightened. An odd wave of discomfort rippled through her, not exactly fear, more like a sensation of being scrutinized. She tried to dismiss it as an overactive imagination born of exhaustion.

"You get settled in your room," Sadie said, drawing her attention away from the crow. "Down the hall, second door on the right. We can talk after you catch your breath."

"Thank you," Emma replied, voice subdued. She grasped the handle of her suitcase again, rolling it over the threshold into a hallway. The walls were adorned with framed sketches of seascapes and forests, each in tinted charcoal. She caught glimpses of small décor pieces—ceramic fox figurines, pressed flowers in glass frames, tiny vessels of dried herbs. Curiosity stirred, mingled with a strange embarrassment at being here under such tragic circumstances.

Her room turned out to be small but inviting. Floral wallpaper in muted earth tones covered one wall, and the bed was dressed in a faded quilt. A tiny wooden desk and matching chair sat near the window, which offered a partial view of the orchard at the rear of the cottage. Emma took a measured breath, closed the door behind her, and let the quiet of the space envelop her.

She began to unpack in small increments. First, she set down a photograph of her parents, placing it carefully on the nightstand. The edges were worn from all the times she had thumbed across them in recent weeks.

Seeing their smiling faces renewed the ache in her chest, the swirl of longing and regret.

Emma blinked back fresh tears, determined not to fall apart on her first night. She was in the habit of laying out the next day's clothes, so she selected a long-sleeved cotton shirt, its faded navy fabric soft and worn. She shook it out, smoothing the sleeves before draping it over the chair beside the bed.

Next, she laid out a pair of simple jeans, the denim thinned from years of wear. She laid them neatly on the seat of the chair, her fingers lingering for a moment before stepping back, as if grounding herself in the small routine amid the unfamiliar.

A knock at the door made her jump. Sadie appeared, holding a mug of tea. "I thought you could use this, dear. It might help you sleep."

Emma tried to guess the ingredients by the scent: chamomile, maybe a hint of lavender or lemon balm. She took the cup in her hands, letting the warmth soothe her. "Thank you," she said quietly.

Sadie's eyes fell on the photograph beside the lamp, and a quiet sadness flickered across her face. "You can talk about them whenever you want. Or not. I understand either way. I miss them, too."

Emma wrapped her fingers around the cup, letting its warmth seep into her skin. Of course, Sadie would miss them—she had also lost a son and daughter-in-law, after all.

Emma fought the sudden welling of emotion. She traced the rim of her mug with her thumb. "I'm not ready. Not tonight," she whispered.

She gave a gentle nod. "Of course. Take your time. We have all the time you need here." She paused, then offered a fleeting smile. "There's soup in the kitchen. If you get hungry, help yourself."

Sadie closed the door behind her, leaving Emma alone

again. She sipped the tea, finding the flavor both soothing and strangely bracing, as though the herbs carried a subtle spark. Quiet settled over the room, broken only by the distant cry of a gull outside.

She found her mind drifting toward the orchard again. She could not explain why it intrigued her; maybe it was the sense that those trees were older than the town itself, standing as silent witnesses to generations. Or perhaps she simply needed something outside her grief to focus on.

After finishing the tea, Emma forced herself to explore the cottage a bit. She slipped down the hall. Lantern light glowed in the living room, now that the sun had nearly set. Her grandmother was nowhere in sight.

A note on the kitchen table read, *Went to gather a few things outside. Be back soon.* Emma's stomach twisted at the idea of Sadie walking around alone in the near-dark, but she supposed Sadie knew Crestwood well enough that it wouldn't be unsafe.

She opened the pot on the stove, inhaling the aroma of vegetable soup. Ladling herself a small bowl, she ate at the table in silence. Each spoonful reminded her of home-made dinners her mom used to make, though the taste was different, layered with herbs that teased the palate. She finished quickly, placed the dishes in the sink, and headed back into the living room. The quiet felt so profound that her own breathing seemed loud.

Drifting to a nearby shelf, she ran her fingers along the spines of the books displayed there. Some were dusty novels, others well-worn volumes with spidery cursive in the titles. She didn't read the spines too closely—fatigue weighed on her brain, and the flickering lamplight made it difficult to see. Instead, she just let the presence of so many books fill her with a small sense of comfort, as if knowledge itself waited within arm's reach whenever she felt lost.

The front door opened, followed by a rush of the cool night breeze. Sadie stepped in, cradling a bundle of wildflowers. "I hope you found dinner," she said, placing the flowers in a small vase on a sideboard.

"Yes, and thank you," Emma said. "It was good." Her tone grew awkward at the end. She wanted to express something deeper, something about how each courtesy from her grandmother eased a little bit of the bruised parts of her soul. Instead, she fell back on politeness.

"You must be tired," Sadie said, noticing Emma's drooping posture. "There will be time to settle into a routine. For tonight, just rest."

Emma murmured her thanks. She returned to the hallway and entered her bedroom, shutting the door with a soft click. A faint glow from the hallway light shone in a sliver at the bottom of the door, comforting in the otherwise dark space. She changed into pajamas, her movements slow and methodical from travel weariness.

Outside, the wind swept across the orchard, blowing through the leaves. She stood by the window a moment, pressing her forehead to the glass. Above the distant treetops, the sky was now a velvety indigo, dotted with faint stars.

She heard the crow again, a faint caw carried on the

breeze. This time, her heart gave a leap. She scanned the gloom outside but could not spot the bird's silhouette. Instead, she saw only the endless rustle of tree shadows. The sensation of being watched bubbled up once more, though she struggled to pinpoint why.

Her reflection stared back at her in the window: eyes too tired, lips parted in an unsteady breath. She hugged herself, wishing the day had not been so taxing. The length of the bus ride, the weight of her grief for her parents' loss, and the strangeness of this new home settled over her, heavy and unshakable.

Finally, she turned from the window and switched off the overhead light. Slipping under the covers, she curled onto her side, her breath unsteady. The mattress was firm, and the sheets carried a faint scent of lavender and sea salt. She held onto the memory of the herbal tea, picturing the steam rising from the mug. For a moment, grief welled up, pressing at the edges of her exhaustion.

The day's tension faded, leaving only the soft, steady rhythm of her breathing. Emma allowed herself a single fragile wish before she fell asleep: that Crestwood wouldn't swallow her whole but instead offer even the smallest spark of healing for the loss. If nothing else, she thought, perhaps the trees would keep her secrets until she was ready to share them with another.

CHAPTER

TWO

Morning light crept through the slim gap in Emma's curtains. She blinked awake, disoriented for a moment, unsure where she was. An unfamiliar quiet displaced the hum of city traffic she used to hear at dawn on the streets outside her home. Then memories of yesterday returned: the bus station, the ride through Crestwood, and finally arriving at her grandmother's cottage.

She inhaled slowly, and for a fleeting second, there was only stillness. Then the grief crept in, sharp and unrelenting, a stark reminder that this unfamiliar home was real—and so was everything she had lost.

She ran a hand through her hair, thinking it might be best to freshen up before facing the careful kindness that Emma just wasn't ready to meet halfway. She climbed out of bed, grabbed her toiletry bag and the clean clothes she had set aside the previous night. Opening her door, she headed across the hall to the bathroom with its hand-painted floral sink and vintage copper claw-foot tub.

Her reflection in the small mirror confirmed her anxious mood. Dark circles sat beneath her eyes, though her hazel irises looked more vivid than usual. Stress heightened the specks of green in them. She washed her face and brushed her teeth, then quickly dressed. As she attempted to smooth down her hair, there was a strange sound in the hallway: a faint shuffle, like small paws on the floor.

It drew her attention enough that she decided not to wait any longer. She quietly opened the door, stepping into the hall. Pale morning light filtered in from a window near the kitchen, illuminating the wooden planks under her feet. The hush of dawn lingered, but she definitely heard the scratch of nails against wood, followed by a low whisper. Emma froze.

Sadie's voice carried from around the corner by the front door. The tone was calm and affectionate, almost sing-song, like a lullaby. Emma inched her way down the hallway from the bathroom, her steps slow and careful, until she reached the corner of the wall.

Sadie was crouched near the front door, a slight smile on her lips as she spoke to a visitor. At her feet stood a creature with rust-colored fur, poised and alert. For a moment, Emma thought it was a stray dog, but then she noticed the pointed snout and bushy tail—it was a fox. A fox standing on two legs, indoors, perfectly calm, as if it belonged there.

Emma's heart thumped in her chest. She had never

been this close to a fox before; wildlife encounters were limited to pigeons or squirrels in a city park. Her weight shifted, and the floor creaked. The fox's ears turned toward the sound, and Sadie glanced in Emma's direction.

"You can go," she whispered to the fox. "I'll see you again soon."

The animal flicked its amber eyes toward Emma. For a moment, she locked eyes with it. The creature looked more curious than startled. Then the fox slipped out through the open door so quickly, Emma almost doubted it had been there at all. Sadie rose to her feet, and nudged the door closed. Nothing in her posture suggested panic or confusion or that anything at all odd had just happened. She turned slowly, studying Emma's expression.

"You're up early," Sadie said in a surprised tone. Her voice carried a faint rasp, as though she had been speaking in whispers for quite some time.

Emma tried to find words. A blur of questions tangled in her mind. "That was a fox," she managed to say. "In the house."

Sadie's eyes widened, but her expression remained calm. "Yes. I gave it a biscuit. Poor thing wandered around looking half-starved."

Emma didn't know what stunned her more: the fact that a fox just visited the cottage or that Sadie seemed to treat the encounter like a neighborhood dog coming in for scraps. She stepped forward and pressed a hand against the wooden door, unsure if she wanted to open it and see where the fox had gone. "Is that... normal?"

Sadie shrugged. "Sometimes animals drift in from the

orchard. We're close to the woods here, and they find their way to friendly doors." She offered no further explanation. Instead, she tapped the door gently. "I keep a small bowl of water near the porch when the weather's dry. Foxes, raccoons, even the occasional owl all pay visits."

Emma listened, her mind swarming with skepticism. "An owl?" She tried to picture a silent bird of prey hopping across the threshold. Maybe Sadie was being metaphorical. Or perhaps Emma was still only half-awake.

Sadie let out a hum that seemed like a polite attempt to end the conversation. "Breakfast is almost ready, if you're hungry. There's bacon and eggs. Or oatmeal, if you'd prefer."

Emma took a moment to gather her thoughts, then nodded. "I'll have whatever you're having," she said. Her voice came out unsteady, caught between confusion and disbelief. Yet the image of the fox lingered, refusing to fade.

In the kitchen, Sadie kept a tidy arrangement of pans and utensils that contrasted with the cottage's otherwise cluttered corners. The subtle aroma of rosemary mingled with the scent of cooked bacon.

Emma noticed a small sprig of herbs on the counter. She recognized thyme, but she wasn't sure about the rest of the herbs. Emma leaned against the counter, deliberately avoiding the subject of the fox momentarily. She bit back the urge to spill the thoughts racing through her mind.

"Did you sleep well?" Sadie asked, patting grease off the bacon piled on a plate.

Emma wanted to nod, but she hesitated. The previous night's rest had been better than she expected, but she remembered dreams of stormy water and dark silhouettes flickering among the orchard's trees. None felt distinct enough to mention. "Well, enough," she said, choosing not to share details. "The bed's comfortable."

Sadie placed crisp bacon and a fried egg on a plate before sliding it toward Emma. Emma murmured thanks, and they moved to the kitchen table by the window. She inhaled the food's warmth, trying to dispel the lingering chill she felt since witnessing her grandmother's odd conversation with a wild animal in the front hallway.

Emma's appetite wavered at first, but the bacon's aroma coaxed her to take a few bites. She searched for something polite to say, some way to bring up the surreal moment with the fox without sounding weirdly suspicious. How did one ask if all the local wildlife dropped by for a chat, or if the fox was a special guest without sounding crazy? Instead, she decided it was better not to ask.

Sadie ate slowly, eyes drifting once to the window, where faint streaks of sunlight filtered through an overcast sky. When she glanced at Emma, she offered a small smile. There was understanding in it, as if she guessed how unsettled Emma was. Still, Sadie didn't offer further explanation about the fox or the orchard. Instead, she reached for a small teapot, poured its fragrant herbal brew into a mug, and passed it across the table to her granddaughter.

Emma folded her hands around the mug's warmth.

The tea smelled faintly of chamomile and something lemony. She sipped it, letting a pleasant flavor spread across her tongue. Behind her, a soft breeze rattled the window, and she noticed a wilted flower in a porcelain pot on the sill. Its petals drooped, and the leaves looked brittle. She wondered if it might have gone without water for too long.

Sadie set down her fork, following Emma's gaze to the windowsill. She stood, humming a tune under her breath. Her voice was low, reminiscent of a lullaby Emma barely remembered from childhood. She brushed past Emma's chair and moved toward the flower on the windowsill. Emma watched with mild curiosity, half expecting Sadie to fill a cup of water or toss the withered thing in the trash.

But Sadie crouched by the sill, humming that soft tune. She stroked the flower's stem with her fingertips, her song quiet and melodic. The petals quivered, and Emma's breath caught. A moment later, the bloom lifted slightly, unfurling pale pink petals that seemed to regain life under Sadie's touch.

Emma's heart raced. The flower straightened, as if a burst of vitality now coursed through its veins. She gripped her mug tighter, her gaze shifting from the petals to the tea in her hands. What exactly had Sadie put in this? Maybe her mind was playing tricks on her. Perhaps the flower had never truly wilted, just curled from dryness. Or maybe Sadie had misted it earlier, and Emma simply hadn't noticed. Still, the movement felt too vivid, too deliberate to explain away so easily.

Sadie straightened, then stepped away from the sill. She stopped humming and observed Emma with a thoughtful look.

"Are you all right, dear?" she asked. Her tone came across as casual, yet her gaze betrayed something else, something wary, or maybe knowing.

Emma swallowed, placing her mug gently on the table. "It looked completely limp a second ago," she ventured, testing the words in the air. Her pulse tapped a nervous rhythm inside her chest.

"Flowers can surprise us," Sadie replied, returning to her seat. She resumed her meal as though nothing unusual had just happened, leaving Emma to wrestle with the moment on her own.

Something about that statement unsettled Emma. She thought of the fox by the door, as calm as a housecat, and now this flower, springing back to life in an instant. She told herself it had to be a trick of perspective or timing. Maybe the soil here had unusual qualities, or maybe Sadie just had a way with plants. But the idea that something else—something more—was at play refused to leave her.

She tried to bring the conversation back to the fox, hoping Sadie might slip and offer a hint about how she had lured the thing in. "You said animals wander in from the orchard," Emma began, selecting her words carefully. "Does that happen often? Like, do I need to keep the door locked?"

Sadie took a small sip of tea, her face giving away very little. "I rarely lock the door in the morning," she answered. "I like to open it wide, to let fresh air in. The orchard is part of living round here, and the wildlife are accustomed to me. They must sense kindness and come right to the door."

"But they actually come inside the house?" Emma pressed, though she tried to maintain a neutral tone. "Foxes are usually shy, right?"

"They are," Sadie said, tapping her nails softly against her mug. "I suspect that one singled me out because it knows I won't chase it off. It also might have been curious about you."

Emma lowered her eyes to her plate. All her misgivings bubbled up, though she couldn't quite voice them without sounding childish. Sadie seemed kindly, wise, and maternal, yet distinctly otherworldly in ways Emma never expected.

A fox would run from most humans. This one had stared Emma down, as if trying to evaluate her. Then her grandmothers seemed to be having an actual conversation with the animal. The entire thing felt unreal.

She finished her meal in slow, deliberate bites. When Sadie offered more tea, Emma shook her head, unsure how much longer she could keep her composure. Unease stirred in her; the flower's eerie revival still fresh in her mind. She had always trusted in logical explanations, but this morning had cracked that certainty.

Sadie stood and stacked their plates. Emma started to help, but her grandmother waved her off with a gentle smile, telling her to rest or explore the cottage. With a quiet nod, Emma wandered into the living room, where the faint scent of herbs lingered in the air.

Her gaze drifted to the shelves lined with old books, some so worn their titles had faded. She recognized a few familiar novels, but many looked handmade, with bits of ribbon marking pages.

Curiosity sparked in her, laced with hesitation. She had the urge to pull one down and start reading, but something held her back—she wasn't sure if her grandmother would welcome the intrusion.

She hovered by the window, hugging her arms around her waist. Outside, clouds drifted across a sky bleached pale by the early sun. The trees in the orchard stood in relief against the horizon.

She tried to convince herself to go exploring beyond the porch, to see if the fox might still be close by, but wariness held her back. It was as though stepping onto that orchard path would open a door she wasn't sure she could close again.

Behind her, Sadie's footsteps brushed over the kitchen tiles. She hummed the same lullaby as before. Emma listened carefully to the soft, melodic pattern, shivers dancing lightly along her skin. Even with the tightness in her chest, she felt an odd comfort in that tune, as if it offered a promise she couldn't yet claim.

At last, she turned from the window and sank into a worn armchair. A dozen thoughts vied for space in her mind. She questioned whether to demand explanations, to ask Sadie outright about what she had seen. She suspected that the truth might be bigger than she wanted to handle at this hour.

Instead, she pressed her fingertips against her

temples, recalling the single moment that refused to vanish from her memory: Sadie's soft humming and the flower springing from near-death to fresh bloom in seconds.

That image grew sharper whenever Emma closed her eyes. She breathed in, slowly, letting the quiet fill her ears. Perhaps she would find the nerve to inquire about it once she adjusted to Crestwood.

For now, Emma opened her eyes and felt the atmosphere of the house settle around her, as though it recognized her presence. She remembered the fox's inquisitive expression, the way Sadie had shown no alarm, the warmth of the morning meal, and especially the bloom that responded to her touch.

As she sat in uneasy stillness, a single, undeniable realization took root: the ordinary rules she once trusted might not apply here at all. Whatever she faced in the days ahead, Emma sensed a shift that stirred both apprehension and a tiny, brave flicker of curiosity.

CHAPTER

THREE

That night, Emma didn't remember drifting off to sleep. One moment, she was curled up in bed, staring at the thin slice of moon through her bedroom window, and the next instant she was plunging into a dream so vivid that it made the air in her lungs taste like salt.

In the dream, she stood on a deserted road. Rain pummeled the asphalt, turning every surface slick. A howling wind whipped through the pines at the roadside, bending their trunks until they seemed ready to snap.

Emma recognized the shape of the road in a distant, disoriented way, though she could not name the location.

Headlights caught the sheen on the pavement, bright and stuttering. She realized with a jolt that those headlights belonged to a speeding car. The engine roared in her ears, merging with the crash of rain. Water droplets clung to the windshield like tiny diamonds in the glare, and for a heartbeat, Emma could not move.

Her parents.

That was all her dream-self knew.

She saw her father behind the wheel, her mother in the passenger seat beside him though their faces blurred under the flickering glow of the storm's lightning. Their voices echoed in the roar of thunder, but the words dissolved before she could understand them. She wanted to scream a warning—slow down, turn back—yet her throat produced only a muffled gasp.

The car lurched on the wet curve, skidding sideways. Light slashed across Emma's dream-vision, and she found herself standing somewhere else entirely: a chaotic swirl of water devouring the road. She heard her own ragged breathing and tasted the brine of salt, as though the ocean had swallowed everything. The thunderclap rattled the air, and the headlights flickered, mesmerizing and terrifying all at once.

She tried to run forward. The wind slapped her face, or maybe it was the weight of her own dread that kept her rooted. The shriek of twisting metal fractured her thoughts. The stormy darkness around her spun into manic shapes, all black tendrils and jagged shards of white light.

She heard chanting—low and distorted, as if carried through murky water. At the edges of her vision, robed figures loomed, their silhouettes shifting in the shadows.

They stood in a circle, though she couldn't tell if they were gathered for some silent ritual or surrounding the wrecked car, passing judgment. Their faces remained hidden, except for the eerie bone-pale glow beneath their hoods. Anxiety spiked in her chest, and her pulse pounded in her ears, steady and unrelenting.

The more she listened to the chant, the clearer it became.

Witch! Witch! Witch!

When she squinted, those silhouettes multiplied, flickering like phantoms each time lightning flared. They were neither entirely human nor entirely illusions. Their presence stirred an undercurrent of dread so profound that Emma's dream-self forgot to breathe. The chanting rose again, screeching and discordant.

She realized she was shaking, though whether from cold or fear, her dream-self could not tell. Her gaze locked onto the robed figures, and in that fleeting moment she realized they were looking at her. She shouted for them to leave her alone or reveal their faces, but the roar of wind drowned her voice.

A flash of lightning seared the horizon. The road vanished. Darkness closed in, swirling with jagged forms like broken glass in a raging sea. She staggered back, blinded by the afterimage. That was all it took—her surroundings splintered into chaos. The shrieking chant escalated, heavy with an otherworldly note. The ground seemed to fracture beneath her feet, leaving her spinning into nothingness.

Then she felt hands on her shoulders, warm and solid. At first, she thought it was one of the robed silhouettes grabbing her. The dream-limbs that tried to fight back felt sluggish, as though she moved through water. She gasped, and the environment flicked to pitch-black.

She bolted upright with a strangled cry. Her real-world bedroom erupted into focus, lit only by a sliver of moonlight. Her chest rose and fell violently. Each breath stung her lungs, as if she had truly swallowed half the storm's rain.

She pressed her palms flat against the sheets, forcing herself to remember where she was—Sadie's cottage, safe in Crestwood, far from the illusions of that nightmare.

Her pulse thundered in her ears. No more rain hammered the roof, and no headlights glared against a waterlogged road. Yet the echoes of the dream persisted, leaving her disoriented and clammy. She wiped her forehead, finding sweat beads at her hairline. She tried breathing slowly, but her heart refused to settle.

A flicker of movement at the window caught her attention. Her entire body tensed with the leftover terror of the dream. The glass reflected the faint shape of her bed, but beyond that reflection, she glimpsed something moving outside.

Her breath stilled. Two specks of light, low to the ground, seemed to glimmer in the darkness. They could have been eyes, or perhaps a trick of moonlight.

She swallowed, forcing her gaze to remain steady. The eyes vanished, leaving her uncertain if she had actually seen anything at all. The pounding in her chest refused to lessen. She thought of the fox from earlier, the one that appeared at the cottage door as calmly as any neighborhood cat. But it was impossible to be sure. The shape at the window no longer took form.

A single whisper—unreal and fleeting—seemed to

echo in her mind. She could not recall the words. The robed silhouettes from the dream drifted at the fringes of her awareness, chanting in an alien tongue she could not decipher. She shook her head once, as though the motion could cast out the memory.

Emma tucked her knees close to her chest, hugging them tight. The bed's quilt, softened by age and repeated washings, offered a small sense of comfort. She tried to recall Sadie's voice, or the gentle tune she occasionally hummed while tending the herbs in the kitchen. Anything to anchor her to the present.

Her bedroom walls felt too close. She flicked her gaze across the shadows, spotting shapes that were only furniture, but in her heightened state, every outline twisted her nerves tighter. The faint scent of lavender from her pillow reminded her of Sadie's bedtime teas, but it did little to calm the lingering tremors of the storm still racing through her.

Finally, she took a deep, trembling breath—in for four counts, hold for four, then out for four. She repeated the pattern, steady and deliberate, forcing air into her lungs and willing her pulse to slow. By the third round, her heartbeat steadied, the panic loosening its grip. She reminded herself: She was at Sadie's cottage, safe from unnatural figures, far from storms and dangerous roads.

She listened for any sign of her grandmother stirring in the hall, but the house remained silent. Relief flickered through her—at least she hadn't woken her grandmother with a scream. Sadie had already been so kind, so patient, and the last thing Emma wanted was to add to her worries.

Still, a pang of loneliness crept in. There were moments she wished she could go to Sadie's room, like a child looking for comfort, but she couldn't bring herself to do it. Admitting how much the dream had shaken her felt too embarrassing.

It wasn't the first time she had dreamed of the storm—she'd relived that night in restless sleep more times than she could count. But tonight, had been different. Sharper. More vivid. The chanting, the shadowy figures... it felt less like a memory and more like a warning.

Emma shifted in bed, pulling the quilt up to her chin. She knew she was safe—rationally, at least—but her body hadn't gotten the message. The tremors still clung to her.

She stared at the window until her eyes burned from dryness, the night wind whispering through the orchard outside. Finally, she forced herself to look away and shut her eyes, even though sleep felt impossible.

She drifted in and out of shallow sleep, never fully resting, until the soft light of dawn crept through the curtains. When she finally opened her eyes, exhaustion clung to her. The dream still lingered, tangled in her thoughts like seaweed wrapped around an anchor. Her body ached from tension.

Moving slowly, she swung her legs over the side of the bed, unsteady and half-numb, then pulled on a cardigan over her pajamas.

In the hall, Emma paused outside Sadie's closed door, her hand hovering near the knob. She heard nothing. Part of her wanted to push the nightmare aside, pretend it hadn't shaken her, but she knew her grandmother would see right through her.

One glance at her reflection in the hallway mirror confirmed it—bleary eyes, pale skin, shadows under her eyes. She looked anything but well-rested.

Then the scent of eggs drifted from the kitchen, along with the quiet clatter of dishes. Sadie was up. Emma's stomach tightened as she stepped away from the door and headed toward the warmth of the kitchen.

Sadie stood by the stove in a pale blue robe, stirring something in a small saucepan. Steam curled from it, but it was the golden scent of syrup and the buttery warmth of pancakes that filled the air. At the sound of Emma's hesitant footsteps, Sadie turned, her expression softening the moment she saw her.

"Morning. I made tea. I think you might need it."

Emma forced a thin smile and dropped onto a wooden stool by the small kitchen table. "Thank you," she said, her voice rough with fatigue.

Sadie poured the tea into a mug and set it in front of Emma, resting her warm palm briefly on Emma's shoulder. The gentle contact pressed against the wall of emotion Emma kept building inside.

"Another rough night?" Sadie asked.

Emma nodded, reluctant to speak. The dream threatened to replay in her mind: wet pavement, thunderous wind, twisting shapes. She pushed the images aside and imagined locking them behind a heavy door.

Sadie pulled out the chair across from her and sat. The

lines drawn across her grandmother's forehead deepened. "I heard you stirring in the night," she said in a quiet tone. "I almost checked on you. Did something happen?"

Emma dragged a breath through her nose, wishing she could dismiss the question with a single shrug. But burying the nightmare would do her little good. She tried explaining the bare minimum. "It was the same nightmare I always have. The storm. The accident," she said, eyes fixed on the tea. "But this time it was different...there were these people...in long robes. I heard chanting."

Sadie's expression softened. "I'm sorry, sweetheart."

Her kindness nearly shattered Emma's fragile composure. She took a careful sip of the tea, hoping it would root her. "It felt so real," she murmured, tracing one finger around the rim of the mug.

Sadie nodded slowly as she turned to the stove to tend to breakfast. "Dreams feel that way, especially after loss."

Emma tried to swallow, but her throat felt tight. She recalled the hooded silhouettes at the edges of her dream, how they seemed to watch her with translucent faces.

"Maybe it's just...my memory playing tricks," she said. She willed herself to sound logical, as though she could banish the nightmare by labeling it pure imagination. "Why would I dream about something so strange like hooded figures?"

Sadie reached out and rested a hand over Emma's. Her palm radiated warmth, a quiet reassurance. "Sometimes our grief draws strange echoes from our sub-conscious. But if there's anything else you remember...or feel—"

"It's fine," Emma interrupted, guilt gnawing at her

abruptness. She gently pulled her hand free, lowering her gaze. "I'm not sure talking about it will help. I'm okay, really. Let's just...have breakfast."

Sadie studied her for a moment, as if trying to read her thoughts, but let it go. Yet Emma's nerves crackled, refusing to let her relax. She remembered the flash of those eyes by the window, uncertain if it was the fox or her fraying imagination. Everything in the cottage seemed to carry that watchful presence in every corner.

Sadie soon produced two plates of pancakes and sausages. The meal was simple but hearty. Emma forced a polite smile and took a bite. The eggs were warm and soft, filling the hollow space in her stomach, though they did little to loosen the tension in her chest.

They ate in near silence. Outside, the early-morning sun climbed over the orchard, casting long, grayish shadows along the trunk of an old oak tree visible through the window. Emma kept her eyes on her plate, pretending not to notice the slow shift of branches in the faint breeze.

Emma latched onto the small, steady things—the scrape of her fork against the plate, the rising steam from her tea, the quiet hum of the cottage around her. But it wasn't enough. The chant from her dream kept looping in the back of her mind, like a song stuck on repeat, its rhythm surfacing every time she blinked, every time she tried to push it away.

When Sadie finished her meal, she set her fork down. Her eyes flicked to Emma's nearly untouched plate, but she didn't comment. "Emma, when you're ready to talk, I'm here," she said simply.

She knew her grandmother was just trying to help but the repeated offers to listen now started to grate on her. Why couldn't she understand she just wasn't ready to really talk? Instead, she rose from the table, carrying her mug. "Thank you for breakfast," she murmured. "I'll clean up."

Sadie gently covered Emma's fingers with her own. "Help me wash up," she offered, voice gentle. "Chores are good for the soul."

They busied themselves rinsing dishes and wiping the table. The mild routine soothed Emma's rattled nerves somewhat. She noticed her grandmother watching her a few times, brow pinched in concern, but Emma pretended not to see.

The day stretched ahead, glaringly bright, too sharp for the weight pressing behind her eyes. Even a hundred pairs of sunglasses wouldn't have dulled it enough. But Emma was determined to push past the fear and anxiety. She had come to Crestwood for a fresh start, and she wasn't about to let a stupid nightmare get in her way.

Sadie began mixing a new herbal sleep remedy to sell at the Central Market and asked Emma to help. Emma agreed, though not without hesitation. Sadie moved through the kitchen gathering herbs. She worked by feel, measuring each herb with the ease of long habit. Her voice was calm as she explained everything she did to Emma.

"Valerian root is the foundation here," she said, tapping the spoon against the rim of a jar. "It calms the nervous system, helps you drift off faster, and keeps you asleep longer. Works by boosting GABA in the brain—

basically telling your body it's time to shut down for the night."

She gave the blend a slow stir. "It's good for easing tension too, helps with headaches and muscle tightness. Just don't overdo it, or you'll wake up feeling like you never left your pillow."

She measured one teaspoon and let it drop into a small ceramic bowl instead of the tea bag. "Too much, though, and it can make you feel sluggish in the morning, so we keep it light."

Next, she reached for the lavender. The scent filled the kitchen immediately, floral and slightly sweet. "This doesn't make you sleep, not exactly." She rolled a few dried buds between her fingers before adding two teaspoons to the mix. "It relaxes the body, takes the edge off restlessness. Helps with tension, especially the kind that settles in your chest." She hesitated, watching the petals fall. "It also balances valerian's earthiness. That root has a way of reminding you it's medicine."

Next came a skullcap, shaking out one teaspoon of its brittle leaves. "And this one," she murmured, tipping the herb into the bowl, "this is for when your mind won't let go of the day. Skullcap calms overworked thoughts, smooths the edges of worry. It's not as strong as Valerian, but it's steadier. More of a gentle quiet than a heavy pull." She paused, tapping the spoon lightly against the rim of the bowl. "It has a touch of bitterness, though. That's why I always tell people—honey helps."

With the blend complete, she measured the mix into a muslin tea bag, pinching it closed and tying it with a length of twine before placing it with the others she had already prepared. "One per cup," she said, brushing a few stray bits of lavender from the counter. "Steep for ten to fifteen minutes—no rushing it. Valerian needs that time to release its strength, and skullcap does better with a long steep, too." She looked up, meeting Emma's gaze. "Drink it warm, about half an hour before bed. If the taste is too strong, honey or a little lemon balm can smooth it out."

She ran a thumb over the twine securing the bag, then set it carefully in the tin with the rest. "Sleep isn't something you force," she said softly. "You just have to let it come. This helps."

Once they had filled dozens of sachets with the herbal mixture, Sadie paused, carefully setting aside seven sachets and pushing them toward Emma. "These are for you," she said, her tone soft but steady. "Take them, keep them close, and use them when you need to unwind. They'll help you sleep; ease that tension you've been carrying."

Emma paused for a moment, her fingers lightly brushing the twine on the sachets. She glanced up at Sadie, her throat tight with an unexpected wave of emotion. "Thank you," she murmured, her voice barely more than a whisper.

The words felt small for all that she wanted to say, the warmth, the quiet care in her grandmother's actions, the comfort of having someone to turn to after all that she had been through. It was all so new, so fragile, and yet it meant more than Emma could express. She settled for those two words, hoping they'd be enough.

Eventually, the tea sachets were ready. Sadie put them in a basket by the front door to take to market. Outside, the orchard shimmered under pale sunlight, and a crow cawed once from a distant branch. The call sent a tremor up Emma's spine, reminding her of how the dream's chanting had echoed.

She inhaled sharply, then released the breath. Heat and embarrassment flooded her cheeks when she realized her grandmother was staring at her. "I'm okay," Emma said quickly, though she felt anything but. "Just...tired."

"I believe you're tired," Sadie replied. She patted Emma's arm. "We'll make a batch of chamomile tea with lemon zest next. You might want to have some later, it will help perk you up."

Emma nodded, grateful for the practical task. They settled into a companionable quiet, working side by side. The hush offered a small respite, yet she could not shake the sense that something hovered at the corner of her mind.

"Could you fetch me the bowl of lemons? I'll start grating the peel."

Focused on the request, Emma withdrew a plump lemon from the little bowl by the sink. A beam of sunlight passed through the window, catching inclusions in the glass and scattering flecks of brightness on the counter-top. For a moment, Emma found the small display of light soothing. Normal.

As Sadie grated the peel, she explained, "We can't put this batch into the market basket just yet though. The zest needs to dry before it can go into the tea bags." She paused, looking over at Emma. "We'll use the dehydrator to speed it up. Just spread the grated zest on the tray in a single layer and set it on the lowest setting. It should only take about four to six hours to dry completely."

Emma helped tidy the kitchen, wiping down surfaces and stacking clean bowls. She felt a bit better. Focusing on simple, tangible tasks offered a welcome break from the grief that had been pressing on her.

"You might want to rest a bit," Sadie suggested softly. "You still look pale."

Emma swallowed, her pulse an uneasy flutter. She wanted to reassure her grandmother with a bright smile and some glib remark. Yet the memory of that dream loomed, too close and too sharp. Her voice faltered. "I'll be fine," she managed, though the unsteady note in her tone betrayed her.

Sadie took a breath as though she might push further, but in the end, she nodded. "If you change your mind..." Her sentence remained incomplete. She let it trail off, gaze flickering with understanding.

Emma went to her room instead, leaving her grandmother in the kitchen. Once inside her bedroom, she stood near the window, peering out at the orchard. The day's light made the apple trees look serene, their leaves dancing in the breeze. No fox or crow lurked at the edge of the yard.

A tremor rippled through her body. She forced herself to imagine the small comforts she had: Sadie's kindness, this snug cottage, and the warmth of morning tea still spreading through her belly. The dream might have rattled her, but she was determined not to let it define her entire day.

Emma sat on the edge of her bed, hugging a pillow close. She drew in a steady breath. She knew Sadie would have listened if she had chosen to talk, especially about the guilt that gnawed at her. But some irrational fear warned her to keep silent.

Maybe she wasn't ready to admit how the dream made her feel. Maybe she worried that acknowledging the strange visuals—especially the robed silhouettes—would make them more real.

Now and then, she heard her grandmother in the living room, moving about. She stepped out of her room and back into the hallway. The aroma of herbs had dissipated, replaced by a faint tang of salt that drifted in whenever the breeze rattled the windows. Sadie had left a note on the kitchen table—*Gone outside to gather a few things. Back soon.*

Emma picked up the note with trembling fingers. She set it aside, exhaling slowly. She recalled the old rules she once relied on to repel nightmares: ground yourself in the present, keep busy, anchor your mind with routine, think good thoughts. That was precisely what she intended to do.

She found the kettle still hot on the stove. It hadn't been long since Sadie had gone out. Pouring herself a cup of sleep remedy tea, she swirled the liquid in the cup and inhaled the fragrance. The memory of that distorted chant tugged at her again, but she breathed through it, forcing the terror to recede.

"It was just a dream," she whispered, gripping the handle of the mug. She repeated the words as if they were an incantation. "The robed figures were only a dream."

Her voice was steel-tinged with fragile hope. In that moment she decided in that moment to cling to the mundane comforts of her life. She had to keep the trembling nightmares locked out of her mind, or she would never find solid footing in Crestwood.

She would continue to do simple things: help her grandmother with daily chores, wander the orchard in the sunlight, keep breathing in and out. Ignoring the uncanny signs felt far easier than trying to unravel them. So, she drank her tea, letting its comforting warmth banish the chill of that storm-lashed memory. And though the memory hummed at the corners of her mind, she convinced herself that the only path to peace was to leave it buried.

CHAPTER

FOUR

Emma had slept poorly again, tossing between shallow bouts of rest and a hollow, jittery feeling that refused to vanish. After breakfast the next day, Sadie suggested a walk into Crestwood's town center, Emma was desperate to escape the cottage's close walls, get some fresh air.

She pulled on a simple sweater, her jeans, and slipped on thick socks and white sneakers. Sadie waited near the kitchen door, an unhurried figure in a slate-blue cardigan. Instead of taking the car, they walked a narrow path that cut through the meadow behind the house, looping around the orchard before meeting the main road.

The cottage was cozy, almost to the point of being claustrophobic, while the outside world offered open space and a breath of fresh air. With each step, Emma inhaled, drawing solace from the steady crunch of gravel under her shoes.

Wildflowers trembled in the breeze, bright splashes of color against a mostly green backdrop. Sadie's presence was comforting, though a hint of guarded caution lingered in her posture. Emma noticed the way her grandmother scanned the path around them on all sides, as if anticipating meeting someone along the way.

A flash of russet fur in her peripheral vision made Emma slow her pace. It was the fox she'd seen in the house the day before. It stood at a distance, ears high. It regarded them with golden eyes, tail swishing.

For a moment, Emma considered approaching it, but Sadie raised a hand to it and the animal darted into the orchard's trees, vanishing into the dappled shadows.

A strange ache tugged at Emma's chest. Everything around her—the animals, the windblown branches of the orchard—seemed to vibrate with an almost electric charge, like the air itself was alive, crackling just beneath the surface. It wasn't fear, but a prickling sensation on her skin, a tightness in her chest, as if the world around her was on the verge of something she couldn't quite grasp. Her grandmother seemed unfazed by it, as though the strange energy in the air was just another part of life, nothing to be concerned about.

Sadie led Emma along a gently curving lane that narrowed at a weathered fence, then intersected with a quiet side street. The buildings clustered close here, their shingles rough and battered by years of salt-laced storms.

Emma ran her fingers along one fence, its wood softened by the damp coastal climate. She caught glimpses of pale curtains drawn tightly across neighbors' windows. In several houses, she saw people peeking through the curtains, then quickly pull them shut. The whole scene felt strange.

"Not many people out yet," Emma said softly. "It's early, I guess?"

"People will show up soon enough—market day draws them in."

She sounded calm, but Emma noted a subtle tension in Sadie's jaw. It added to the knot of unease already coiling in Emma's belly. She tried to match her grandmother's composure as they approached the next bend, where a few shops clustered around an old-fashioned signpost.

The main road was wider, paved with worn stone tiles that gleamed in the sunlight, and the wind grew stronger, carrying with it scents of pine trees and moss.

Here, Emma finally spotted other people. Two elderly men in cap-and-scarf attire stood outside a small bakery, quietly talking over steaming cups of coffee. Their voices cut off abruptly the moment they noticed them passing.

One man gave a slow, respectful nod, while the other lingered with a curious, cautious stare, as if weighing whether it was proper to say something. The first man nudged him, and he finally bowed his head as Emma and her grandmother approached.

Sadie smiled warmly at them. "Hank. Ernie. How are you gentlemen on this fine day?"

Hank, the first to recover, shifted his weight nervously. "Oh, Miss Sadie, we're doing well. Doing well, indeed.

Lovely day, ain't it? Perfect for a walk, or, well, a cup of coffee." He cleared his throat, his hands trembling slightly as he adjusted his scarf.

Ernie, still a bit hesitant, gave a quick nod and added, "Yes, yes, Miss Sadie, couldn't be better, really. Just, uh, enjoying the peace and quiet, as we do." He chuckled nervously, glancing at Hank for support before looking back at Sadie and Emma. "Always nice to see you, Miss Sadie."

Both men looked at Emma for a moment, unsure how to address her. Sadie stepped in with a smile, her tone warm but casual. "Gentlemen, this is my granddaughter, Emma," she said, her voice carrying a sense of ease that seemed to relax the men a little.

Hank gave a slow, respectful nod. "Ah, Miss Emma. Such a fine young lady," he said softly, his voice carrying a slight tremor. "It's a pleasure to meet you."

Ernie followed suit, his words a bit rushed. "Yes, yes, a real pleasure, Miss Emma. We're glad to make your acquaintance." He gave a quick, nervous bow of his head, his hands shifting from his scarf to his cup as if seeking something to hold on to.

Sadie chuckled gently, her eyes twinkling as she observed the men. "They're just a little...excitable. Don't mind them, sweetie."

Emma forced a polite, quick smile, her pulse jumping at the sensation that she was on display. She lowered her gaze, pretending to focus on a stray pebble in the road, only to feel her heart pound even faster. Emma felt the men's stares on her as she and her grandmother continued onward.

Within a minute, they reached a cluster of shops with colorful awnings. The bright tones of the canopies didn't fully mask the peeling paint on the walls beneath. Some store windows were dusty, others carefully polished. The entire effect was a patchwork of pride and neglect, as though the town yearned for a past glow but could not quite let go of outdated habits.

A narrow street led them to the Central Market where small stalls were arranged under a wide, sloping roof for produce and artisanal goods. Sadie paused at the edge, scanning the scene. At least a dozen locals milled about, chatting in low voices near the stalls.

Emma's nerves spiked, anticipating more scrutiny. Despite her fluttering apprehension, she inhaled the heady scents of freshly baked bread and ripe apples. That mingling of comfort and unease unsettled her. She wondered if Sadie felt it too, or if her grandmother had grown immune to curious glances.

They walked on, passing a stall piled high with vegetables. A younger vendor offered a hesitant wave, then silently looked away. Every rustle of clothing, every footstep on creaking boards, made Emma's skin prickle. She tried to stifle her self-consciousness, forcing a small nod at two townsfolk who glanced her way.

Their whispered conversation stopped abruptly, leaving a heavy silence that settled over Emma, making her feel tense and uncomfortable.

She stepped closer, and Sadie gently tucked a hand

under her elbow, guiding her through the rows of baskets filled with early-fall harvest. Near the far end stood a table heaped with apples, their glossy red skins reflecting flecks of sunlight. A gray-haired woman stood behind it, her face lined with wrinkles but softened by a warm, beautiful smile. She caught sight of Sadie and lifted her hand in greeting.

"Morning, Sadie," The older woman spoke, her voice raspy yet calm. She surveyed their baskets, her eyes sweeping over the tea sachets. Then, her gaze shifted to Emma, and she fell silent, studying her with quiet intensity.

"Annette, this is my granddaughter, Emma," Sadie said quietly. No further explanation followed.

Emma tried for a polite smile and dipped her head in greeting. Annette's brows lifted, and her eyes flickered to the sky. Overhead, a flock of starlings soared in a smooth spiral, chattering in a melodic wave of sound.

Emma noticed the hesitation in the woman's expression, a reserved curiosity as she watched the birds. It reminded Emma of how someone might stare at a lit fuse, uncertain if it would spark or fizzle harmlessly. The woman didn't speak for several seconds, then offered the faintest nod.

"We're gonna have a good harvest season," Annette said. "Food lasts us for the winter, if the weather holds. Long as the storms stay away."

Annette glanced at Emma, her eyes sharp and guarded, as if measuring her reaction. There was subtle wariness in the way she looked at her, a quiet caution, like she wasn't sure how much Emma understood. Was Annette talking about the storm that had caused her parents' accident?

"Sold anything yet?" Sadie asked, filling the awkward gap.

"Some," Annette replied. She shot another appraising look at Emma, then fussed with her stack of fruit. "Folks come and go."

Emma cleared her throat, struggling to think of small talk. Something about the entire stall—its neat arrangement and Annette's watchful stare—made her want to step back. Yet she felt pinned in place by her own unease. There was no overt hostility, but the air bristled with the suspicion that Emma somehow carried an invisible label.

A word flashed in her mind—*witch*—whispered low and sinister, as if it came from somewhere deep and hidden. Other words followed but she couldn't make them out clearly; she couldn't tell if the voice said *trouble* or *new*, but the feeling that came with it was sharp and uneasy, and she wasn't sure which was worse the voice that seemed to invade her mind, unbidden or the words it said.

She looked around at the others, their faces calm and unaware, nothing in their expressions to suggest they'd heard the whisper too. It made her feel small, as though she were the only one touched by something no one else could sense. A chill ran through her, and, for a moment, she wondered if it had really been there at all.

Sadie selected three pears, placing them in a canvas bag she carried. The vendor accepted coins in exchange and murmured a vague thanks. The women chatted as

Sadie set up her tea sachets for sale at Annette's stall. When she'd finished, she said goodbye to her friend, then nudged Emma away from the stall, guiding her toward the main thoroughfare.

They wove between a few more stalls, where locals displayed knit scarves or homemade jams. Everywhere Emma turned, she caught a flicker of someone's gaze.

An older couple paused to murmur behind their hands. A young woman near a display of pastries watched her, then pretended to be busy. Emma's skin crawled with the sense that she was under constant surveillance. She considered pulling up the hood on her jacket, but the day was fair, and that would only seem more suspicious.

They followed the gradual slope of the street until it opened onto a modest square lined with old-fashioned lampposts. Here, quilted banners hung overhead, drifting in the breeze. The lively colors contrasted with the demure townsfolk. Even the group of crows overhead felt subdued, as if the birds themselves recognized the tension.

At the far corner of the square, an arched sign pointed to the local café. Emma noticed a few customers at an outdoor table. Their conversation died the moment they spotted her.

One of them called, "Sadie," in cautious greeting, but the rest said nothing. She could not help feeling as though she and her grandmother had walked straight into a silent play.

"Let's rest for a moment," Sadie said, gesturing to a bench near the lamppost.

Emma nodded, relieved for a chance to steady her

nerves. They sat side by side. The bench's wooden slats pressed into Emma's back. She rolled her shoulders, exhaling slowly to release the day's stress.

A breeze whisked through the square, ruffling the corners of the banners overhead. The drifting cloth stripes made a soft flapping sound. Emma became acutely aware of the layered scents around her: warm bread drifting from a bakery cart, faint perfume from passing strangers, and the ever-present salt tang of the sea. Sadie gazed toward a point near the far edge of the plaza, where several people had gathered to talk. Her expression was unreadable, lips set in a calm line.

Emma dared a soft question, mindful of curious ears. "Do you come here a lot?"

Sadie lifted a shoulder. "Every week."

Emma had been trying to make sense of the way the townspeople treated her grandmother—with a kind of cautious reverence, as if they respected something about Sadie they didn't fully understand. It wasn't fear, exactly, but more like the careful distance people kept when they sensed something other.

Emma thought about the fox she had seen and how it had seemed to study Sadie with an almost knowing look. She remembered the little plant, how it had withered and died, only to spring back to life under her grandmother's touch.

At first, Emma had brushed it off as nothing more than an oddity, something she hadn't seen clearly. But now, watching how the locals acted around Sadie, she was starting to understand. There was something in the way they treated her—a reverence that wasn't just for her age or because she was a good neighbor, but for something deeper, something they respected and maybe even feared.

Emma's gaze drifted to a group of bystanders who stood whispering near a sculpture in the center of the plaza. Their glances skittered across Emma's face. She looked away, hating how vulnerable she felt, caught in the crosshairs of a small-town rumor mill that had her grandmother squarely in its sights without any concrete explanation.

"Sadie," Emma said quietly, "So they are staring at me because I'm with you? "

Sadie reached over and squeezed Emma's hand. Her fingers felt warm, reassuring in a world of quiet tension. "Yeah," she answered, voice low. "They're probably wondering if you share the same... abilities that I do."

Emma's mind churned. She was unsure if she should interpret abilities as mere talents for gardening or something more arcane and mysterious.

Before she could speak, the voice invaded her mind again, sharp and insistent. *She's a witch.* Emma froze, a cold shiver running down her spine. The air felt heavier, and Emma's mind reeled, recalling the odd moments she'd tried to dismiss—the way Sadie had an actual conversation with a fox who seemed to be communicating back, the plant in the kitchen that came back to life when her grandmother spoke to it. The dreams warning her of a witch.

Emma had tried to brush them off as strange coincidences, but now, looking at her grandmother, it all made sense in a way she hadn't been ready for. She couldn't brush off the voice in her head as easily, though. It was persistent—like an uninvited guest at a dinner party who just wouldn't leave.

She looked at Sadie, bewildered. "They think you're a witch, don't they?" she asked, her voice barely above a whisper, as though the words themselves were a burden.

Sadie's eyes softened, but there was no surprise in her expression. "How do you know that?" she asked, a note of curiosity creeping into her voice.

Emma hesitated, unsure whether she should tell the truth. But it slipped out before she could stop it. "I... I heard it. A voice. It's been whispering *witch* to me. And...I kind of had a dream where some creepy monk-like figures in dark robes kept chanting witch, too. I think they were talking about you."

Sadie pursed her lips, studying her closely for a long moment. Then she nodded slowly. "If you can hear a voice like that...and have dream premonitions... then you must have a gift of your own, too." Her tone was serious, and there was a quiet pride in it.

Sadie let the silence stretch between them for a moment before standing and motioning for Emma to join her. "Come on," she said, her voice calm. "Let's see if there's anything else we need from the market."

Emma felt a bit unsettled. It was strange how easily Sadie seemed to brush off her question, as if it hadn't been anything significant. Emma was left feeling awkward, not sure how to push for more. So, she followed, trying to shake off the discomfort.

They made their way along the edge of the plaza, passing another stall lined with jars of jam that gleamed in the sunlight. The vendor, an older man with a stocky build and weathered face, nodded politely at Sadie but didn't say anything. Emma forced a small, polite smile. The man glanced at her briefly, assessing, then quickly returned his attention to his jars.

She overheard a faint snippet of a conversation. Two townspeople whispered near the next stall; the word *witches* audible between whispers.

The speaker caught Emma's glance and turned away, as though embarrassed at being overheard. Emma's stomach churned. She tried to remind herself that not everyone in Crestwood was out to judge her grandmother...or her. Possibly some were just curious or protective after hearing rumors. Yet the gnawing sense of foreboding still bloomed in the pit of her stomach.

Steering her away from the eavesdropping pair, Sadie stopped at a stand displaying crocheted scarves and woven hats. The middle-aged merchant behind the table forced a tight-lipped smile. Sadie handled a scarf, deftly turning it over in her hands to check the stitching.

Emma noted the quiet proficiency with which her grandmother moved, as if she had done this for years and refused to let small-town gossip rattle her. That calm radiated outward, and Emma tried to absorb a bit of it, reminding herself that she was here of her own accord, that she had a right to be in Crestwood if she genuinely wanted a place to belong.

The merchant cleared her throat. "Lovely day for a

walk, Sadie," she offered. Her smile wavered when she looked at Emma.

"It is," Sadie agreed, placing the scarf back on the table. "We're taking advantage of the mild weather."

The woman nodded. "Good to see you." She pressed her lips together, avoiding further chatter. Emma dipped her head in a silent goodbye, wishing she could vanish into the crowd.

Once they moved on, Emma leaned closer to Sadie. "How do you just... ignore it?" she asked, voice tight with the frustration of feeling so exposed. "Everyone stares at us like we might do something terrible."

Sadie's mouth curved in a gentle smile. "I've grown used to it," she said. "Besides, ignoring them means they grow tired of staring eventually." She gestured toward a small café sign a few paces ahead, then guided Emma into the narrower street. She paused at the threshold, giving Emma a moment to gather herself. "Are you all right?"

Emma nodded, though her heart pounded. She was not certain if she was all right or if she was just determined not to let the townsfolk see her rattled. "It's... odd," she said. "I'm not sure what to do."

Sadie's eyes warmed with empathy. "Let them wonder," she answered quietly. "You have no obligation to prove yourself to people who only see what they wish to see." She cast another glance around the street, then pressed her palm lightly against Emma's arm in an affectionate pat. "Now, come along."

They wandered farther into the heart of Crestwood, away from the bulk of stalls. The narrow roads twisted between older structures that leaned together, their eaves nearly touching overhead. Emma noticed flaking paint and crooked shutters, a testament to the town's age beneath any attempts at modern charm. She slipped her hands into her sweater pockets, forcing herself to relax. Sadie's unhurried presence helped.

Her thoughts circled back to the orchard, its trees, and the intangible magic that occasionally seemed to hover around her grandmother. Simple as it sounded, Emma yearned for a place where she was not an object of scrutiny.

Her gaze swept across each shop sign, from the chipped lettering on a tailor's storefront to a café with windows tinted by the afternoon sun. She paused near one window, glimpsing the reflection of her own face, eyes too wide. She tried to school her expression into something confident, but the tension in her neck refused to fade.

When they turned a final corner onto a modest side street, the crowds faded to only a few passersby. A row of squat cottages lined the pavement, with little gardens squeezed in front, edged by picket fences. One fence was draped in tangles of ivy. Another had an overgrown rose-bush, pink petals drooping as though exhausted by the day's chill.

Emma took in the sight, letting the quieter surroundings soak into her senses. She peered down at a loose stone, gave it a light kick, then exhaled a tremulous laugh at her own anxiety.

The last hour felt like many. She wanted to retreat

back to the orchard, but she also wondered if facing Crestwood's suspicious eyes was necessary. Possibly this was all part of accepting Sadie's world. That realization both intrigued and unsettled her.

Sadie came to a halt near a weathered bench under a small apple tree. It was not as grand as the trees in the orchard, but its branches offered a scrap of shade. "We can stop here," she said, setting down her small canvas bag. She rummaged inside and pulled out the pears she got at the market. Handing one to Emma, she gestured for them to sit. Emma obliged, settling on the bench. The wood groaned softly beneath them.

They ate in thoughtful silence, the crisp sweetness of the pear momentarily calming Emma's nerves. A pair of sparrows hopped along the grass, pecking at scattered seeds. Sadie's gaze followed them. Despite her composed demeanor, Emma detected a hint of weariness etched in her brow, as though she bore the burden of the town's scrutiny without complaint but felt its sting.

Emma took a bite of the pear, its sweetness fresh and juicy, with a hint of tartness near the core. The flesh was soft and smooth, with a slight grainy texture, and the skin added a subtle firmness to each bite. She peered at Sadie. "Do the whispers and sideways glances ever stop?" she asked quietly.

Sadie wiped her fingers on a handkerchief, then slipped it into her pocket. "They may quiet down if you stay here long enough," she said. "Or they might never stop. Many of these people cling to old stories, old fears.

The best you can do is live your life in the open, as honestly as you can."

The day's warmth began to fade, leaving the air cooler against Emma's arms. Clouds drifted high above, hints of a pale blue sky filtering through. She studied a trailing vine along the cottage wall across the street and deliberately tried to still her racing mind. For the smallest moment, she found a measure of calm, sitting there beside Sadie, chewing on sweet pear flesh.

"We can stay here a bit longer, or we can head home," Sadie said gently.

Emma turned the fruit in her hand, feeling its sticky juice sliding across her palm. She looked at Sadie, searching her grandmother's face for any sign of regret or embarrassment about the confrontation in the market. Sadie's eyes reflected concern, but also a steady resolve. It was as though she had chosen, long ago, to bear this fate without self-consciousness.

"We can go," Emma replied, her voice soft. "I've seen enough for one day."

Sadie stood. Emma followed, tossing her apple core into a nearby trash bin. Quietly, they retraced their steps toward Crestwood's central streets, though they avoided the busiest market stalls. Occasionally, someone nodded a greeting that Sadie returned, no words exchanged. Emma felt as if she wore an invisible net that caught every glance, every rumor-laden whisper.

At last, they reached a calm intersection where fewer people gathered. It was more forgiving here, aided by the sun moving across the midday sky.

Emma's heart still thrummed with something like dismay, overshadowed by the sense that she was tiptoeing through a dormant beehive. The knowledge that she might be labeled a weird newcomer bothered her, but the possibility that these stares were connected to witchcraft unsettled her even more.

She wondered if Sadie felt the same swirling tension or if she actually thrived on it in this coastal town.

FIVE

Several days later, Emma hugged her cardigan close to her chest as she walked the winding streets of Crestwood, determined to break free from the cottage for even a little while.

The morning sky hung low and gray, but the promise of a warm cup of coffee propelled her forward. Occasional glimpses of other pedestrians, shoulders hunched against the wind, reminded her that she was far from alone in this little town.

Still, the tension she'd felt in recent days weighed on her. Perhaps the local café would give her a welcome reprieve.

She soon found the café's storefront, its weather-beaten sign swinging over the door—Seabreeze Corner, letters chipped but still legible in stylized script. Flashes of bright paint around the window frames hinted at cozy decor inside. The scent of espresso enveloped her the moment she stepped in, a subtle invitation to leave her worries on the threshold. Soft lamps cast golden pools of light over small round tables, each with neatly folded napkins. Emma exhaled in relief, feeling the sea chill evaporate from her skin.

An older woman behind the counter offered a polite nod, though Emma noticed the hint of curiosity in her eyes. She returned a small smile before placing an order for a plain latte.

Her muscles struggled to loosen as she waited for her drink. She still remembered how the entire town had seemed to watch her every move last time she was there. She'd caught whispers about Sadie's name and glimpsed suspicious stares.

Despite her best efforts to erase the memory from her mind, the unease lingered. She reminded herself why she had come here: to find something resembling normal life amid all her grief.

Clutching the steaming latte, she slid into a table in the corner, hoping the subdued chatter around her would distract from her thoughts.

The café's interior was small but inviting, with a few local artworks decorating the walls. Modern touches showed in the gleam of the espresso machine, while an old-fashioned chalkboard listed pastries in various pastel chalk colors.

She spotted only a few customers spread across other tables: a pair of elderly friends trading gossip, and two teens tapping on their phones. No one paid her more than a passing glance.

Settling in, Emma retrieved a battered book on marine

biology from her messenger bag. A pang echoed through her chest at the memory of her parents, whose shared fascination with ocean life had once fueled family trips to aquariums and beachside tide pools.

She had picked up this book before leaving home— well, it wasn't home anymore. The place and all her parent's belongings were now in the hands of lawyers settling their estate. As dull as that was, she was deter- mined to keep at least a piece of their passion alive. Truth be told, it was a way to hold onto Mom and Dad.

Thumbing through the pages, she studied sketches of coral reefs and tiny fish, letting the quiet comfort her. She sipped her latte, letting the scents of coffee and steamed milk chase away the gloom that so often wrapped around her at Sadie's cottage.

At first, she managed to sink into the text, reading about coral polyps and the intricate interplay of marine ecosystems. The focus she felt was a rare gift, a small moment of serenity in a sea of chaos. She hoped to project that calm outward—maybe if she looked like any other teen quietly reading, no one would question her presence. She needed to vanish into the background, if only for a single morning.

The gentle sound of the entrance door's bell pulled her from a paragraph about clownfish behavior. She slid her gaze over the top of her book, feeling an unsteady jolt of awareness.

A figure with bright, strawberry-blond hair hurried in, carrying the energy of a gust of wind that had found its way indoors. The newcomer wore cuffed jeans and a hoodie in a bold neon shade of pink. She gave a friendly wave to the person behind the counter, then spun around to scan the tables. Her gaze locked on to Emma's corner.

Emma stiffened, instinctively lowering her eyes to the page. She pretended to read the same line about coral symbiosis, heart fluttering with the worry that this bright-haired teen might approach her. So far, she hadn't invited a conversation with anyone in Crestwood.

She feared it would stir up questions about Sadie, or about the nightmares that haunted her nights. Yet she caught movement in her periphery. Emma looked up too late to act disinterested.

"You're new here," the girl said, voice lilting with curiosity. She slid into the seat across from Emma before an invitation was given, though her grin sparkled like she didn't care about formalities. "I saw you with your nose in that book, all serious. Thought I'd say hi while I have my coffee, if you don't mind."

Emma blinked, momentarily unsure how to respond. She noticed the girl's eyes flick briefly to the marine biology cover, then to Emma's face. There was something disarming about her open manner. Still, Emma found herself on guard, uncertain what rumor might float around if they spoke.

"Um, hi," Emma managed, setting the book down. A flicker of guilt hit her for being so tense. This might be an ordinary teen, not someone prying into witchcraft or orchard secrets.

"Gale Bullock," the girl said, pointing to herself. "And you are?"

"Emma Turner," she answered quietly. Her voice caught, so she cleared her throat. "I— I just moved in with my grandmother."

Gale nodded in a show of acceptance, leaning forward with her elbows on the table. "I know," she said over the faint hiss of the espresso machine. "Word travels fast here. Don't worry, I don't care about the rumors." She tapped the rim of Emma's latte cup. "What I do care about is how you can drink a plain latte without a mountain of whipped cream. That baffles me."

Emma let out a small laugh, caught off guard by Gale's abrupt teasing. "I guess I like the taste without the extra sweetness," she said. "You probably thinking I'm a bit of a plain person, I know."

"Nothing about you seems plain," Gale replied, eyes shining with curiosity. "You've got that thoughtful vibe and a whole lot of unreadable energy. I'll forgive you for the lack of whipped cream."

Gale's directness caught Emma off guard, but there was something disarming about it—something that made her want to listen rather than pull away. She watched Gale fish a sugar packet from a bowl on the table, tear it open, and pour it into a paper cup of her own coffee. Gale stirred vigorously, flamboyantly making a show of how sweet she wanted it. Emma tried to suppress the grin that tugged at her lips.

"What brings you to Crestwood so early in the day?" Gale asked. "I figured you'd be home or out in your grandmother's orchard." She paused, then nodded to Emma's book. "Or maybe you need to do serious research on fish because you plan to be a stowaway on a boat in the harbor."

The mention of Sadie's orchard prickled Emma's nerves. It still felt too personal to admit that the orchard fed her nightmares with its eerie calm, or that strange glimpses of robed silhouettes wouldn't leave her mind. So, she forced a light shrug. "No big reason. I just wanted coffee and quiet."

Gale's expression turned mock-scandalized. "In this place? Wrong choice." She giggled, the sound bright enough to lift some of the weight from Emma's chest. "Seriously, though. There's a weird vibe swirling around Crestwood right now, creepier than usual. You must've noticed. Neighbors watch each other from behind curtains, the air feels off." She sucked in a dramatic breath and finished with, "Like the calm before a storm, you know?"

Emma's pulse kicked up a notch, suspicion fluttering inside her. That was an unnervingly accurate description of how she felt whenever she stepped outside Sadie's cottage. She clasped her hands together to keep from fidgeting.

"Yes, I— I guess there's some tension," she agreed carefully. She debated how much to reveal and decided to keep it vague. "I'm still getting used to it."

Gale eyed her with a quirked brow. "Weird how this town is always hush-hush about things. Everyone has secrets. You learn to tune it all out, or you go crazy. Me, I like to pretend half the rumors are about me. Spice up my reputation." She smirked. "That's why I appreciate random newbies minding their own business. Nothing personal, but I think we might get along just fine."

Emma breathed out, relief spreading through her body. This conversation felt refreshingly normal after days of worry. Gale's sarcasm seemed to slice through the gloom, reminding Emma that not everyone sat in judgment. Suddenly, Emma's phone buzzed in her bag, the quiet vibration startling her. She fumbled to turn it silent, cheeks warming at the interruption.

"Let me guess," Gale teased. "It's your grandmother tracking you down? Or maybe you've got a secret fiancé texting, telling you to come meet him in the orchard?"

Emma laughed. "No fiancé, secret or otherwise," she said. "I just graduated high school." She checked her phone. Spam call.

"Yeah? Me, too." Gale stuck her fist out, waiting. Emma blinked at it for a moment before hesitantly lifting her own and tapping it against Gale's.

"So," Gale said, stretching her arms over her head with a dramatic sigh. "What's next for you? University? A job? The Peace Corps to have an adventure while saving the world?"

Emma huffed a quiet laugh. "I was hoping you'd tell me."

Gale dropped her hands and shrugged. "No clue. Kind of just... rolling with life, I guess, and see what opportunities present themselves. I figured college would be a waste of time if I don't know what I want to do."

Emma nodded. "Same."

They sat there for a moment, the weight of their

aimlessness settling between them, not heavy, just there. "Guess that means we figure it out together."

Emma exhaled, something easing inside her at the thought. "Yeah. Guess so."

Gale sat back, drumming her fingers on the table. She nodded at the biology book. "I love that you're into fish. Or is it ocean stuff in general?"

"Ocean stuff," Emma answered quietly, running her fingertips across the worn cover. "My parents... Well, they studied marine wildlife. It's an interest I picked up, too."

A flicker of understanding crossed Gale's face, and her teasing smile softened. "That's pretty cool," she said, voice gentler now. "We have decent tidepools around the cove, or so I hear. I'm not a big shell collector or anything, but maybe I'll take you sometime if you're up for it. Could be fun."

Emma blinked at the casual offer. She sensed genuine warmth behind Gale's words, not pity. For the first time in what felt like ages, she allowed a surge of hope. Maybe she could form a connection or two in Crestwood that wasn't tinged with suspicion. "Yeah," she said softly. "That sounds nice."

Gale nudged her cup across the table, as if extending a peace token. "Just think about it," she said in a conspiratorial hush. "Because I also know the best store for window-shopping. It's further down by the harbor. They have cheap clothes, but they're weirdly tasteful. Up for an adventure in style?"

Gale's ideas came fast and unfiltered, leaving Emma grasping for a foothold in the conversation. A day spent browsing racks of clothes and sipping sugary frappés felt worlds away from her grandmother's quiet living room and the orchard that never seemed to stop humming in her thoughts. She pictured herself among normal teens, chattering about shoes instead of illusions. It was almost too appealing to resist.

"That could be fun," Emma admitted, letting her smile break free. The words carried a spark of real anticipation.

She sipped her cooling latte, focusing on the swirl of foam patterns on the surface. A shopping trip might be the perfect antidote to the heaviness nesting in her chest.

Gale's grin spread wide. "Great. Hand over your phone. Let's swap numbers. We can figure out a time to go."

She slid her own phone, decked out with bright stickers, across the table. Slightly flustered, Emma dug out hers as well. She typed in Gale's number, copying the digits from the pink phone screen. There was a silly joy in the exchange, like a reminder that she could still be a normal teenager forging new friendships in a new town. The phone felt reassuring in her hands as she saved Gale's name, adding a smiley emoji next to the contact without giving it much thought.

Across the table, Gale blew on her coffee, eyes shining with amusement. "If you ghost me, I'll come hunt you down in your orchard," she joked. "You can't hide forever."

Emma shook her head in mock exasperation. "I promise I won't hide. The orchard is pretty big, though."

Gale's eyes flickered with something like curiosity, a spark that suggested she was more aware of Crestwood's strangeness than her breezy jokes let on. "You should show me around sometime," she said, sounding far too casual. "I've never ventured too deep back there myself."

Caught off guard, Emma fidgeted with the corner of her book. "I'm not sure how interesting it is," she said carefully. "Just old apple trees, a few ancient oaks and some tangly paths."

"Old and tangly can be cool," Gale insisted, draining the last of her coffee. She lowered her voice as though sharing a secret. "A lot of things in this town are old and tangly, you know. Doesn't mean they aren't worth exploring."

Emma's heart gave a small flutter. It was like Gale had read her mood, teasing out the tension underlying Emma's daily life. Part of Emma wanted to warn Gale that the orchard gave her chills at night, that she dreamt of robed figures drifting among the trees. Another part of her savored the simplicity of this moment—two new friends bonding over coffee.

A clatter from the counter drew their attention. The older woman cleaning a spill glanced in their direction, and Gale offered a quick wave as if to show that all was well.

Emma remembered the cautious looks she had gotten in the market before. Here in the café, no one seemed to whisper about witches or curses. Emma felt a small surge of gratitude for simple normalcy.

Eventually, Gale stood, tucking her phone into the pocket of her jeans. "I have to head out," she said, pulling the hoodie tighter around her torso. "Dad roped me into running errands. But hey, text me. Let's actually plan that shopping trip. Trust me, you and I can find the strangest outfits and we'll look amazing, or at least we'll laugh a lot."

Emma couldn't hide the grin that tugged at her lips. "Sure," she said, voice hushed but sincere. "Thank you for... for talking to me. It's been nice."

Gale rolled her eyes good-naturedly. "I'm super nice, especially when I see someone who looks like they need a break from reading about fish." She slung her backpack over one shoulder, then paused, the teasing aura lifting for a moment. "Seriously, though. If people give you trouble about your grandma or anything else, you let me know. I'm pretty good at shutting down rumors." The last line had a protective note that made Emma's chest tighten with appreciation.

"I will," Emma managed, fiddling with the edge of her latte cup. The gratitude she felt went beyond the surface. She wondered if Gale could guess how lonely she'd been these last several weeks.

With one last wink, Gale turned and wove around the tables toward the door. A gust of briny air blew in as she opened it, fluttering the corners of Emma's pages. Then she was gone, leaving Emma to realize how empty the café felt without her bright presence.

In under twenty minutes, a stranger had shifted Emma's entire mood. She glanced down at her phone, fresh contact glowing on the screen, and let out a long exhale.

She closed the marine biology book, gathering her

things. Outside, the gray sky promised rain, but she felt a flicker of hope she hadn't experienced since arriving. Gale's invitation echoed in her mind: minted with humor, offering a glimpse at what normal friendship might look like. Emma savored that possibility as she stood, slinging her bag over her shoulder.

She cast a final glance around, noticing the small joys—warmth, coffee aromas, the hum of voices unburdened by suspicion. She left a tip on the table and with latte in hand, left the cafe, letting the salt air greet her once more.

The future still felt uncertain, layered with unseen tension in Crestwood's corners, but she held onto her phone and Gale's number like a talisman against the gloom.

Emma realized that the dread clouding her chest had softened. A single conversation, full of witty banter and open acceptance, had made Crestwood seem less hostile and more like a place she might learn to call home.

She thought back to Gale's words, about the orchard being old and tangly but potentially worth exploring. Maybe there was more than fear in that orchard too. Maybe there was a chance for growth if Emma let herself take the first step.

She kept her head high, latte cup warming her palms, and allowed herself a small, genuine smile as she slipped into the narrow streets. The memory of Gale's laughter buoyed her forward, a bright note piercing the haze of doubts in her mind.

For the first time in days, Emma felt a spark of excitement at the idea of venturing out again—this time, not as a wary onlooker, but as someone who might actually belong. And for that fleeting moment, the cold wind on her cheeks didn't feel like a warning, it felt like a push forward, a reminder that something new was waiting ahead.

CHAPTER

SIX

Emma adjusted her messenger bag across her shoulder and stepped into Crestwood's public library. She breathed in the familiar scent of old books and worn leather, with just a hint of ink lingering in the air.

The quiet was filled with the soft rustle of pages turning and the occasional scratch of a pen on notebook paper. Sunlight streamed through tall windows, casting warm patches of light on the wooden floor, where shadows shifted as people moved between the towering shelves.

A faint memory flickered through her mind—walking behind her father in a university archive, the scent of old books surrounding them. The thought made her heart ache with longing. She forced that thought aside and focused on the library's interior.

Rows of tall shelves ran from one end of the wide reading room to the other, each labeled with faded letters. The space was quiet enough for her to hear every shuffle of feet on the worn wooden floor. A clock ticked softly behind the main desk. The quiet felt hollow in a way that made her neck prickle.

She noticed a woman standing behind the desk, carefully arranging a stack of returned books. At first glance, the librarian appeared modest—her brown cardigan hung loose around her thin frame, her hands moving in neat, measured motions.

When she looked up, Emma caught a glimpse of dark hair pinned back in a simple style. A thin chain glinted at her throat. If not for the strange tension in her shoulders, Emma might have assumed she was just another quiet caretaker of old tomes.

"Welcome," the librarian said. She slid a heavy volume onto the desk. Her voice was soft, polite, yet a thread of intensity ran beneath the words. "Looking for something in particular?"

Emma swallowed, keenly aware that she was the only patron in sight. She managed a small nod. "Hello, I— sorry, I was just hoping to find some books on marine ecosystems. My father," she added, the words catching, "used to study them. I thought I'd continue... reading up on those topics." She cleared her throat to fill the silence that yawned between them. "My name is Emma."

The librarian's eyes sparkled with subdued interest. "Catherine Fry," she replied, smoothing a hand over her cardigan. "It is nice to meet you." She studied Emma in a way that felt uncomfortably close, as though she was sizing up more than a casual inquiry.

Catherine inclined her head toward the far shelves.

"We keep biology texts on the left side, two rows in. But marine ecosystems... that might mean venturing into the older shelves." She gestured to an area near the far corner, a stretch of dim aisles that looked less traveled.

Emma nodded and offered a tight smile. "Thank you." She could not quite bring herself to hold Catherine's gaze for more than a moment. A peculiar warmth pressed on her, as though the librarian's stare weighed heavily against her sense of privacy. To distract herself, Emma fixed her eyes on a posted sign listing the library's open hours.

Catherine's voice cut into the quiet again. "Were you close to your father? If you don't mind my asking."

Emma blinked at the sudden question, her pulse quickening. Even though she had come here partially because of nostalgia for her father's research, the directness surprised her. She hesitated, not wanting to come across as rude and uncertain how much to reveal to a stranger who asked too many personal questions. "Yes," she said softly. "He and I... shared an interest in sea life."

"I see." Catherine leaned forward, resting her elbows on the desk. Her dark hair fell across her shoulders in a gentle wave. She inspected Emma with an intensity that made Emma's cheeks warm. "Family bonds are... important," she continued in a voice so quiet Emma almost strained to hear it. "Sometimes we want to hold on to them, especially when the rest of the world seems to... weigh us down."

Emma's stomach lurched. The woman's tone felt far too personal, as though she probed for a deeper confession. Unsure how to respond, Emma nodded briskly. "I'm sure that is true," she managed. In the silence that followed, she thought she sensed the faintest movement of air around her. She forced herself to speak again. "I wonder if I can just go find the books myself."

Catherine didn't reply right away. Her gaze lingered on Emma's face for a moment, then drifted toward Emma's bag. Emma wondered if the woman might ask to search inside it for borrowed items. The librarian held a subtle power in that single look, enough to make Emma's skin prickle with unease.

"Of course," Catherine said, stepping back. She clasped her hands, the faint hint of a smile touching her lips. "Let me know if you have trouble locating what you need."

"Yes, thank you," Emma murmured, turning swiftly before the woman could press her with more personal questions. She stepped deeper into the library, relieved to put distance between herself and that gaze.

She wandered down the first aisle, scanning rows of hardcover spines. They glowed dully in the overhead lights. The library definitely showed its age: many books featured chipped edges or fraying covers, and the faint smell of must and old paper was more pronounced away from the main desk.

She ran her finger along the shelves, noting titles about local ecology, maritime legends, and a few about sea flora and fauna. In the relative silence, her mind drifted to the reason behind Catherine's curious interest.

Had the librarian heard rumors about Emma's family?

There was no shortage of gossip in Crestwood, especially after the tension in the marketplace that first day with Sadie.

She continued deeper into the labyrinth of shelves, ignoring the uneasy fluttering in her stomach. If she found a volume or two on marine life, she might distract herself with Dad's passion, at least for a few spare hours.

Her fingertips soon brushed the cracked spine of a promising text titled Coastal Marine Systems. She tugged it free, coughed against the small puff of dust that swirled into her face, and flipped through the brittle pages.

Graphs of tidal patterns and reef illustrations lined the heavier sections, reminding her of calmer family moments back when her parents led her through aquariums and tide pools. That memory weighed on her heart.

She shoved it down, determined not to grow teary in the middle of the library. She tucked the book under her arm and kept searching.

A few shelves over, she spotted a smaller tome labeled *Seashore Biodiversity*. She reached up and grasped it, then jumped in surprise at a soft click behind her. Slowly, she turned. No one stood there, but she could have sworn she heard a shoe against the wooden planks. Her heart thumped harder as she cast a quick glance down the aisle.

Had Catherine followed her?

She inhaled and willed herself to relax, stepping out of the row and glancing down the long corridor. The only movement was the faint flutter of the overhead lights. She reminded herself that libraries often had strange creaks and that old buildings settled. She strengthened her grip on the books and made her way to a cluster of reading tables in a corner well away from the main desk.

The table's surface gleamed with an old polish. She placed the books down and studied the swirling dust motes in a ray of sun streaming through the tall window. Then she sank into a chair, letting the library cradle her while she opened *Seashore Biodiversity*.

Her gaze drifted over minimal text, focusing on pictures of starfish, kelp, and rock crabs. She should have felt comfort in these familiar images, but her mind kept returning to Catherine's eyes.

Something about the librarian's stare unsettled her, a hint of prying too close for comfort. It reminded Emma of the suspicious glances she encountered in the market, except Catherine's concern felt more... pointed, like a needle seeking a soft spot.

She tried reading a handful of paragraphs, but she found herself turning pages without truly absorbing the words. Eventually, she sighed and closed the book.

Though she longed to remain anonymous, a gnawing sense of unease twisted at her core. She found it hard to focus on marine facts with the knowledge that Catherine might appear at any moment to ask more personal questions.

Reluctantly, Emma decided to check these two books out and head back to the cottage. Once she got home, she could curl up in her bedroom, make tea, and read in peace. Sadie might even have some interest in hearing about Emma's father's fondness for ocean research—if Emma could be brave in discussing the subject openly. The thought of her grandmother's gentle warmth bolstered her. She gripped both books tightly and rose from the table.

As she approached the center aisle, she spotted a flicker of gray fabric near a distant shelf. The presence vanished almost as soon as she saw it. For a moment, she wondered if she had glimpsed the edge of Catherine's cardigan slipping around the corner.

Biting her lip, Emma strode briskly for the main entrance. Why was she so nervous? The library was public; Catherine was only doing her job. Yet Emma could not quell the discomfort clawing at her every step.

When she reached the check-out station, she saw nobody behind the desk. She paused, uncertain if she was meant to ring a bell or hunt for the librarian. A small sign read, "Be back soon." She let out a slow breath, straining her ears.

A distant rustle came from beyond the desk, possibly from a side office or a hallway. Emma considered leaving a note, then realized she had never learned the self-checkout system—if one even existed. She drummed her fingers against the book covers, glancing around.

Her heart lurched when Catherine slipped out of a door near the back wall. This time, the librarian's expression was unreadable, her dark brows drawn together in that same probing concern. Emma tried to keep her posture relaxed, reminding herself that she was only here for books, nothing more.

Catherine offered a faint smile that didn't reach her eyes. "Reading in the quiet corner?" she asked, moving behind the main desk. Her cardigan fluttered at her hips when she turned, the fabric catching the overhead light. "You found something suitable?"

Emma lifted her chin. "Yes, these two," she said. She laid them on the desk with a decisive tap. "Thank you for your help."

Catherine ran her fingertips across the covers. A polite nod followed, yet something in her manner made Emma's pulse speed up again. Catherine pressed her lips together. "Coastal Marine Systems," Catherine read aloud, her voice soft. "That one has a few references to local tides, I believe. Perfect for continuing... your father's legacy, wouldn't you say?"

Emma swallowed. The words *legacy* and *father* on this stranger's tongue sounded off. She yearned to pry the books from Catherine's hands and leave. "I suppose so," she managed to reply, forcing a polite edge into her tone. She watched Catherine step sideways to a computer terminal for the checkout process.

Catherine typed Emma's name into the system, then paused, her eyes flicking toward Emma's messenger bag again. "Do you live near the orchard?" she asked, so casual it felt rehearsed.

Emma tensed at the mention of the orchard. She wondered who had told Catherine that detail. Crestwood was small, so perhaps the knowledge of Sadie's cottage on the orchard's perimeter was common. "Yes," she answered. "It belongs to my grandmother."

Catherine's smile sharpened, though it had no warmth. "That orchard is... interesting. The trees have a certain aura about them." Her voice dropped to a near whisper, her gaze pinned on Emma. "Do you ever feel that, lingering among the branches?"

Emma's throat tightened. The question came so unexpectedly that she nearly fumbled for words. "I—it is a peaceful spot," she ventured, refusing to reveal more. She clutched the strap of her messenger bag, knuckles whitening.

"Peaceful." Catherine let the word hang in the air. The corners of her mouth tilted, an expression hovering on the edge of condescension. She typed a few strokes, then lifted the first book, as if verifying the barcode. "Did your grandmother mention me?" she asked mildly, pressing a stamp to an inside flap. "We have... chatted about some of her herbal wisdom in the past."

The candid question tightened the knot of tension in Emma's chest. If Catherine truly spoke with Sadie about herbs or local remedies, Emma had never heard of it. She shook her head. "No. I mean, not that I recall."

Catherine's fingers stilled on the second book, her gaze flicking to Emma's face. "You seem... unsettled. Are you sure nothing is bothering you?"

Emma felt the library's hush press in, as though all the shelves had ears. Her pulse pounded in her ears.

She forced a light shrug she hoped looked casual. "I'm only in a hurry. I need to get home soon," she answered, which was not wholly untrue. The idea of retreating to Sadie's cottage now felt like a rescue.

Catherine rose to her full height and passed the stamped books to Emma. Their covers slid on the desk with a gentle rustle. "Of course," the librarian said. "Here you go. Be sure to come back if you need more."

Her voice carried an odd note that set off every alarm in Emma's mind. She nodded stiffly, whispered a quick thank you, and cradled the books protectively to her chest.

As she turned to go, a strange awareness sifted through the air behind her, as if Catherine's stare was a physical touch dragging across her back. She moved faster, refusing to glance over her shoulder.

The library foyer stretched before her. She wove between two tall shelves near the entrance, still unsettled by the faint echo of Catherine's voice. She sped through the final steps leading to the door, grateful when her hand closed on the metal handle. Pushing it wide, she emerged into the afternoon light.

Outside, the sky had shifted to a colorless gray that clung to the rooftops. Passersby moved along the sidewalk with subdued expressions, carrying grocery bags or strolling without urgency. Emma took a few shaky breaths, letting the tang of the sea breeze ground her. She pressed the book spines against her rib cage, not caring if they rubbed her slight sweater the wrong way.

She redirected her steps toward Sadie's cottage. Each footstep tapped out a slow, nervous rhythm on the pavement. The feel of the library lingered on her skin. It was almost as though some intangible presence had followed her outside. She glanced behind her once, seeing only two older men stepping into a nearby shop. Catherine was nowhere to be seen.

An unsettled pang took hold of her chest. She recalled

Catherine's quiet questions about the orchard's aura and her father's legacy, the direct mention of Sadie's knowledge. It all felt too precise, too knowing.

How much did Catherine really understand about the orchard—or about Emma?

That prying conversation left her more rattled than she cared to admit. She turned her attention to the books she held, eyes scanning the spines. Perhaps it was her imagination that made the atmosphere feel heavier, but she could not dismiss the lingering weight.

A breeze tugged a loose strand of hair across her cheek, and she brushed it aside with an impatient jerk of her fingers. She told herself not to jump to conclusions, that Catherine was only being curious or kind. Yet the memory of that woman's unwavering gaze made her heart pound again.

The pressure behind that stare had felt oddly charged, like a magnet seeking steel. She hastened her pace, eager to trade the gloom of the library for the relative safety of her grandmother's cottage.

At the next intersection, she paused to wait for a slow-moving vehicle to pass. Then the final stretch of road leading out of Crestwood's center stretched ahead, lined with a few more shops and weather-beaten fences.

The sea wind picked up a little, carrying the faint call of gulls. Emma pulled her sweater closer for warmth, though she suspected the cold in her bones came more from nerves than the weather.

She tried to calm herself by focusing on an old memory: trailing behind her father as he led her through tall library shelves in another town, one that smelled more like cleaning solution and fresh ink.

He had possessed such excitement in his voice when pointing out sections about deep-sea creatures. The recollection untangled a bit of her anxiety. She clung to that comfort, letting it remind her there was still knowledge and wonder in books. She would read these borrowed volumes at home, glimpsing a piece of the life her father had once loved.

Turning the final corner past a cluster of low-rise buildings, Emma found the sidewalk quieter, the scattered foot traffic thinning out. Beyond the rooftops, she could see the outline of distant trees. Just a short walk remained.

She tightened her grip on her books and exhaled slowly, preparing herself to share small details of the outing with Sadie if asked. She would keep Catherine's invasive questions to herself for now, though. There was no sense in stirring Sadie's worry or fueling more rumors she could not prove.

As she approached the wide curve that marked the old fence line, the breeze shifted direction, blowing the ocean's brine into her lungs. She slipped a hand into her messenger bag, finding the place where she kept her phone. The weight of the device steadied her slightly, a reminder that she was not truly alone.

She could call Gale if she felt too uneasy. Gale's cheerful and sarcastic laughter might cut through the tension in a single moment.

Still, Emma decided to wait. The library experience was fresh, and she wanted to gather her thoughts. Each echo of Catherine's voice in her memory suggested that the librarian was not as mild as she seemed.

Emma reached the outskirts of Crestwood, where neatly spaced lamps began to dwindle. The path toward Sadie's cottage beckoned, partially framed by bristling orchard trees in the distance. The late-afternoon sun dipped lower, adding an orange hue to the horizon. As she moved along the fence, she felt a dull ache in her shoulders.

She stepped around a loose stone, recalling how Catherine had said, "We have chatted about some of her herbal wisdom in the past."

Emma could not imagine Sadie casually trading knowledge with the librarian.

Sadie was private. She trusted few neighbors, and Emma had never once heard of Catherine.

Could the librarian have approached Sadie in secret, drawn perhaps by rumors of the orchard's old magic?

The notion made Emma's pulse flutter with unwelcome visions. She pictured Catherine rummaging through Sadie's herbs, her eyes scanning every corner of the cottage for glimpses of hidden spells. The image made Emma's breath feel tight.

Her foot struck a dent in the pavement, jarring her from her thoughts. She readjusted the books in her arms and focused on her breathing. The last stretch of road ahead was lined with stunted bushes, opening onto the meadow that extended to Sadie's land. A swirl of leaves tumbled across the asphalt, stirring with the late-day breeze.

The air remained unnaturally still afterward, as though the wind had paused for reasons unknown. Emma cast one last glance over her shoulder.

Far behind her, a few rooftops of Crestwood peeked above the gentle slope. No silhouette in a cardigan followed her, yet Catherine's presence remained in Emma's mind.

She gripped the spines of her borrowed books. The knowledge that she would soon be home felt like a welcome solace. She meant to spend the evening quietly, nibbling on whatever Sadie made for supper and perhaps confiding her unsettled feelings to her grandmother if the moment felt right.

At last, Emma stepped onto the narrower lane that led to Sadie's cottage. The research books were getting heavier with each step, but she refused to shift them. Their bulk acted like a shield from the uncertainty that had trailed her since leaving the library doors.

Whatever Catherine truly wanted—if she wanted anything specific—remained unclear.

Only one fact was certain: kindness didn't always hide behind a quiet voice and gentle smile.

One day, she told herself, she might discover what truly lay behind Catherine's intense stares. For now, she would keep her distance.

She lowered her gaze to the pebbled path, listening to the crunch underfoot, and resolved to stay on guard. The orchard rose in front of her like a protective labyrinth of branches. In the half-light, the trees formed a silhouette that shielded the cottage from the rest of the world.

As she slipped through the orchard gate, the final rays of sun licked the horizon, scattering a mellow glow between the trunks. The weight of the day's unsettling moments pressed on Emma's heart, but she strengthened her resolve to face them head-on, with Sadie's reassurance if needed.

She reached for the doorknob of the cottage, mindful of how the short walk had transformed her jitters into quiet purpose. The gentle darkness of early evening enfolded her as she entered the cottage, books in hand. The orchard seemed to welcome her home.

CHAPTER

SEVEN

Emma could still sense the library clinging to her long after she and Sadie finished dinner. The memory of that librarian's too-intense gaze refused to fade. Emma left the table, her bowl of stew half-finished, feeling stifled by a tension she could not name.

Outside, dusk settled over the horizon, and the last streaks of orange sky were fading into a deep, inky blue. The windows in Sadie's cottage rattled gently with the breeze that carried the salty tang of the sea. It felt as if the entire evening waited for her to do something. Anything.

She noted unease in Sadie's shoulders. Her grandmother was usually calm, the sort of presence that made Emma feel safe when the rest of Crestwood seemed to narrow its eyes. Yet even Sadie's expressions had been tight since Emma came home from the library earlier that day. They had shared a simple meal of hearty stew, but every bite left Emma feeling restless.

"I need a walk," Emma said quietly. She made herself sound certain, even though her heart felt ready to pound out of her chest.

Sadie's eyes flicked up from the bowl of stew she had barely touched. Her brow furrowed. "Don't stray far, Em," she said. "And not too late. You know how the orchard can be after dark." There was gentle concern in her warning, but Emma also heard a note of resignation. Sadie never seemed able to keep Emma contained once her mind was set.

"I'll just loop around," Emma promised. "I... I won't go too far."

Sadie let out a soft sigh and gave a faint nod. She watched as Emma pulled on a light sweater, eyes full of caution, though no further protests left her lips.

Outside, the cool evening air greeted her skin like a promise. The wind carried a hint of salt from the shoreline, but it also carried something else, an undercurrent of magic she could not fully ignore.

She closed the cottage door gently. The orchard stood before her; rows of trees shadowed in the dim light. Some distant part of her mind recalled her grandmother's repeated warnings about wandering the orchard's fringes after nightfall, yet the shimmering pulse in the air pulled her forward. Instead of heading for the small garden path behind the cottage, she veered farther, letting intuition guide her.

Every few steps, she glanced over her shoulder, half-expecting to see Sadie's silhouette lingering at the doorway. But the cottage windows glowed softly, with no sign of her grandmother stepping out.

The orchard, however, felt more alive than ever. Leaves rustled overhead in a subtle whisper. A pair of crows flapped into the sky, cawing a lament that made Emma shiver. She draped her sweater more securely around her body, aware that the temperature was dropping rapidly.

She navigated the orchard's winding rows until she reached an old gate that led beyond the property. The gate squealed when she pushed it open, the hinge stiff from disuse. Her pulse thudded with the certainty that she was crossing into uncharted territory.

Beyond lay the Enchanted Woods, or so locals called them—tall pines that towered against the night, forming a corridor of looming shapes. Her breath quickened at the sight of them rising like dark pillars in the moonlight.

She remembered Gale implying, in that teasing tone of hers, that Crestwood was a little strange. That thought comforted Emma. Besides, she had grown tired of letting fear steer her choices.

The forest floor muffled her footsteps. The dense bed of pine needles and scattered moss created a soft crunch that contrasted with the quiet swirl of wind above. A restless moon hung in the sky overhead, half-obscured by shifting clouds. Each time the moon peeked out; it revealed more of the trail.

Emma pressed forward, guided by an impulse she kept trying to label as curiosity. Still, a prickling on the back of her neck suggested something else, as if the air was summoning her closer.

It was not long before she spotted a kind of small

clearing she had never seen on her previous walks. A faint glow illuminated the open space, as though the moon had conspired to slip its silver beams through the canopy at exactly this spot. Emma stopped at the edge of the trees, her breath catching as she heard soft chanting.

She hid behind a wide tree trunk, heart hammering. Step by step, she edged forward, her curiosity warring with caution. She could just make out a figure in the center of the clearing, arms raised, voice low but steady.

He wore dark, simple clothes that clung to his lean form, and though she was not close enough to see the details of his face, her pulse raced at the sight of him. He had dark hair curled slightly around the back of his neck, and when he moved, his posture reflected a kind of poised grace that seemed part of the very night air.

Emma's body tensed, ready to bolt if this situation turned menacing. A swirl of gentle luminescence wound around his arms, pulsing as he spoke words she could not immediately decipher. Then, his voice grew clearer, and Emma realized he was reciting an incantation:

"In quiet hush, in midnight's glow,
Let storms inside me cease to blow.
By moon and breath, release this strife,
Grant gentle peace to guide my life."

He ended on a soft exhalation, and for a single breath, the glow around him intensified. The faint light rippled outward, passing through the air like a small wave. Emma felt the wave as a warm brush against her skin, easing a knot of tension in her chest she had not even known she carried. She blinked in astonishment, pressing her fingertips to her racing pulse.

Over the past weeks, she had witnessed Sadie humming and singing little verses, but this... this felt different. She sensed no threat, only a tender yearning for calm, something that resonated with her own anxieties.

The figure lowered his arms and sank to his knees, panting lightly as though the incantation had cost him considerable effort. Emma's heart squeezed in sympathy. She watched his shoulders rise and fall in an unsteady rhythm.

He dragged a hand through his hair, eyes closed for a vulnerable moment. Then, as if sensing her presence, he tensed.

She almost stumbled backward; sure he would turn hostile at the first sign of an intruder. But she could not bring herself to flee. The air crackled, charged with some unspoken tension. Emma took a resolute step into the clearing.

His head snapped up. The faint moonlight caught the sharp angles of his face. Her breath caught again, and she felt oddly exposed under his gaze. He was... gorgeous, in a way that made her heart flutter.

Long eyelashes framed eyes that glimmered with a trace of residual magic. His lips parted slightly, but he didn't speak. Instead, he studied Emma with a mixture of alarm and something softer.

Emma's mind raced. She recalled Sadie's caution about walking in the woods alone. Yet this quiet figure didn't resemble the menace she had imagined. He seemed real, anchored in the forest. The slight tension in his jaw revealed he was as uncertain as she felt.

She took another tentative step, unable to shake the sense that the clearing itself was holding its breath, waiting for her choice. Her cheeks warmed under his unwavering attention, but a small voice inside her refused to let her run after coming this far. He had performed a spell for peace. She was in no danger.

Was she?

Emma inhaled. The crisp scent of pine and damp earth invaded her senses, mingling with the faint trace of magic that clung to the clearing. His gaze was intense, yet it carried a flicker of uncertainty and maybe relief that someone else dared approach him.

Emma's mouth felt dry, and her heart kept galloping. She wanted to say something about how the clearing looked bathed in silver or how she felt the gentle pull of his incantation. But the moment left her speechless, pinned in place by the swirl of questions racing through her mind. Who was he?

A breeze rippled through the clearing, ruffling the leaves overhead. Moonlight glimmered across his face, highlighting the slight sheen of sweat that beaded at his temple.

He had said those words—invite peace—and for a single, breathtaking instant, Emma felt a calm presence drift over her fear, as if his incantation had found a home in her own chaotic thoughts. Oddly, she sensed that same calm in him as well, though she could not explain how.

A subtle cord seemed to tremble between them, as if the orchard's hidden energy had reached this far into the Enchanted Woods to bind them in a single heartbeat.

Finally, she took one more step into the clearing, the pine needles rustling beneath her feet. Her sweater slipped off one shoulder, and she hastily pulled it back up, hyperaware of just how close they already were, though several yards of moonlit grass separated them.

He rose to his feet in a fluid motion. He stood tall, though not threatening. His broad shoulders lifted with one last shaky breath before he steadied himself. They locked eyes for a second time, tension rippling in the silence. Emma felt electricity gather along her skin, as if the clearing itself thrummed with anticipation.

For a heartbeat, neither spoke. She watched his expression shift from wary alertness to a kind of puzzled fascination. mind flicked to warnings about illusions and nightmares, yet she sensed no deception in his posture. There was only the undeniable awareness that they were two strangers, drawn to the same forest for reasons neither understood.

Still, neither of them spoke. The forest air hummed with a silent question. Emma's mind raced with half-formed thoughts—her grandmother's caution, Catherine's unsettling stare, her own throbbing curiosity. She watched the man's throat bob, watched the tension in his jaw. A spark of moonlight caught in his eyes, and she saw uncertainty and longing reflected there.

She didn't run.

They simply held each other's gaze, hearts pounding

in time with the breeze. Her next breath shook, but she refused to look away. She had never felt more alive—or more on edge. And in that pulsing quiet, rich with tension, the tree branches bowed low toward the ground, as if somehow marking the meeting under the restless moon.

CHAPTER

EIGHT

The man broke the silence first. His voice carried warmth, but beneath it lay a curious edge, as though he sensed potential danger but still chose to meet it head-on. "I'm sorry if I startled you," he said quietly, stepping past a half-buried tree root. The moonlight softened the outline of his lean frame, though Emma caught a flicker of tension in his shoulders. "I didn't think anyone would wander this far into the woods at this hour."

Emma tightened her grip on the branch behind her. A moment earlier, she had glimpsed a swirl of faint lights coalescing around him, leaving her unsure of what she had seen. She had interrupted him chanting something that sounded like a prayer or a plea. It felt like an intimate moment she should've have interrupted whatever the heck he was up to.

"I don't usually come into the woods," she said. She wanted to remain composed, but her voice wavered. "I heard..." She almost admitted she had heard an odd hum that had drawn her here, but she hesitated. Her throat felt too tight. "What were you doing out there?"

He studied her carefully. In the shafts of moonlight that broke through the canopy, she saw a line of strain at the corner of his mouth. "Would you believe me if I said I needed the quiet?" He didn't smile.

She believed him, but there was more to it than just a need for solitude. A subtle energy prickled along her arms, alive and restless. Right now, she could feel it around him —a charged, unspent force humming in the air. Still, she refused to flinch.

"I think you're looking for more than quiet," she said, her voice steadier than before.

His eyes flickered toward the low brush along the clearing's edge. For a moment, Emma worried that he had seen something lurking. Then, he exhaled. "I was trying to keep control," he admitted, though that admission felt incomplete.

"Control over what?" she pressed.

A flash of what could have been frustration or embarrassment flickered in his gaze. "Spells don't always do what I want," he said. "Or maybe it's me who doesn't always do what I should." His tone carried self-irony, as though he had joked about this before. "Tonight, I thought if I focused more, I could settle the chaos inside me. You saw me chanting. I bet it looked strange to an outsider."

Emma hesitated. Spells? He said the word so matter-of-factly, as if magic was something real. As if it wasn't just a metaphor for something else. He'd said it like he really believed he could do magic.

The thought unsettled her, but she kept her expression neutral, not wanting to hurt his feelings by challenging him outright. Maybe he meant something else, some personal ritual, a way to center himself. That made more sense.

Didn't it?

But she couldn't explain away the faint silver light—which wasn't fog, at all—curling around him, shifting as if it responded to his words. Emma struggled to make sense of what she had seen. It had to be a trick of the moonlight, an illusion brought on by the eerie stillness of the clearing. Yet the air carried an undeniable charge, like something waiting to be acknowledged.

She hesitated, choosing her words carefully. "I'm not sure what I saw, if you want to know the truth.

"You don't believe in magic, do you?" His gaze flicked downward for a fraction of a second before returning to her face. "I don't let people see me practice. You weren't supposed to be here."

Emma stiffened, trying to ignore the question about whether or not she was a believer. It was easier just to leave. "I can leave if that's what you want."

His expression shifted, something indecipherable passing over it. "You don't have to leave."

The wind stirred through the clearing, carrying the scent of damp earth and pine. He swiped hair off his face and stared at Emma. She had the strange sensation that this moment had been waiting for them, that it was meant to happen.

"If anybody else in Crestwood had stumbled on me

here, they'd either run or stare like I was insane," he murmured. "I think you might be a little different."

Emma didn't know how to respond. Magic wasn't supposed to be real. But she couldn't ignore what she had seen so far. But then she thought of Sadie. Of the way the old woman had coaxed a wilting plant back to life with nothing but a few murmured words. Or the fox that had locked eyes with Emma days ago, watching her too knowingly before vanishing as if it had never been there. A strange certainty settled over her. Maybe she *had* seen something impossible.

Instead of answering, she challenged him. "So...you can do magic, then?" The word felt foreign in her mouth, like she wasn't sure she believed it even as she said it. "I assume that's what you were doing, right?"

He half-laughed, but no real humor came out of his mouth. "Yes, it's magic," he said. "I don't want to cause trouble in town when I practice so I come out here. The forest is quieter."

Emma recognized the lonely edge in that statement. She wondered if he had always carried such burdens alone. Her mind drifted to her own restlessness, how she suddenly had this shimmering pulse she felt but couldn't see. He smiled, but tension lined his jaw.

His eyes flicked to her face. "What drew you out here, anyway?"

She pressed her lips together. She could claim curiosity, but the truth ran deeper. A gentle force had guided her steps. She had walked beyond the orchard, ignoring her usual misgivings about the dark, hoping to find relief from the swirl of unease that had followed her since her visit to the library. She felt silly admitting it out loud, but what the hell. Why not just tell him what she felt?

"There was something I could feel," she admitted, her voice quieter. "Like a pull on my heart. I don't know how to explain it, but it led me here." She glanced away, suddenly self-conscious. "I thought maybe I was imagining things, but there have been a few things I can't explain." Her eyes flicked back to him, searching his face. "Nothing's making sense at the moment."

He tilted his head as he considered her. Another breeze rustled the branches overhead, scattering faint beams of moonlight that moved across the clearing's grass. "Sometimes, you need to just let what seems impossible in. It can mess with your sleep sometimes, though...knowing there are powers out there that shape our lives...our destinies."

Her heart panged with a flicker of empathy. She reminded herself that she knew nothing about him, that caution was wise. Yet a faint sense of kinship hovered in the air. She decided to keep pressing. "Is that why you chanted that incantation? To make sleep easier?"

He stiffened, edging forward as if uncertain whether he wanted to close the distance between them or retreat. "Sometimes," he said carefully. "I have powers that are... difficult to control. I have nightmares about it sometimes. I try to anchor them, keep the nightmares from spilling over into when I'm awake. When I chant, it helps calm me. Keeps my magic under control."

The tension in the clearing thickened, pressing against Emma's chest, but it no longer felt like fear. At some point, her racing heart had steadied. Now, she was simply aware of him—the quiet power lingering around him, the way the air seemed to hum with something unseen. In the corner of her vision, certain details about him shimmered, as if just beyond her full understanding. A part of her wanted to step back, but she refused.

"I am not here to judge you," she said, voice low. "I don't even know your name."

He regarded her, a flicker of hesitation crossing his face. There was wariness there, but also something resigned—like he knew he couldn't take back what she had already seen. His shoulders shifted slightly, tension coiling beneath the surface. "I didn't mean for this to get complicated," he admitted, voice low.

Emma let out a short, humorless breath. "Then stop making it complicated." The words came out sharper than she intended. She was done with cryptic half-answers, the ones whispered in the library, the ones lingering in the orchard, the ones he seemed determined to give now. "Just tell me... who are you?"

His jaw tightened, and for a moment, she thought he might brush her off again. Instead, he exhaled slowly, as if weighing his options. "You might regret asking," he murmured.

Emma's pulse kicked up, but she refused to flinch. "I'll take my chances."

Something in him shifted. He took a slow step closer, and in the dim light, she caught flecks of gold in his eyes. "My name is Ian Williams."

A muscle in his jaw twitched, and a strange light flickered behind his eyes. He leaned back, crossing his arms in a loose but guarded stance. "Your turn," he said.

"Emma Turner," she said. The simple word tumbled out too quickly. She breathed in, searching for something else to add, some reassurance that she was not an intruder. "I live near Crestwood," she said, proud that her voice didn't quake. "My grandmother is Sadie Turner."

He studied her more closely now, as though memorizing the shape of her face. "Emma," he repeated, his tone musing. Silence stretched taut between them again, charged with a conflicting sense of caution and magnetic pull.

She wet her lips nervously. "So, Ian," she ventured. "How often are you out here...keeping the nightmares at bay?"

His shoulders dropped a fraction, releasing some of his tension. He looked down at the grass. "A lot," he replied. "It rarely helps as much as I hope it will, but it's all I have." He sounded younger for a moment, less guarded, and Emma felt an unexpected ache in her chest. "The illusions the incantation produce are supposed to protect me but sometimes...they don't seem to. And they can cause... trouble."

"Illusions?" she asked, curious.

"Did you see the silver light around me as I cast the spell?"

She nodded, glancing at the small ring of disturbed leaves where the swirl of his magic had been. Pale moonlight made them shimmer, as though they had been dusted in starlight. "So, that's what that was," she said carefully. "I did see them; rather... intense."

He stared at her. "They are," he admitted. "That's what I'm trying to control. Some illusions get away from me, some of them lock out the nightmares. Others try to take control of me. I don't always know how to manage them. That is why I came out here tonight." Another brief pause. "Do you know about illusions?"

Emma shifted her weight, uncertain how to respond. She didn't understand the strange magic swirling in Crestwood. Before coming to Crestwood, she didn't even know magic was a real thing. "I'm... I don't know anything about magic. All I did was wander beyond the orchard fence and run into you. Well, there's my grandmother who I'm pretty sure does something sort of magical. But I thought she was just...eccentric."

His gaze sharpened. "You live by the orchard?" The question pinned her, as though he recognized something significant in her mention of orchard fences.

She didn't like the sudden weight of his focus. Yet she would not deny it. "Yes, my grandmother Sadie's cottage is right next to the orchard. But I prefer the forest. It's my Zen place."

He gave a nearly imperceptible nod. "There is a different kind of energy there," he said. "It helps me think." Then his lips quirked in a faint apology.

Emma nearly let out a nervous laugh, but she smoothed the sound away. "We all have reasons to search, I guess," she said.

Emma noticed how still the night had become part of

the conversation, as if the forest itself was listening. She could feel the subtle shift in his presence, like an unseen force testing the space between them, searching for fear or awe. But whatever it was, it passed over her, meeting no resistance—like wind against stone.

To her own surprise, she felt steady. Her gaze lingered on him, the tension in his stance, the way his arms remained close to his chest, as if bracing for something. And then, barely perceptible, a tremor. A fleeting sign of uncertainty beneath all his guarded strength.

She inhaled a steadying breath. "I should get back," she said. "It's late."

"Do you want me to walk you back?" he asked.

Emma lifted her chin. "I can get home on my own," she said, her tone steady. "I can take care of myself."

Even as she said it, she remembered the unease she'd felt stepping into the trees. However, she'd come this far, drawn by something she couldn't name, into a moment she hadn't expected. She still didn't understand what she had witnessed, but she wasn't running from it. And that had to count for something.

He watched her carefully, then dipped his head in a semblance of a nod. "I'm sure you can," he murmured. "And I suspect you may not be scared easily."

She answered him with a brief smile, though her heart fluttered again. She knew there was more to their strange connection than chance. This meeting bristled with the kind of tension that felt like an open door to something unknown. It both excited and unnerved her. "I guess not," she said, echoing the words she had spoken earlier.

He inhaled deeply, as if gathering the nerve to speak, but instead, his gaze flicked to the faint markings his chanting had left in the grass. Whatever words he might have offered, he swallowed them. Slowly, he unfolded his arms. The air around them thickened, turning the clearing into a pocket of subdued light.

On impulse, Emma glanced at the sky. The moon had climbed higher, its silvery light filtering through the branches and painting delicate lines across the ground. A quiet unease settled over her. She wondered if it was as late as she feared.

She bent to pick up her bag, dusting off a stray leaf from the flap. "Well," she said, clearing her throat. "I should go."

He took a half-step forward, then paused. "Yeah. Guess so."

She wanted to ask a hundred things. She wanted to stand there until dawn, picking apart the mysteries behind his eyes. But a heavier caution tugged at her thoughts. She should go. "Yeah," she said simply.

They stood in silence a few moments more, letting that last flutter of introduction settle between them. Emma's pulse sped up. She pictured the orchard's winding path, waiting to guide her back to Sadie's house.

A pang of regret twisted in her chest because she knew that, come morning, she would probably question the reality of everything she saw and felt tonight. She would wonder if she had fallen under a fleeting illusion. But the steady edge of her senses told her this was genuine, or at least as genuine as it could be when two strangers meet by moonlight and share glimpses of fragile truths.

Finally, she slung the strap of her bag over her shoulder and took one step backward. "I guess... I'll see you 'round," she ventured, not sure if it was a promise or a question.

Ian offered a cautious nod, though his gaze flicked over the clearing again, as if checking for watchers. "Hopefully," he said. His voice lingered with a quiet note of uncertainty. "Take care, Emma."

She ran her thumb over the bag's worn fabric, then turned. A strip of grass parted under her boots, and a swirl of faint moonbeams guided her across the clearing. She didn't look back until she reached the tree line. When she glanced over her shoulder, she caught a final glimpse of Ian standing in that circle of pale light, arms at his sides. He watched her, guarded intensity woven into his stillness. Something flickered in the air around him, a trace of silver that might have been leftover magic.

Then Emma turned and slipped through the trees, letting the forest's hush swallow her footsteps. The name Ian repeated in her mind, anchoring itself there with quiet insistence.

Emma.

Ian.

Their cautious exchange of names felt like a first enchantment all its own, a subtle shift that promised something she could not name. She followed the faint path leading back toward the orchard, unsure how she would sleep tonight with her thoughts so thoroughly awake.

CHAPTER

NINE

Morning light filtered through the cottage's curtains, and Emma blinked awake with a dull ache in her chest. Instantly, last night came to mind—the Enchanted Woods, Ian's unsteady inhale nudging the quiet air, his incantation lingering like a half-remembered melody. And those gorgeous eyes and face.

She pressed her hand to her forehead. The encounter felt so vivid that she half-expected to find a faint glow still clinging to her skin. Instead, she saw only the humble furnishings of her grandmother's guest room: an old wooden dresser, a few framed photographs of her parents, and the corner of her backpack jutting out of the closet. All ordinary yet now set against the backdrop of a single extraordinary meeting.

Her pulse fluttered with nervous excitement. She had spent half the night replaying every moment—how Ian's eyes caught the moonlight, how the faint runes around him had pulsed before fading. There was something about him that stuck with her, something just out of reach. He wasn't just mysterious; he felt like a puzzle she suddenly needed to solve.

Every word they'd exchanged ran through her head, tangled with the strange sense that she'd brushed up against something she wasn't meant to see.

Ian had been careful with his answers, like someone used to keeping things to himself, but there had been something else too; a flicker of interest, like maybe he hadn't expected her to hold her ground. That thought sent a restless energy through her. She wasn't sure what unsettled her more—the strange magic she'd witnessed or the realization that she wanted to see him again.

Curiosity burned in her, but so did a quiet thrill. Had she imagined that pull between them, or had he felt it too? The question made her stomach twist in a way that wasn't entirely unpleasant.

At one point, she had nearly written a note to Sadie about the whole thing, hoping for some kind of explanation. But the thought of the look on her grandmother's face made her tuck the idea away.

Early that morning, she had slipped out of bed, thinking maybe Sadie was already up—but her door was still closed, so Emma let it be. She paced through the cottage, fingers brushing over the worn wood of the kitchen table, and the cool metal of the sink.

No matter what she did, Ian was still there in her thoughts, his voice, his presence, the way the air had shifted around him. And now, in the quiet morning light, she had no idea what to do with any of it.

The muffled clink of teacups in the kitchen signaled that Sadie was up, likely stirring her usual brew of herbs. Emma rose, legs still stiff from her tense walk in the woods the previous night. She grabbed her hoodie from the chair, slipped it on, and made her way to the kitchen, ignoring the sheen of morning sweat on her neck.

The scent of rosemary and sea salt greeted her the moment she stepped in. Sadie stood at the stove, gently tapping a wooden spoon against a small pot of steaming water. Sprigs of fresh rosemary bobbed on the surface, their delicate green needles curling in the heat. A swirl of salt crystals had settled at the bottom, giving the water a faint brine smell that reminded Emma of the ocean's edge.

"Sleep well, Em?" Sadie's voice was calm, though Emma sensed an undertone of watchfulness. She realized it might be more difficult to hide her restless night than anticipated.

"More or less," Emma lied gently. "I... just have a lot on my mind."

Sadie hummed in response, pouring the infusion into two small cups. She held one out and offered a soft smile. Emma accepted it, careful not to spill the hot liquid. The tang of salt mingled with the woodsy aroma, tickling her senses in a pleasant, if unusual, way.

They sat at the small wooden table in the corner, where the morning sun spilled through the window, illuminating the dust motes dancing in the air. Emma sipped the infusion, letting it warm her from within. Sadie took a measured breath, gazing over Emma's face as though searching for answers Emma wasn't yet ready to volunteer.

The silence lingered until Sadie cleared her throat. "You seem unsettled," she said softly. "More than usual."

Emma traced her fingertips along the chipped rim of her cup. She wondered how much to reveal. Memories of Ian's quiet intensity tugged at her, urging her to confide in Sadie. But something held her back—a mix of excitement and protectiveness. She didn't want anyone tearing away the heady mystery too soon, even if that someone was her own grandmother.

"I... had a strange walk last night." Her voice sounded small in the stillness. "I stepped into the woods and went a bit farther than planned. Nothing bad happened, I promise." The last part spilled out in a rush, as though she expected Sadie to scold her.

Sadie placed her cup down, the faint clink echoing. "I could feel some stirring in the air," she said. Her gaze sharpened with gentle worry. "A shift in the orchard's ambiance, and beyond."

Emma looked up quickly. "You felt that?"

"Mmm. Intuition, especially related to family." Sadie paused, pressing her lips together. "You didn't see anything... suspicious, did you?"

Images of Ian and the swirl of silver light spooled through Emma's mind. She took another sip of the briny tea and willed her pulse to steady. "Nothing I couldn't handle," she finally replied, hoping the vagueness would suffice.

Sadie's eyes narrowed slightly, but she chose not to press further. Instead, she reached into a small wooden box on the counter and took out a handful of dried leaves. She scattered them into a mortar, added a couple of pale petals, and began to grind them with confident, measured motions. As she worked, she spoke with quiet deliberation.

"There are plenty of young men in Crestwood," she said, pressing the pestle into the herbs to release a fragrant aroma. "Some harmless, others less so. The fishermen's sons, for example, spend half their nights by the docks. They mean no harm, though they've a reputation for mischief after too much ale."

She paused, glancing at Emma. "Then there's Gareth, who fancies himself to be a traveling bard. He plays music well enough, but he'll spin a tale just to see a girl blush. He's not a bad guy, just a bit of a fool sometimes."

Emma managed a faint laugh. She had heard rumors about Gareth's flirtations down at the local café. Though Candace, the barista, often teased that Gareth's guitar got more kisses than any woman he pursued.

"Then there are those who skirt the edge of power they shouldn't toy with," Sadie continued, "Crestwood is old, Em. We've got families whose gifts run deeper than they let on. There are people here who value their privacy. Others chase illusions for their own ends."

"Privacy? You mean secrecy, don't you?" Emma asked. "They're not the same thing."

Sadie's hands stilled for just a moment, her gaze flicking up to Emma, and a small, knowing smile tugged at the corner of her mouth before she resumed grinding the herbs.

"Always knew you were a sharp cookie," she said. "And you're right. Privacy and secrecy are not the same thing. Privacy is about boundaries, keeping something for yourself, deciding what parts of your life you share and what parts you don't. Secrecy, though... secrecy is about control. It's about keeping something hidden because of what might happen if it were known."

She dusted off her hands and reached for another bundle of herbs. "Crestwood is filled with secrets," she admitted, "but if you pay attention, you'll notice the people who have them."

Emma leaned against the counter, watching Sadie work, the rhythmic motion of her hands not quite masking the weight behind her words.

"Sadie," Emma said, letting her gaze roam to the small window overlooking the orchard. Rows of trees parted the golden light in neat lines. "Suppose I did meet someone out there. Someone who could do...magic. How would I know if they were dangerous or not?" She tried to keep her tone neutral, but her heartbeat thudded in her ears.

Sadie set the pestle aside. "Did you meet someone in the woods, Emma? A young man—someone with a talent for illusions?" Concern and understanding blended on her face. She sighed softly. "I suspected as much."

Emma's pulse quickened. "I... yes. His name is Ian. He seemed serious. Intense. But I wasn't scared of him at all." She hesitated, recalling the gentle wave of calm that brushed over her when he had finished his chant. "He was practicing magic, but it didn't feel dangerous. Just a bit strange."

Sadie lifted an eyebrow, pressing her palm flat on the table as though grounding herself. "If it didn't feel dangerous, what did it feel like?" she asked.

Emma struggled for the right words. "It was...sad. I think he was looking for comfort. Like he was trying to quiet something inside himself." The memory of Ian's voice, low and pleading as he recited that incantation, nearly made her shiver again. "He wasn't a threat."

Sadie pressed her lips together, carefully choosing her next statements. "There are talented men and women who practice magic in Crestwood, some with good hearts, some with wounds they refuse to heal. You must be cautious, though. Magic doesn't reveal a person's true intentions."

Emma studied her grandmother's face. She saw no immediate disapproval, a worried acceptance that magic was weaving Emma deeper into Crestwood's tapestry than anticipated. "I'll be cautious," Emma promised. "But I can't deny... I'm curious."

"I see that," Sadie whispered, her features softening. She resumed grinding the herbs, releasing a gentle wave of earthy fragrance into the air. "Curiosity drives many toward knowledge. Just don't let it overshadow your sense of self-preservation."

They lapsed into a simpler conversation after that, sipping the rest of their tea and mulling over the day's mundane tasks. Sadie mentioned needing to restock certain supplies in her herb cabinet, maybe a trip to the local stalls if it stayed sunny. Emma responded absently, her mind compulsively wandering to the forest and that memory of silver light curling around Ian like a cat seeking warmth.

LATE MORNING SUNSHINE found Emma in the living room. She flicked through one of Sadie's dog-eared books about local flora, trying and failing to focus on the passages describing foxglove toxicity. She let the book slip shut, drawing her knees up on the creaky armchair and pressing her face against them.

The memory of Ian's eyes refused to fade. That unwavering gaze had been neither cold nor truly warm—more akin to a silent question, as though asking if she could witness his vulnerability without recoiling.

Her chest fluttered with what felt like the first stir of real excitement since coming to Crestwood. A pang of guilt followed; she recalled her parents' accident again, how grief had overshadowed every step she'd taken in this sleepy seaside town. She wasn't used to anticipating anything with eagerness, but now her thoughts sparked with an energy that both thrilled and frightened her.

Footsteps approached, and she looked up to see Sadie in the doorway. Her grandmother's expression had a new briskness. She held a small woven basket in one hand, lines of practicality returning to her forehead.

"I have an idea," Sadie said. "It's a lovely day, and

you've spent enough time indoors. Perhaps we ought to take a walk through the orchard."

Emma noticed the subtle shift in Sadie's tone—like the older woman was deliberately steering Emma away from thoughts of men and illusions. Her grandmother's gentle attempt to distract her wasn't as transparent as she thought it was, but it was well-meaning.

"The orchard?" Emma asked, tension easing from her shoulders a fraction. She glanced outside again, noting the speckled shadows dancing under the apple trees. "Sure, if you want."

"I do," Sadie replied, smiling. "There's a small clearing behind the older rows. I'd like to show you around, point out some carvings, maybe gather some herbs that grow near the base of the trees. This orchard is more than just a place for trees and fruit. It has a history—our family's history."

Uncertainty tightened in Emma's chest. She recalled the strange symbols she had spotted before, etched into certain trunks, the fleeting sense of being watched by silent boughs. Sadie had never invited her for a formal tour. They had ventured among the trees casually but never with the promise of exploring deeper corners.

"That sounds good," Emma replied. Her palms were sweating, but she stood anyway, unwilling to let Sadie see her nerves. "Should I grab a jacket? It's sunny, but the orchard can be chilly in the shade."

Sadie nodded, adjusting her basket. "If you like."

Emma grabbed her coat from the closet and met Sadie at the back door, where she stood with a basket hooked over one arm. Outside, the wind stirred against the windows, hinting at a breezier afternoon.

As Emma reached for the doorknob, she realized part of her desire was to feel it—the quiet pulse of the orchard's magic, that subtle hum that sometimes sent a shiver over her skin.

Sadie turned to Emma and offered a small but encouraging smile. "Ready?"

Emma blew out a breath. "Yes. After you."

"Tell me a bit more about the clearing in the orchard," Emma asked. She glanced at Sadie's basket, noticing the intricate pattern of silver charms woven into the rim.

Sadie's expression turned pensive. "We call it the orchard's small heart. A ring of apple trees encircles the space, and in the middle, the ground is covered in soft grass year-round. Your ancestors often performed blessings there, nothing grand, just small ceremonies to protect the orchard. I thought you might like to see it up close."

Emma felt a subtle pulse in her chest, as though some hidden part of her recognized the tug. She couldn't help recalling how Ian's incantation in the woods had similarly pulled her forward, how her own curiosity seemed tied to energies in ways she barely understood. Perhaps it made sense that Sadie wanted to show her the orchard's deeper spaces, too.

They passed the threshold leading to the back patio, and pastel sunlight brushed against Emma's cheeks. She saw the orchard's rows stretching out in gentle arcs, some trees heavy with apples, others more gnarled and barren.

A few wildflowers dotted the edges, stirring in a lazy breeze.

From here, nothing looked extraordinary, just an old orchard. Yet Emma knew better. She'd felt the orchard's pulse before.

Sadie turned briefly, resting a hand on the doorknob. "Would you like to walk through the orchard now, Emma?" Her tone was warm, a gentle invitation that held a promise of shared understanding.

Emma opened her mouth, the memory of Ian's face still flickering in the back of her mind. She closed it again, nodded, and stepped forward. She would deal with her warlock thoughts later; for now, she would follow Sadie's lead.

A smile touched her grandmother's eyes. "Good. Let's explore."

TEN

Out in the orchard, bright streaks of midmorning sunlight filtered through the canopy of apple trees, and the tang of damp earth rose into the still air. Sadie walked outside, moving carefully across the uneven ground.

Emma followed, her heart fluttering with a quiet unease as the orchard seemed to breathe around them. She marveled at how she had only seen random trees before when she visited with her parents; now the orchard felt so connected and alive. It was a bit weird.

Birds soared overhead in perfectly timed arcs, their calls echoing between the trunks. The sudden rush of wings made Emma pause. She tilted her head to watch the birds wheel in a fluid circle, then settle on a distant row of branches.

She could not quite shake the sense that those creatures were performing a serene dance designed to capture her attention. Sadie gave a mild shrug, explaining in a measured tone that flocks sometimes lingered here, drawn by old seeds or leftover scraps of fruit. Yet Emma sensed more than random chance in their flight.

A tingle prickled the back of Emma's neck, rippling through her body in a surge of electricity that made her breath hitch. The world around her sharpened, as though she were experiencing it in more dimensions than she ever had before. Colors deepened, sounds stretched into something layered and for a moment, she swore she could feel the pulse of the earth itself.

She reached out, pressing her fingers against the rough surface of a tree. The texture was real, but more than that—beneath her fingertips, she felt something thrumming, alive in a way that defied logic. It wasn't just wood and sap; it was energy, movement, awareness. The connection sent a rush of something wondrous through her, something impossibly vast yet deeply intimate.

Then she pulled her hand away. Instantly, the world dulled. The extraordinary sensations faded, leaving only the ordinary warmth of the afternoon and the gentle rustling of leaves.

Had she imagined it?

The power that had coursed through her just seconds ago felt like a dream slipping from memory. She swallowed hard, unsure of what to make of it.

And yet, she couldn't quite shake the feeling that something had just woken up inside her.

Sadie continued deeper into the clearing. The grass parted around her ankles, revealing patterns of exposed roots along the earth. Emma glanced over her shoulder, where the cottage's white stone walls and weathered roof peeked through the orchard's outer edge.

A half-dozen apple trees, gnarled but still lively, surrounded them. Many bowed with age, their trunks knotted, bark chipped. Others stood taller, leaves trembling with a breeze Emma could not feel on her cheeks.

Sadie stopped beside a wide oak tree bearing faint unfamiliar carvings, curved lines and pointed crescent shapes. On the tree, Emma also saw loops that reminded her of a language she had glimpsed in one of Sadie's journals she found open on her desk.

As she moved closer, the patterns became clearer. Some looked freshly cut, as if someone had run a blade along the bark only days before. Others seemed ancient, half-consumed by the tree's healing growth. Emma bit her lip. A swirl of nerves unfurled in her stomach.

She had dreamed of symbols like these. In nocturnal visions that blurred reality, she had seen slender ribbons of light twisting into shapes she could not name. Confronted with them now in broad daylight, she felt a strange blend of excitement and unease. She could almost hear an echo in the orchard's hush, beckoning her to make sense of what she was seeing.

"What are these things?" Emma asked.

"Runes," Sadie said, running her fingers lightly over one of the older carvings. "They're used for many things—marking boundaries, storing intentions, even holding echoes of the past."

Emma studied the symbols, their edges worn smooth in some places, sharp in others. Storing intentions. The phrase settled in her mind, heavy with meaning.

"And these?" Emma gestured to a cluster of interwoven markings that seemed to hum beneath her fingertips.

Sadie's expression grew thoughtful. "Some amplify magic, making spells stronger, more precise. Others offer protection—wards that guard against what shouldn't cross certain thresholds. And some," she hesitated, her palm hovering over a delicate spiral of runes at the base of the trunk, "some are meant to transform or disguise, weaving illusions into the air, changing what people see—or what they remember."

A chill curled around Emma's spine, despite the afternoon warmth. She reached out but stopped just short of touching one of the symbols, uncertain if she was ready to feel whatever history it held. She was still struggling with the hyperawareness she'd just experienced, trying to make sense of it.

"Who carved them?" Emma asked, wanting to press her palm against the tree trunk.

The bark would feel warm under her skin, as the morning sun soaked into it. But she wasn't ready to feel everything around her in more vivid detail again, like someone had turned up the volume on the world.

Sadie paused, crossing her arms against the mild breeze that occasionally swept through the orchard. Her expression remained gentle, but Emma caught tension in the line of her shoulders.

"Your ancestors carved the old ones," she said, voice

low. "Some families pass down traditions in diaries or song. We Turners have left clues in the orchard for generations." She paused, letting the breeze carry her words. "Are you curious about them?"

Emma's pulse quickened. She wanted to dig further, to ask precisely what these runes meant—were they messages, or something else entirely?

More importantly, she wanted to ask what was happening to her.

Why was she feeling all these strange sensations?

Were they real?

If they were, then whatever was happening meant her life was about to change in ways she couldn't imagine. If they weren't, did it mean she was delusional from grief?

Each time she thought of a question, her mind buzzed with memories of strange happenings in this orchard. Things she couldn't possibly know or remember because she was so young when they happened. Like the time when she was five and she heard the wind in the orchard sigh her name. She brushed the memories off as grief-fueled imagination. It was easier to do that than accept her family was anything other than ordinary.

The birds lifted off again, swirling in unison, their calls echoing across the orchard. This time, Emma watched them with silent wonder. They didn't scatter in chaos but rose in a synchronized pattern, as if some hidden hand guided their flight. She could not decide if it comforted or unnerved her. Sadie followed her gaze.

"It always amazes me," Sadie said. "They must find plenty of seeds, or enough vantage points atop our branches." She offered Emma a small, knowing smile. "Crestwood is full of small wonders, you know."

Emma answered with a forced laugh. "Well, even small wonders can be overwhelming," Emma managed, letting her fingers trace the carved lines on the bark. She felt the slight indentation where the symbol dipped inward. The texture reminded her of newly healed skin. "I feel like I'm missing half the story whenever I look around here."

Sadie's eyes flickered with empathy, but she offered no immediate clarification. Instead, she turned slightly, drawing Emma's focus to another tree a few paces away. The trunk there bore swirling runes that looked like roiling waves. Emma suppressed a shiver, recalling how her parents had vanished in a terrible storm. The orchard's carvings conjured that memory as a sudden ache in her chest. Her hands fell back to her sides.

"Let me show you something." Sadie moved carefully around some low, tangled roots. She sighed; her voice hushed. "Look at the base of this one." She indicated the tree with a tilt of her chin.

Emma crept forward. A scattering of pale flowers had taken root in the grass by the trunk. They were white, with lavender-tinted edges, and gave off a faint but pleasant perfume laced with something cool and faintly sweet, like rain-soaked herbs. Beneath their small petals, a sequence had been etched.

Emma bent close enough to see that the lines over-lapped. Perhaps ages ago, a carver had started a pattern, only for the bark to grow over part of it. She stared at the half-hidden shape, wondering if it once spelled a name.

"It almost looks like an inscription," Emma said, her throat dry. "But I can't read it."

Sadie nodded, kneeling to brush away a fallen leaf, revealing a little more of the inscription. Her posture seemed composed, though her eyes glimmered with something like regret.

"Many of these markings hold personal significance—names, prayers, or blessings. Some might be warnings." Her voice trailed off. "Over the years, the orchard has been a place where family members could leave their mark."

Emma inhaled, forcing herself to speak. "Did...did my parents carve any runes on these trees?" The need to touch any runes her parents had carved overwhelmed her. Not because she believed they were magical but because she wanted to connect with something living her mom and dad had touched.

Sadie rose to her feet, dusting bits of bark from her hands. She wandered over to an apple tree, the lower part of the trunk covered with runes. "These." She pointed at a cluster of runes carved in a circle. "These." She pointed at the carvings, the ancient script curling and weaving into a pattern of delicate knots and intersecting lines. Some were simple, their edges softened by time, while others remained deep and deliberate, as if etched with certainty.

"These are binding runes," Sadie said quietly, her voice carrying the weight of memory. "They're meant to tie people together—not just in love, but in life. A promise. A connection that can't be broken, even by time."

She ran her fingers over the grooves, tracing them with the care of someone who had done so many times before. "Your parents carved these," she said, glancing at Emma. A faint, wistful smile crossed her lips. "On the day they told me they were expecting you."

Emma's breath caught in her chest as she went to the tree and pressed her palm flat against the bark.

"They wanted the trees to remember," Sadie said. "To hold the moment long after they were gone." She paused, her voice quieter now. "And they do. Even now."

Emma swallowed hard, stepping closer. The runes, once just strange shapes in the bark, suddenly felt like something more. A message left behind. A promise carved in wood. "It's a lovely memory."

"It's more than just a memory," Sadie replied. "Love is strong magic. Sometimes, in extraordinary circumstances, the orchard chooses to act on that magic." She studied Emma's face, eyes softening at the flicker of confusion that must have been obvious. "It is not simply about what we carve. It is about the intent behind it, the bond between us and this land. You can think of it like a partnership, though not everyone believes that."

"What do you mean the orchard can choose to act?" Emma scoffed. "They're trees."

Uncertainty trembled in her chest. She kept recalling her dreams and the strange sensations she kept feeling every time she got near the orchard. Something whispered to her that the orchard was more than a cluster of trees. That they were alive, watchful.

The notion hovered between comforting and unsettling. She hated that she could not label it as wholly one or the other. She hated, even more, that she felt like she was going crazy.

Sadie took a measured breath. "Trees can react to the energy we carry, particularly in families with... a certain heritage. Messages take root in living wood. If there is enough synergy, something stirs and those with special abilities awaken to their powers."

She paused, hesitating as though unsure how much to reveal. "Your parents once believed that but, sometimes, it's easier to choose a simpler life when you know that awaking to the magic...complicates things."

Emma's heart clenched. She recognized the gentle sorrow in Sadie's expression. Although part of her wanted to question more about what they truly believed and why they abandoned these orchard traditions, she also feared dredging up anything that might complicate her already fraught life. A swirl of frustration accompanied her curiosity.

She tried to shift the focus. "Well, it's a lovely idea anyway, these runes." She let her finger follow the lines of the swirl nearest her. When she felt a faint vibration thrum beneath her fingertip, she jerked her hand away.

Sadie offered a slight nod. Her gaze drifted to the tree's crown, where leaves rustled in a mild breeze. "You feel it, too. I knew you would. Those who carved these runes knew it was important to document their presence in the orchard, to create a connection with these trees that we can feel today. Other families did the same. Some used their own symbols, some used the runic alphabets. The orchard has seen them all."

Emma swallowed, absorbing the gravity of Sadie's words. She thought about illusions she had glimpsed in her peripheral vision over the last weeks, things she dismissed as fatigue or grief. A prickling sensation ran up her arms. The orchard stood at the crossroads of something bigger than either of them, though she could not define it. It left her in a state of fragile wonder.

Emma let silence settle, and the orchard responded in kind. She noticed how the runes on the bark cast tiny shadows in the sun's shifting light. The gnarled tree trunk seemed to stand as a sentinel, protecting centuries of stories pressed into it. A gust of wind swept through the clearing, rustling leaves and scattering a handful of petals from the tiny white flowers. The birds sang again, as if stirred by an unseen cue.

"Sadie," Emma said, "about the fox I saw you talking to the first day I was here. It seemed like it understood everything you said. Foxes usually steer clear of humans, so why is that one so attached to you?"

Sadie's mouth curved in a thoughtful smile, and she took a half-step closer to Emma. "As with all living creatures, it's all about trust. Sometimes a fox is just an animal. Sometimes, it's... a messenger. Magic exists in the space between belief and proof. Your instincts are guiding you to pay attention. Perhaps it is only a curious fox. Perhaps it is more."

Emma frowned. The answer did nothing to clear her confusion. She let it go, knowing they were both skirting around something bigger. Sadie knew more than she was willing to say—at least right now—and Emma wasn't ready to hear it anyway. The orchard's quiet felt almost expectant, as if it wanted them to talk more about its deeper secrets, but neither of them did.

Emma glanced at the carved runes again, letting her hand linger on the trunk. She could feel a subtle hum, as if the orchard's heartbeat pulsed under her fingertips.

In a small surge of boldness, she tried to focus her mind, wondering if the swirl in the bark would shift or glow. Nothing happened. Emma's breath escaped in a slow exhale.

Was it crazy to hope for some dramatic sign to prove she wasn't going crazy?

Sadie cleared her throat softly. "I brought you out here because I wanted you to see a fraction of why this place matters, not just to me but to everyone in the Turner family, past, present, and future. There may come a time when you need to learn more about these carvings, or the orchard's past." She paused; her voice wisely calm. "When you're ready, I will help you. I promise."

Emma's chest tightened at the gentle note of reassurance. She realized she wanted to cling to Sadie's words, to the idea that answers waited whenever she chose to seek them. Yet she also felt a flicker of dread over what those answers might be.

For a moment, she pictured illusions running wild, tree runes blazing with raw power, or the fox leading her somewhere she could not return from. She blinked the visions away.

"Help me with what?" Emma asked quietly, her voice shaking. This was getting stranger by the second. "I know you want to help me after...after what happened. And I appreciate it. Truly." She walked closer to the older woman, though she stopped just shy of an embrace. Something in her needed to maintain distance, uncertain of which boundaries felt safe to cross right now.

Sadie nodded, then gently backed away and gazed toward the orchard's far boundary, where more weathered trees with more runes stood. The flock of birds, which had settled for a moment, took off once again in a flurry of gray and brown. Their piercing cries resonated like a chorus above the treetops. Emma could not tell if the orchard guided them or if they simply soared of their own accord.

Emma grew keenly aware of the sweet wildflower aroma underfoot, the fragrance thick enough to be almost dizzying. Wind ruffled her hair, but the leaves on the trees seemed to remain motionless, as if waiting for the next step in an unspoken ritual.

Emma felt her heartbeat slow, each thud matching the quiet pulse she could almost sense through the soil. She shifted her stance, placed one hand on the carved bark, and let her curiosity and anxiety merge into a single breath. She realized that, beneath her tangled nerves, a faint undercurrent of longing tugged at her. Longing for clarity, for belonging, for a tangible connection to something larger than grief.

Sadie stayed near, silent, supportive in her presence. The birds overhead quieted, forming a languid circle near the orchard's perimeter. Their wings caught flashes of sunlight between the leaves, flickering like bright signals. Emma listened to their cries grow distant, then fade into the hush. She breathed in the orchard's thrumming quiet, no longer sure if she imagined the sense of living magic around them or if it was truly there.

She spotted the fox again, gazing at her through the underbrush of the blackberry and gooseberry bushes that ringed the orchard, unafraid. She thought of the swirl of illusions she had seen in her restless dreams—half-formed shapes that dissolved upon waking. She felt weird, almost tipsy, like she was drunk.

A knot of emotions tangled in Emma's throat, but no words formed. She realized that, for now, it was enough to stand here and wonder if the orchard was not as simple as she had once believed. Each carved line on the bark, each swirl of birds overhead, and each subtle shift in Sadie's posture hinted that there was more going on.

Gradually, the light breeze died down, and the orchard fell quiet. Emma didn't move away from the tree. Sadie stayed at her side, letting the calm settle around them.

Neither spoke. The smell of earth and blossoms hung in the air, and somewhere in the distance, a fox might have been watching, but Emma could not see it.

The orchard waited, and so did they, both poised in a tension that felt as delicate as the runes etched into living wood. Emma wondered if she would ever find the courage to unravel it fully. For now, she stayed still, letting the orchard's heartbeat reverberate in her mind until it was the only sound she could hear.

ELEVEN

The days at the cottage settled into a routine, or at least, Emma tried to believe they did. Most mornings, she woke to an empty house. Sadie was always gone early, likely in the orchard, though Emma never knew exactly what she was doing out there. Left on her own, she made breakfast—something simple, toast or eggs—before figuring out how to fill her day. Some mornings, she walked into town, a habit that became easier now that Gale had made it her personal mission to keep Emma from spending too much time alone. They met for coffee at the small café where Gale gossiped about the town and made sarcastic comments about the older patrons who eyed Emma like she might hex their next latte.

Other days, Emma spent hours at the library, losing herself on books on marine biology. She liked the quiet, the scent of old paper, the way the soft scratch of pages turning made the world feel steady. Reading about ocean life made her feel connected to something familiar, something safe. She traced the diagrams of coral reefs, let her mind drift to memories of her father explaining tidal patterns or her mother describing deep-sea creatures with the same awe other people reserved for myths. But no matter how absorbed she tried to be in what she was doing, the sense that something was off never completely left her.

It was always there, just beneath the surface. More than once, she saw Sadie with the fox. But what unsettled her wasn't that it was always nearby—it was how it walked beside Sadie, not like a nervous wild animal or a pet on a leash, but like they were old friends out for a stroll. It was becoming increasingly difficult to brush off the fact they were walking together, side by side, as if they were having a conversation.

She watched them once from the kitchen window, standing on the pathway. They turned toward each other, and for a long moment, Sadie simply listened, her expression serious, as if the fox was telling her something important. Its mouth never moved, but the weight of the exchange was unmistakable. Emma wanted to explain it away.

Sadie talking to animals could mean a lot of things, none of them good. What if this was a sign of dementia, her grandmother slipping into something she couldn't be pulled back from? And yet... that didn't explain the fox's behavior—the way it watched Sadie, its golden eyes sharp, aware, as if it truly understood every word she said and had a few things to say itself. Emma told herself she was imagining things, but the doubt remained, curling around her thoughts like mist at the orchard's edge.

One afternoon, Emma paused in the doorway, unsettled by the soft glow that filtered through the afternoon light. Sadie stood at the small kitchen table; bent over something Emma could not fully see. After a moment, Emma realized it was the worn silver amulet that Sadie often carried in her pocket. The amulet's lid lay open, and for the first time, Emma caught a glimpse of her own photo tucked inside. Sadie's fingers trembled slightly as she whispered words Emma could not make out. Even in the gentle hush of the cottage, Emma felt a tug of power ripple through the air. It reminded her of what she had sensed during odd moments in the orchard, a subtle charge that made her heartbeat quicken.

Sadie looked up as if she had sensed Emma watching. A small smile curved her lips, and she closed the amulet, slipping it back into her sweater pocket without a word. Emma hesitated, wanting to ask about the whispered incantation, about why Sadie had been speaking to a locket with her picture inside. But uncertainty twisted in her stomach, and she swallowed the question. She wasn't ready to hear the answer. The tension of the past few days still sat heavy on her, and Sadie's quiet displays of power only made the mysteries of the orchard—and everything else—harder to ignore.

Sadie glanced up as Emma stepped into the kitchen, then reached into her sweater pocket and pulled out a small slip of paper. "This came while you were upstairs," she said, handing it over.

Emma took the postal notice, her eyes skimming over the familiar Crestwood shipping depot address.

"I believe that's the notice about the boxes the lawyers said they were going to send. Looks like they finally arrived, Sadie said, setting aside the dish towel she'd been holding.

Emma's stomach flipped with anticipation. Those boxes held pieces of her old life—photos, books, little things that still carried the scent of home. "I'm going to pick them up now," she said quickly, already reaching for her coat.

Sadie frowned, glancing toward the window. "It's getting foggy," she murmured, her voice edged with concern.

Emma pulled on her coat and grabbed her keys. "I'll be fine," she assured her. "It's just a quick drive."

Sadie hesitated, then exhaled, her fingers brushing over her sweater pocket as if checking for something inside. "Just... be careful. I have a feeling something's coming," she said, her voice quiet but firm. "I don't know if it's good or bad yet."

Emma paused for half a second, then forced a small smile. "I'll be back before supper."

Without waiting for a reply, she stepped outside, the air was heavy with the scent of the ocean and the creeping chill of approaching fog. She climbed into the 15-year-old Ford Mustang Sadie had bought for her and gripped the steering wheel a little too tightly. It was just a short drive, a simple task, nothing strange. She told herself that again as she pulled away from the gravel path, leaving the cottage behind.

By the time she reached the two-lane highway, the fog had thickened, curling low across the asphalt. Emma switched on her headlights, leaning forward to peer through the mist. The trees lining the road stood in dark clusters, their skeletal limbs stretching upward, twisting in ways that made her stomach tighten. She told herself not to be ridiculous. It was just the weather, just another ordinary drive. But with every passing mile, the unease in her chest deepened.

Her thoughts turned to Sadie's repeated reminders that Crestwood was older and stranger than it seemed. She remembered the orchard at dusk, how the air would flicker with possibilities she could not name. A knot formed in her throat. She tried to keep her eyes glued to the road, focusing on the rhythmic hum of the car's engine.

Nightmares had plagued her since she arrived: images of her parents from the night they died, swirling with glimpses of unnatural shapes in the orchard's darkness. The accident that took her parents had never fully left her mind, and now, she had stepped into a world where magic might be real. Or she might be going crazy.

She gripped the Mustang's steering wheel so tightly her knuckles blanched. The fog grew thicker, and visibility dropped. Another bend in the road materialized. She slowed to a crawl, scanning the shoulder for oncoming headlights. The air smelled of wet pavement, pungent earth, and her own anxiety.

"It's just a short drive," she whispered to herself. The leftover tension made her voice tremble. She glanced at her phone, propped nearby, out of some instinct to check for any missed calls. The screen was dark except for faint reflections of the headlights.

As she turned another narrow bend, movement exploded at the edge of her vision. Before her mind could piece it together, a deer bolted out of the fog. Its hooves slid across the road; eyes wide with panic. Emma's breath locked in her throat. She stomped the brake. The wet asphalt had no mercy. The Mustang's tires screeched, and the frantic shape of the deer loomed at the hood.

She heard a single, sickening thud.

Emma's world froze. The car skewed sideways, then stopped. She fumbled to shift into park, lungs seized in horror. The headlights illuminated the deer lying at the roadside. The animal's sides heaved, struggling for breath, and its legs kicked weakly against the glare. Emma's heart hammered. Her seatbelt felt constricting, and she wrestled with the buckle until it released. Shoving the door open, she stumbled out onto the damp asphalt.

The deer lay just past the shallow ditch, eyes blinking in pain. One slender foreleg bent at an unnatural angle. Blood matted its fur along the shoulder. Emma's breath came in hard gasps. She reached for her phone, thumbs trembling so badly she dropped it on the road. The device clattered. She snatched it up and tried to dial 911, but her mind spun. She could barely make the keypad function. The fog pressed around her, thick as a shroud, and the night closed in.

Finally, she managed to hit the call button. It rang once, then the operator's voice buzzed in her ear, barely making sense. Emma opened her mouth to speak, but only a ragged sound emerged. Her thoughts muddled; she ended the call in desperation. She tried Sadie next, hands shaking violently. The phone slipped from her sweaty grip. It fell in the grass, and Emma let out a broken sound that hovered between a cry and a cough.

She fell to her knees near the deer, feeling helpless. "Oh, no. Oh, no, no, no," she whispered, voice cracking. The animal's breath rattled, its chest still rising and falling, though each movement looked excruciating.

In the distant quiet, she heard an engine approach. Emma looked up, heart pounding. At first, she feared it was another car that might slam into them, but then she recognized the battered shape of Sadie's old truck. Headlights swept over the roadside as Sadie parked and jumped out, face drawn with urgent concern. Emma could not form words. All she could do was stare, tears gathering at the corners of her eyes as her grandmother hurried to her side.

Sadie crouched next to the deer. The older woman placed one hand gently on Emma's shoulder, then carefully moved forward. "Em, it's alright," Sadie murmured. "I can fix this."

"How can you? She's almost dead." Emma started, but her voice collapsed, drowned by her tears. She could barely process the scene, the metallic tang of blood, and the deer's laboring gasps.

Sadie didn't bother answering. She pulled the silver

amulet from her pocket, letting it rest loose in her palm. She knelt next to the animal and pressed her free hand lightly over the deer's flank. The creature jolted, eyes rolling in terror. Sadie whispered words that Emma could not fully catch, her tone steady and unhurried, as if reciting a lullaby. A thin mist swirled off the road, drawn by an inaudible current that circled Sadie. In the glow of the headlights, Emma saw the amulet's surface glimmer.

A peculiar warmth radiated through the air. Sadie's gaze was calm and steady, the same quiet determination Emma had noticed earlier that day when Sadie whispered over that amulet in the cottage. Emma's tears caught in her throat. The deer let out a pained breath. Sadie began chanting more clearly, and Emma made out fragments of her voice: gentle words that resonated with the night. The pulse of energy grew, and a faint shimmer appeared around Sadie's hand, as though the air itself had turned luminous.

Emma inhaled sharply. Beneath Sadie's touch, the deer's wounds sewed itself together in a slow but undeniable motion. Torn flesh fused. Blood flow halted. The animal's ragged breathing eased. Emma wanted to recoil in shock, but she felt rooted in place, unable to shatter the magic of that moment. Her entire body shivered with adrenaline, and confusion flooded her senses.

Sadie released a trembling exhale. She gently lifted her hand from the deer's side. A thin line of freshly knitted fur remained, a ghostly ridge that hinted at the damage that had existed mere seconds ago. Emma watched the deer blink, then lift its head. Its ears twitched, uncertain, as if testing for pain. None arrived. With a trembling effort, it scrambled upright on all four legs.

Emma's eyes could not move from the newly healed foreleg. It looked solid, strong, as though no bones had cracked at all. A silent wave of awe rippled through Emma's chest. She expected the deer to hesitate, but the creature jerked away from Sadie's hand, then bounded several steps toward the dark woods. It turned once, ears angled back, then sprang off into the swirling fog.

Emma pressed both hands to her mouth. Her heart pounded so fiercely she thought she might collapse. The final threads of panic still threaded her veins, but they fought against a dawning realization that she could not escape. She had witnessed impossible healing, real magic revealing itself in cold, undeniable clarity. The silver amulet glinted in Sadie's hand, continuing to glow faintly before dimming to normal.

Sadie slid the amulet back into her pocket, then turned toward Emma. Concern and relief battled in her expression. "Are you hurt?" she asked, voice quiet. She stepped closer, pressing steady hands on Emma's arms.

Emma shook her head. Words remained tangled in her throat. She could still see the blood, the horrifying limp, and then that shimmer of magic. She forced out a shaky breath. "I... I hit it so hard. It should be... that deer should be..." She could not finish the sentence, but Sadie's eyes said enough.

Sadie put an arm around Emma's shoulders. The older woman's warmth seeped into her, offering more comfort than any phone call or blanket could have. Emma leaned against her, tears sliding down her cheeks, and let the surge of adrenaline recede. The fog swirled around them in uneasy eddies, though it felt less suffocating than before.

They stood by the roadside for some time, quiet except for the rumble of Sadie's truck engine that was still running. Eventually, Sadie guided Emma back toward her car. The driver's side door remained open, headlights still cutting through the darkness. Emma glanced at the stains on the asphalt—traces of blood that proved the collision had happened. Any lingering doubt about Sadie's healing gift melted at that moment. The knowledge that something truly supernatural pulsed beneath Crestwood's ordinary exterior took root in Emma's mind.

"Let me check your car for damage. Then we will head home and talk." She left no room for contradiction, though her gentleness remained. Emma simply nodded, heart still rattling in her chest.

The hood was crumpled like an accordion, the grill was smashed in, the front bumper was gone, and one headlight was cracked. Emma wasn't sure the car was even drivable. Sadie double-checked for serious fluid leaks. Emma smelled oil in the air. At last, Sadie turned to Emma, took the younger woman's trembling hand, and squeezed gently.

"I'll call Ernie. He'll tow the car to his garage and repair it if he can. Hitting a deer can total a car." She took a breath then put her hands on Emma's shoulders. "You terrified me tonight. After you left, I felt the amulet stir. I knew something was terribly wrong, so I followed you."

She stroked Emma's pale check and sighed. "Come. Let's go home. I'll make tea."

Emma felt too unsteady to argue. She let Sadie guide her to the passenger's side of the truck and open the door so she could slide in. Sadie climbed into the driver's side and put the car into gear and pulled onto the damp road. Emma stared at her hands, uncertain how to form the questions bombarding her mind.

She had watched Sadie heal a seriously wounded deer, as simply as if she had bandaged a scraped knee. She'd stitched together torn flesh in the span of a heartbeat. Emma could not deny it now: the illusions in her dream, the orchard's mystery, the fox's uncanny behavior, her grandmother bringing a nearly-dead flower back to life seemed to be mere hints at the power around her. The reality of magic was beyond her understanding, but it was undeniable now.

She licked her lips, voice emerging in a whisper. "Sadie... what you just did. It was..." She faltered. She didn't know if she wanted to say it was magic or a miracle. She only knew that the rules of possibility had shifted forever.

Although her shoulders tensed, her voice stayed gentle. "I know. Let's get back to the cottage and I'll explain," Sadie said calmly as she drove.

Emma finally let out a breath as the house lights became visible through the fog, promising that the turn onto the cottage's gravel drive was close. She stared out the windshield at the soft glow from the living room window as Sadie pulled the truck into the driveway.

Emma tugged stiffly at her seatbelt, then stepped onto the gravel, her legs wobbly.

Sadie was beside her in a flash, guiding her up the path to the cottage. Emma glanced at the older woman's pocket. She half expected the amulet to glow again, responding to unasked questions. But it was still. The night air carried the faint smell of sea salt and dead leaves. It felt different than before, heavier with truth and magic.

They entered the cottage. The warmth inside wrapped around Emma, who shivered as she shed her jacket. Sadie hung her own coat on the peg near the door, then spread her palms over the small heater in the corner.

After a lengthy silence, Emma finally forced words out, voice tight with fatigue and wrought with complicated relief. "You healed it. You saved that deer. That was…was real magic." She shuddered at her own use of the word, the label she had resisted for so long.

"I tried to guide your awakening to my powers a little more gently," She laid a hand on Emma's shoulder, squeezing in silent support. "But yes. Magic is real, Emma. And it is only a fraction of what runs deep in our family's veins."

Emma fought tears again, though she could not say if they were born of shock, gratitude, or something else. The deer's recovery had been more than remarkable. It was raw, undeniable proof of magic.

She took a shaky step forward. "Why didn't you tell me sooner?"

Sadie drew in a slow breath. "I hoped showing would be better than telling. You weren't ready to believe me until now. Besides, I tried to spare you the full weight of it until you had settled in a little more. You have been through so much—losing your parents and moving in with me. I wasn't sure when you would be ready to hear the truth about what I am." She gave Emma a sideways glance. "More importantly, you weren't ready to hear the truth about what you are, either."

Emma closed her eyes. Echoes of the collision still rang in her ears. Even the memory of that thick blood on the ground, now vanished, made her stomach turn.

Sadie touched her arm with heartbreaking gentleness. "We will talk when your mind and heart have had a moment of rest," she said. "I promise I will answer what I can. For now, let me make you some tea."

Emma nodded, overwhelmed and exhausted. She let Sadie guide her to the small chair in the living room. She thought of how, at the roadside, Sadie arrived within minutes of the accident, as though the amulet itself had called for her. Turning her head, Emma glimpsed that same amulet now resting on a side table, the chain coiled. She realized it was both a tether and a warning, a symbol of the bond between them that ran deeper than she had ever imagined.

Sadie busied herself with the kettle and teacups. The ragged sense of fear still pumped through Emma's veins, but a strange, quiet acceptance was unfolding too. She had crashed into something far beyond her old life, and though she was terrified, she was also brimming with a new sense of certainty. This time, there was no denying the reality. Magic had touched her life in an impossible way, and there would be no going back.

When Emma closed her eyes, she saw again the deer's flank knitting together under Sadie's hand. When she opened her eyes, she saw Sadie's gentle silhouette in the kitchen. Outside, the fog pressed close, wrapping the night in a silent vigil. The deer lived, saved by a power Emma would do anything to understand. She would ask Sadie questions—real, difficult questions—and discover what it meant to inherit magic that could mend broken bodies and unravel illusions. For now, she simply let the sense of relief come, breathing in time with the delicate swirl of steam from her waiting cup of tea.

TWELVE

Sunlight pressed gently against the thin curtains of Emma's bedroom, stirring her awake before she felt ready to face another day. Her eyes ached from the night's turmoil, and a dull throb still pulsed at her temples. She had barely slept. Each time she drifted off, she saw the deer's ravaged body on the roadside and relived the memory of Sadie healing it. That surreal image looped through her dreams. No matter how she tossed or turned, the same whisper returned: She had witnessed magic, and it could not be undone.

She sat up, blinking to clear her vision. She needed an extra moment to gather her thoughts. Everything had changed last night. For weeks, she had wrestled with a haunting sense that Crestwood's weirdness was more than coincidence. Now she had no excuse to cling to denial.

Emma sighed and ran her hands through her tangled hair, pushing it back from her face. She glanced around the small room, searching for some anchor of normalcy. The bedside table held a mug of cold tea, a half-finished novel she had abandoned days ago, and a small silver amulet Sadie had given her. Her grandmother had insisted on its protective properties, though Emma had yet to decide whether she believed in such things. After last night, part of her wanted to hurl that amulet out the window, because it represented a reality she was not sure she was ready to accept. But she found her fingers closing around the cool metal shape, searching for comfort that proved elusive.

She rose to her feet, determined to confront Sadie without letting her doubts fester another day. Last night, it had taken every shred of composure not to collapse in hysterics when she saw the impossible happen in front of her eyes. She felt the same swirl of disbelief and anger returning now as she walked down the hallway. She had cornered Sadie with half-formed questions before, but never with the raw urgency that coursed through her in this moment.

In the living room, the first wash of sunlight filtered through threadbare curtains. Sadie stood across the room at the wooden bookshelf, her back to Emma. She seemed lost in thought, absently tracing a fingertip along the spines of well-thumbed volumes. When she turned, her eyes carried a tired warmth that made Emma's chest tighten. Emma felt a strange pang of guilt, as though she were intruding on some private moment. But she couldn't let sympathy stop her. She needed clarity.

Wordlessly, Emma stepped into the living room and

placed herself between Sadie and any possible escape route. She fought an urge to fidget with her hands, refusing to let anxiety drive her. A ball of tension settled at the base of her throat, and she inhaled slowly to steady herself.

"Tell me," Emma said, voice taut. "No more half-answers or trying to wave off my questions. I saw what you did last night. That—" She paused, remembering the wounded deer's labored gasps. She forced herself to press forward, "That was impossible. And you... you didn't even hesitate. So, I need to know how."

Sadie closed the book she held, set it on a side table, and turned fully toward her granddaughter. Morning light cast soft shapes across Sadie's face, revealing lines of worry beneath her calm expression. "I was afraid this would happen before you were ready," she said softly. "I can see that you are upset."

Emma made a small, choked sound, too angry to find the right words. "Of course I'm upset. You keep telling me to trust my instincts, and then you do... magic. I nearly crashed my car because I hit a deer in the fog. Next thing I know, you arrive like an ambulance that wasn't called, and then you—" Her voice quavered. "You healed it, Sadie. You healed a living creature in seconds. I'm not imagining that. So, tell me the truth right now. Did my parents know about this? About you?"

Sadie exhaled, glancing toward the window where the orchard lay. For a moment, Emma wondered if she might try deflection again: a mild suggestion to sit, a gentle promise to explain in due time. Instead, Sadie faced Emma directly, shoulders set with quiet resolve. "They knew some," she said. "Your mother and father both dabbled in magic. Not to the extent I do, but they had gifts. Small ones. They chose to turn away from them." Sadie paused, searching Emma's face. "I don't know if they feared it or simply believed they could lead simpler lives without the power that ran through their veins. Regardless, they left magic behind."

That admission was even sharper than Emma's worst fears. She gripped the back of a nearby chair, knuckles whitening. "So, you're saying my parents had powers, too?" She thought of her mother's sudden bursts of panic that used to send curtains billowing across closed windows which she thought must have been drafty to begin with. She remembered her father's playful attempts to blow out candles that refused to die until he uttered some silly phrase. She thought they were trick candles. Emma had always chalked it up to standard family jokes, weird flukes best left unexamined. Now, those memories rushed back in vivid flashes. She pressed her lips together, unsure if she felt betrayal or awe. "They never told me."

Sadie collected a crocheted shawl from the chair's arm and fiddled with the fringe. "They likely meant well. They wanted to protect you from the burdens that come with being... different. I only wish I had convinced them otherwise. But that is all in the past."

Emma didn't move from her spot. Anger, grief, and surprise churned in her chest, forming a single knot of emotion she could barely unravel. "So, after they died," she said, her voice trembling, "you brought me here. You let me see strange things—like that flower you revived. And you gave me half-hints. But you never explained what I was really noticing."

Sadie set the shawl aside, her gaze steady. "I worried that if I told you immediately, it would shatter what little peace you had left. You were grieving, Emma. Please understand that I have tried to give you space. The orchard has a way of revealing itself gradually to those who carry Turner blood. I hoped you might find a gentler path toward acceptance." She paused, a faint sigh escaping her. "Last night forced the matter. I could feel something was terribly wrong, and I used the power of this amulet to get to you. I had no choice but to show you what I can do."

Emma let out a disbelieving laugh. The mention of the amulet made her grip tighten around the wooden chair. "Every time I think I'm getting hold of my life, you drop another impossible truth. What else haven't you told me? How powerful are you? This morning, I can barely breathe, because I've realized I live with a witch. My grandmother is a witch." She let the words hang. It sounded ludicrous. It also made a searing kind of sense.

Sadie's face softened, a blend of compassion and regret in her eyes. "I am a witch," she said evenly. "Far from the only one in Crestwood, but certainly one of the most... knowledgeable." She pressed her hands together. "Most of the time, I use my abilities for healing and protection. This orchard, this town—they hold old energies that can be used for good or twisted for ill."

"So, you're telling me," Emma said, voice shaky, "that

Mom and Dad not only knew, but they had small powers. Then they walked away. And I…" Her pulse pounded. "I have them too, don't I? Some kind of magic in my veins. This isn't a random fluke. The orchard feels different to me, the runes I've seen… all of that is because I'm your granddaughter?"

Sadie's silence spoke volumes. Emma closed her eyes, reeling from the confirmation. For so long, she had doubted her own senses, refusing to label the orchard or the hidden runes as supernatural. Yet the more she reflected, the more she recognized how blind she had been.

Her breath came faster, and an unexpected wave of relief rippled through her. The word "magic" still frightened her, but it also felt like an answer to every inexplicable moment that had haunted her since arriving. She was tired of feeling foolish for sensing presences no one else admitted existed.

She let out a ragged exhale. "Prove it to me," she said, more fiercely than she intended. "Healing that deer was amazing, but maybe I was in shock or hallucinating from adrenaline. Show me right now that this is real. Do something. Make me see it with my own eyes while I'm calm."

Sadie tilted her head thoughtfully. Shadows of hesitation lingered in her expression, but she nodded. "Very well. Your heart demands certainty." She walked toward the center of the living room, gently shifting a stack of old newspapers from a wooden coffee table. Then she cradled her hands together, palms upward.

Emma found herself taking an involuntary step closer,

curiosity trumping any lingering fear. She felt her pulse thrum with anticipation. She detected the faintest crackle of energy in the air, a buzzing sensation that raised the hair on her arms. Dust motes danced in the morning light, swirling as though stirred by an unseen breeze.

Sadie drew a slow breath. Her posture straightened, lending her an aura of quiet command. "What I'm about to show you is elemental manipulation in a contained form," Sadie explained. The hush in the room deepened, and Emma could almost feel the walls listening. "Focus on my hands. Let your mind rest on the space past my fingertips."

Before Emma could question further, a shimmering pulse flickered across Sadie's skin. At first, it looked like a swirl of candlelight reflecting across her palms. But then it brightened, coalescing into a soft, radiant glow that hovered above the flesh. Emma's breath caught. This was no trick of reflection. The light grew into a small orb, faintly pulsating like a tiny sun. It was warm and soothing to behold, casting gentle beams around the living room. Every dusty corner came alive with golden illumination.

Emma's eyes widened. There was no rational explanation she could conjure in explaining this. It was undeniably magic. She stepped forward, arms folded as though she feared if she reached out, her trembling fingers might disrupt the delicate orb. Yet she desperately wanted to touch it, to feel its warmth. A swirl of awe and intimidation rushed through her veins.

Sadie kept her focus, palms steady. "This orb is harmless in its current state. If you step forward, you can feel it.

It's a thin concentration of energy. Not enough to cause harm." She spoke in a low voice, pitched soft enough to avoid shattering the fragile hush.

Emma swallowed. She inched closer until she was near enough to see slight ripples within the orb, dancing like sunlight on water. "It's... real," she whispered. She raised her hand, hesitating just below the glowing sphere. The energy radiated gentle heat that reminded her of summer sun on her face. She pulled back at the last moment, unsure if touching it would burn or jolt her.

Sadie lowered her hands, letting the orb float for a moment as if suspended by an unseen current. Then she exhaled, almost inaudibly, and the light winked out. The corners of the room settled back into their usual dimness, though to Emma, the entire cottage seemed bathed in a new clarity. Magic existed. The older woman who had soothed her nightmares for weeks was, in fact, something far more powerful than a kindly grandmother who gardened herbs, brewed tea and whispered odd lullabies at dusk.

Emma's heart pounded. Awe mingled with the sting of betrayal. But a surprising swell of pride also bloomed. This power was hers by blood, presumably, if she let herself claim it. She pressed her shaky fingers to her mouth, noticing that her cheeks felt warm.

Finally, Sadie straightened and turned to face Emma. Her voice held a hint of regret. "That is a glimpse of the gifts our family holds. Your parents tested a few spells. Then they turned from it, deciding it was not the life they wanted for you. But your bond with magic, Emma, runs deep. You have seen how the orchard reacts to you, how the runic markings call to you. I can't ignore it anymore, and neither can you."

Emma let out a hollow laugh. Tears of confusion pricked at her eyes. She brushed them away impatiently. She never wanted to be the naive girl who cried at every revelation. "And you really think I... I can do something like that?" She gestured to the empty space where the orb had hovered. "I don't even handle stress well. Last night, I was a mess after I hit that deer. I can't imagine controlling something as delicate as a ball of light."

"You're already coping with more than you realize, but we must awaken your powers before you can use them," Sadie said. She took a step closer, resting a hand on Emma's arm. The contact felt comforting in a way that Emma could not put into words, as though she could sense the same gentle power that had shaped that orb of light. "This morning you woke up ready to talk about all of this, despite the fear you felt. That is strength. Magic isn't always about grand gestures. It's about understanding the forces around you and channeling them with respect and purpose."

Emma's breath came quickly. She felt the faint impression of that orb's glow in her memory, an imprint that seemed to pulse along with her heartbeat. She pivoted and stepped away from Sadie, needing a moment to let the enormity settle. The cottage's cozy clutter, once comforting, now felt like evidence of hidden powers and mysteries she had spent weeks stumbling upon. Her gaze caught on a battered old trunk near the hallway. She wondered if it contained more secrets waiting to be unveiled.

She glanced back at Sadie, who waited patiently, fingers clasped at her waist. "How do I deal with this?" Emma whispered. "I'm not sure I know how to be... me, if I admit that witchcraft is real. My parents obviously had reasons to walk away from it."

Sadie's expression softened. "You deal with it one day at a time. I don't want to force you down either path. This magic belongs to you as much as it belongs to me, but the choice to embrace it or set it aside is yours. All I want is for you to make that decision with full knowledge, not under a cloud of secrecy."

Emma swallowed, eyes flitting to the small table near the window. "I don't know if I can walk away," she admitted, voice raw. "Off and on, I've sensed something stirring here. Even if I pretended none of this happened, that orchard won't just disappear. I can't unlearn what I saw last night. I can't unsee this demonstration. It's real now."

Sadie stepped forward, her presence exuding a tenderness that tugged at Emma's chest. "You have time," she said gently. "No path must be chosen today. But magic shapes itself around our intentions, so your curiosity will guide you. If you wish to learn, then I will teach."

Emma nodded, though the gravity of embracing witchcraft made her pulse flutter. She might never be the same. Yet a part of her felt oddly liberated. For weeks, she had crouched in uncertainty, haunted by illusions of confusion and grief. At least now, the confusion had a name.

She ran her thumb over the amulet chain still gripped in her palm. The metal was cool against her warm skin, and she felt new appreciation for what it might represent: a tether to her grandmother's legacy, and the spark of a power in her own veins. She inhaled a shaky breath, steeling herself for all the revelations that would surely follow.

Stepping around the coffee table, she collected her thoughts and spoke quietly. "I'm still angry you kept this from me. But... thank you for telling me. Thank you for showing me that orb. I can't pretend it's not real anymore."

Sadie offered a solemn nod. "I understand your anger, Emma. Truly. I only hope we can navigate what comes next together."

Emma dropped onto the edge of the couch, shoulders bowed under the weight of her new reality. She lifted her gaze to Sadie, who stood a few paces away in a golden patch of sunlight.

"All right," Emma said, voice determined. "We'll figure it out. Together." She scanned the living room walls, still half-expecting to see after-images of that orb dancing in the shadows.

She closed her eyes for a moment, the morning sun warming her cheek, the memory of magic pulsing beneath her ribs. The quiet allowed no retreat to ignorance. Whatever awaited her from this point on, Emma would meet it with eyes open, heart pounding, and magic stirring patiently underneath her every breath.

THIRTEEN

Emma had grown tired of second-guessing her own reality. All week, her pulse had raced with something beyond any normal explanation. Afterward, Sadie's revelations about the Turner family gifts had left Emma reeling. She felt half amazed, half betrayed. Rather than dwell on anger, she needed to ground herself in something tangible. If Crestwood hid centuries of magic beneath its gentle facade, perhaps the local archives would confirm what she sensed everywhere she went.

She set out for the library in the late afternoon, glancing at the sky as she slipped on her coat. Pockets of clouds glowed a dull silver, hinting the sun would soon hide behind the horizon. She reminded herself that she was not going there to chase rumors; she only wanted evidence—some historical records or legends that might validate the swirling questions in her head.

Sadie had offered no protests when Emma announced

her plan to visit the library alone. In fact, her grandmother had gone uncharacteristically quiet, as though anticipating Emma's restlessness. Emma took that silence as permission. By the time she reached the library's front steps, her heart pounded with a stubborn mix of curiosity and unease.

The exterior of the library, an old building with gray stone walls, conveyed a sense of timelessness. Its windows yawned with dark glass, and the once-grand wooden doors hung slightly crooked. Minimal foot traffic wandered in or out. Emma took a moment to notice the weathered plaque near the entrance, identifying the structure as the Caldwell Memorial Library. A pair of carved owls flanked the sign, as if silently warning visitors to tread carefully.

She pushed inside, bracing herself for a briny gust that followed her through the door. She paused near a small bulletin board plastered with community notices—lost pets, crafts fairs, and the occasional cryptic advertisement for "Mrs. Porter's herbal cures." Her gaze lingered before she reminded herself she had come here with a purpose. She moved deeper into the library, toward the area labeled "Local Archives." Her boots made a soft thump against the old wood, and the echo rippled in the quiet. If anyone else roamed these halls, she neither saw nor heard them.

A single desk lamp burned on a table near the far corner. A sign on the wall identified it as a dedicated research station. Beyond that stood a row of tall shelves, each stuffed with thick tomes on Crestwood's history, old genealogies, and records detailing maritime tragedies. Emma's gaze flicked to a couple of volumes that bore spines titled "Crestwood's Founding Myths" and "Legends of the Coastal North." She selected the first, cradling it in her arms, and pulled another about rumored cult activity in the region centuries ago. Her pulse quickened at the mention of "cult." Perhaps the orchard's runic carvings and Sadie's calm might connect to old groups who once practiced magic in secrecy.

Emma carried her fledgling stack to the research table, setting them down carefully. Each book smelled faintly of musk and old glue. Flipping open the first volume, she ran her fingers down a list of contents. Mentions of local superstitions, hidden curses, and ominous references to "family lines burdened by ill fortune" caught her eye. She traced the words, recalling how Sadie had revealed the Turner lineage's connection to magic just days earlier.

The hours might have slipped by without Emma noticing, so focused was she on scanning each passage. More than once, she found references to a "Turner orchard" rumored to be enchanted or protected by wards. Her thoughts kept drifting to the orchard at dusk and the eerie illusions she had half-glimpsed among the trees. At last, she found a short excerpt describing how some families in Crestwood whispered about witches, particularly ones capable of healing mortal wounds or controlling storms. That passage sent a chill up Emma's spine.

Her next find was an account detailing a decades-old rumor of a sinister figure who once frequented the library's sub-level archives, searching for references to "binding spells." The text offered little more than speculation, but it left Emma unsettled, especially when she recognized the layout note: Caldwell Memorial Library. She remembered her brief interactions with its current librarian, Catherine, whose mild smiles and unnerving stares had set Emma on edge from the beginning. No matter how sweetly Catherine welcomed her, Emma sensed a lingering tension beneath every word. Now reading about a figure rumored to dabble in advanced magic in this very building, Emma felt a small knot of anxiety coil in her stomach.

She pressed on, flipping pages faster than she could fully absorb them. Her desire to find something concrete warred against her creeping sense of dread. None of the dusty tomes provided absolute proof, but all the hints and half-veiled accounts chipped away at her attempt to remain skeptical of the supernatural. She was about to slide out another volume when a soft floorboard creak broke her concentration. She startled, glancing around the corner of the tall shelves. She saw no one.

Exhaling to steady her nerves, Emma resumed turning pages. The quiet of the library magnified every sound— the rustle of a skirt in another aisle, the distant clock ticking near the main desk. She made herself focus on the text. The poetic language described how certain families in Crestwood had once "sealed away unspeakable powers" in hidden places. She wanted to mark half the pages with sticky notes, but she had no pen, so she kept track mentally.

There again was the faintest rustle of fabric. Carefully

peering around the edge of the bookshelf, Emma scanned the aisle. The library's overhead bulbs cast elongated silhouettes, but she spotted nothing unusual. Frustration built in her chest. She was already jumpy from the subject matter, and the quiet sense of being observed made her pulse race.

Determined not to let fear distract her, Emma tucked a stray hair behind her ear and returned to the text. This time, however, the hair on her arms prickled. Another presence lurked—she was certain of it. The next instant, a voice emerged behind her, low and soft.

"You have an affinity for local folklore," the person said. "Is the subject for a school project?"

Emma nearly dropped the book. Heart hammering, she turned to see Catherine standing on the other side of the tall shelf. She had materialized so smoothly that Emma wondered if the woman had been there for minutes, merely waiting. Catherine wore what looked to be her usual attire—a cardigan buttoned neatly over a blouse. Her expression bore a polite smile, but Emma thought she noticed a predatory gleam in the librarian's dark eyes.

"I—" Emma fumbled for composure, reminding herself she had every right to browse these volumes. "I'm just researching some old stories around Crestwood." She tried to keep her voice neutral, betraying no mention of magic. "I read that the library's archives have plenty of historical records."

Catherine inclined her head, the overhead light catching the frames of her glasses. "They do. Though not many people bother." She slid a fingertip along the bookshelf, her posture calm. "What topics intrigue you most? Certainly, you're not reading about old curses for casual fun."

Emma forced a casual shrug, ignoring the dryness in her throat. "Just curious about local legends, that's all," she said. She tried to gather the tomes subtly, as if preparing to leave.

Catherine's soft chuckle sent a ripple of unease through Emma. "Legends, curses, folk magic. It is a fascinating tapestry, yes?" She let her gaze sweep over the titles in Emma's arms. "Crestwood's cozier than it appears. Plenty of families with secrets. You must find them interesting."

Something in Catherine's tone tightened the space between Emma's ribs. She refused to show intimidation, yet she couldn't deny the weight of Catherine's scrutiny. The older woman seemed too invested in whatever Emma was looking for. "Sure," Emma replied, attempting a friendly smile that felt stiff. "I might write an article or something. My grandmother used to mention local folklore."

"Mmm," Catherine acknowledged, her expression unreadable. "Well, if you need assistance, do call. My desk is at the front." She paused, letting the faint hush fill the gap between them, as though she expected Emma to volunteer more information.

Emma swallowed and took a step back, bracing the thick tomes against her chest. "I appreciate it," she said. "Though I think I have enough for now."

Catherine's eyes flicked to Emma's arms, as if measuring how many books she had collected. "Yes," she said quietly. "It seems you have quite a bit to mull over."

Emma dipped her head in a polite farewell, then turned, feeling Catherine's gaze follow her. Every hair on the back of her neck prickled. She half-expected Catherine to block her path or press her for more details, but the librarian simply stood there like a crooked shadow that refused to vanish. Emma steadied her breath, forcing her legs to carry her toward the checkout desk.

Once Catherine was out of sight, Emma allowed herself a shaky exhale. She reminded herself that there was no law against research. If Catherine suspected Emma's budding knowledge of the orchard's magic, she gave no outright sign, but the tension in that encounter felt suffocating. Emma glanced over her shoulder, half-fearing the librarian would materialize again.

The main checkout counter stood in gloom, an ancient desk lamp casting a small circle of yellow light. Emma set the books down. By the desk sat a ring binder filled with sign-out slips for local archives. She hurriedly filled in her name, scribbling titles of the volumes. Part of her wanted to run, but she forced a calm pace, at least outwardly.

All was silent until Catherine emerged again, gliding behind the counter. Emma tensed, pushing the books across. She expected intrusive questions, but Catherine merely pressed the covers gently, double-checking the library stamps. With quiet efficiency, she slid them back to Emma.

"I trust you'll handle them with care," Catherine said,

voice low enough to make the hair on Emma's arms lift. "Some of those pages are quite... delicate."

Emma nodded; throat dry. "I will." Without another word, she scooped up the books. She heard a slight rustle of fabric as Catherine moved, but she refused to look up. She gave a tight nod, then walked briskly toward the exit. Her steps echoed with each stride.

Pressing open the heavy door, she stepped into the outside world. The late afternoon light had faded into a soft gray hue, and the temperature felt sharply colder on her cheeks. She paused on the library's stone step, inhaling a gulp of fresh air, the crisp tang of autumn cutting through the lingering tension in her shoulders.

She clutched the stack of books, eyes darting across the empty sidewalk. No one lingered near the lamppost, no drifting figure spotted behind the library's windows—yet she couldn't shake the prickling certainty that Catherine might appear at any moment, silent and prying. Forcing her mouth into a firm line, Emma clung to her newly borrowed volumes. Each book promised details—some hidden, some partial—that might help her understand the orchard, her grandmother's powers, and her own future path.

Despite the wind's chill, her temples felt hot, as if her body still buzzed from the encounter. She told herself this was progress: she had tangible sources to read, a plan to anchor her swirling thoughts. Yet her mind refused to calm. Even the distant cry of a seagull made her heart jolt.

She descended the library steps, shivering once as she pulled her coat tighter. In the failing light, Crestwood's narrow streets felt especially still, shops closed or near closing. The sea breeze gathered in force, carrying the hint of salt and damp leaves. The weight of the books in her arms served as a reminder of what she sought—truth, or at least a clue pointing her toward understanding magic.

Emma paused near a row of empty benches, letting a swirl of dry leaves skate across her boots. Hassling Sadie with a barrage of questions this evening felt inevitable, but she had to cross-reference these tomes first. She craved knowledge, a glimpse of how her family's orchard came to hold such potent secrets. She needed to see if any record tied the orchard's runes to the rumored witches who once lived in Crestwood.

Clutching the books tighter, Emma started down the sidewalk, deciding that lingering outside the library would only feed her nerves. The path back to Sadie's cottage stretched before her, and she exhaled slowly, letting the taste of sea air ground her. She would read until her eyes burned if that was what it took. A strange flutter of resolve settled in her stomach. Maybe learning more about Crestwood and its hidden lore would give her the answers Sadie couldn't provide.

When she reached the corner outside the library's boundary wall, the cold wind nipped her cheeks. She drew the books closer to her chest, feeling her pulse drum in her ears. The crisp autumn air seemed to whisper questions she couldn't answer yet. She scanned the deserted street one more time, but no figure emerged from the looming gray silence. Even so, she knew in her gut that Catherine's watch was far from over. Every fiber of her being insisted that the librarian's mild expression and soft voice were only a mask, hinting at trouble Emma was barely ready to name.

Outside, the crisp autumn air stung her cheeks, but she could not dispel the uneasy sense that Catherine's watch would not end at the library doors.

FOURTEEN

A few days later, Emma trudged along the narrow street that wound through Crestwood's modest downtown, listening to the gulls squawking overhead. The briny smell of low tide drifted around her, mingling with the sugary waft of pastries from a nearby bakery.

Gale's text had arrived earlier in all caps—something about an afternoon outing to chase the gloom away. The invitation felt perfectly timed. Emma woke that morning reeling from the sense that she would go crazy if she stayed one more day cooped up in Sadie's cottage. Lately, every knocked-over chair or innocuous beam of light put her on edge. Crestwood's weirdness pressed around her like a band tightening around her chest, and she hated that she'd begun jumping at any hint of movement.

Now, Gale hopped off the curb ahead, a splash of color in the otherwise subdued street. Her short hair was pinned back with mismatched clips, one a neon green star, the other painted with tiny daisies. She wore a snug hoodie plastered with witty pins—one read "Support Local Coven," another read "Nope, Not Today." Emma clenched her tote bag closer, fondness sparking in her chest. It was impossible to feel entirely hopeless when Gale's energy lit up the atmosphere.

"Catch up, Em," Gale hollered, pausing in front of a display window showcasing whimsical dresses. Plastic mannequins posed stiffly, each wearing bright floral prints more suited for a spring runway than Crestwood's cloudy seaside. "You're moping all the way back there. At this rate, we'll miss the lunch specials."

Emma fell in step beside her, trying not to dwell on the fact that the last special she'd eaten in a café was overshadowed by the memory of anxious stares. "Sorry," she said in a low voice, adjusting the bag's strap on her shoulder. "Been in my head too much."

"You?" Gale teased, nudging Emma's arm. "It's not as if strangeness has ramped up in your life or anything." Her eyes danced with mischief, though Emma caught the flicker of genuine concern beneath Gale's humor. "Look, if we can't find anything interesting in these shops, I say we grab a milkshake and talk about that good-looking status update you owe me."

"Status update?" Emma frowned slightly, though a small smile tugged at the corner of her lips. "I never promised any such thing."

"Hon, you act like I didn't see your eyes drifting off to another dimension the last time we hung out." Gale sang the words, hooking her arm through Emma's and steering her down the sidewalk. "Crestwood might be quiet, but not that quiet. Something's in the air, and I'm not just talking about the sea breeze."

Emma opened her mouth to deny it, but the words dried up. She thought of Sadie's careful warnings, and that unsettled twist in her stomach whenever she remembered Catherine's watchful stare. Then her mind darted to that other presence in her life: the guy in the woods with the quiet intensity. She hadn't gone looking for him in the woods since that jarring night, yet she felt him lingering in her thoughts. Pressing her lips together, she tried to shove aside the tangle of confusion.

"Maybe I do have stuff on my mind," Emma admitted quietly, following Gale toward a row of shops that sold novelty items—postcards of Crestwood's harbor, seashell jewelry, crocheted mermaid dolls. "I'm just not sure I can talk about it freely. It's... complicated."

Gale stopped short, spinning on her heel so that Emma nearly collided with her. "I'm your friend," Gale said, voice lighter than the concern that flashed in her eyes. "I'm not about to run blabbing your secrets to the entire soccer team. Or whatever remains of it around here."

Emma snorted. She recalled Gale joking about the local teen cliques when they'd first met at the café. The memory eased her tension enough to follow Gale into a boutique that smelled faintly of lavender and lemon. Clothing racks lined the walls, each loaded with bright garments meant for a more carefree place than Crestwood.

Stitched banners hung from the ceiling, proclaiming summer sales on floral dresses.

Gale darted over to the nearest rack, humming approval at some bohemian-style tunic, then pointed toward Emma. "Nuh-uh, no skulking by the door. Come help me judge these horrendous ruffles."

Emma approached, letting a subtle sense of normalcy kick in. The soft overhead lighting and cheerful fabrics felt worlds apart from magical illusions and talk of curses. She brushed her hand over a pastel blouse covered in tiny, embroidered seahorses. The design was whimsical and unexpectedly charming. "This is... actually sort of cute," she murmured, flipping the price tag. "Though I'm not sure I see myself wearing it."

"Honey, you'd rock that, but I'm not sure seahorses scream your brand." Gale sighed dramatically. "Anyway, as I was saying about your brand. Tell me about the hush-hush weirdness. You used the words 'gorgeous guy in the woods' last time we chatted."

Emma raised an eyebrow. "I never said those things."

"Oh, you definitely implied them," Gale sang back, wiggling her eyebrows. "The dreamy eyes, the cryptic aura, the totally enthralling vibe that probably has half the town swooning. I'm onto you, Em."

A flutter of heat rose in Emma's cheeks, and she tugged the pastel blouse off the rack as an excuse to look away. "You're making things up now."

"Fine, fine. You owe me specifics, though." Gale paused to inspect a black sundress. She smirked, brandishing it in Emma's direction. "Not that you have to talk about it here, but I'll pry it out of you eventually."

Emma recognized that stalling with banter would only go so far. She thought to herself that Gale was safe to confide in—at least somewhat. They drifted from the clothing section to a small corner with racks of costume jewelry. Silver bangles rattled as Gale tried a pair on. The tinkling sound reminded Emma of the faint clinks in Sadie's cottage whenever jars of herbs knocked together.

Truth pressed at her throat, an intense swirl of half-kept secrets. She lifted her gaze and caught Gale watching her in the store's dressing mirror. "Okay," Emma said at last. "Let's grab those milkshakes you promised. Then I'll fill you in on something."

Gale's grin flashed bright. "Deal," she said. "I'm about to talk your ear off about all the snarky rumors swirling in this place, so brace yourself."

They paid for a pair of silly socks—Gale insisted on matching sets embroidered with starfish—before stepping back into the crisp air outside. Emma felt a slight tension coil between her shoulder blades, as though invisible eyes tracked them. She tried to brush off the unease, letting Gale's chatter fill the space.

Five minutes later, they arrived at a small diner that perched at the corner of Maple Circle. Two enormous potted ferns framed the entryway. Inside, a bored-looking waitress pointed them to a booth by the window, where neon letters flickered overhead: "Shakes & Sundaes." The seats were lobster-red vinyl, and Emma slid onto one side while Gale took the other.

"Chocolate or vanilla?" Gale asked, drumming her fingers on the laminated menu. "Or something adventurous like salted caramel?"

Emma smoothed the menu across her lap. "Chocolate, I think," she managed. "I could use the extra sweetness."

When their shakes arrived—taller than expected, crowned by generous swirls of whipped cream—Gale lifted hers in a mock toast. "To the strangest summer Crestwood has ever seen," she declared, slurping at the straw. "Tempted to add a shot of espresso to mine, but I'll settle for sugar-induced mania."

Emma stifled a smile. The chocolate was rich and cool, comforting in a way. She watched people bustle past the diner's window, some carrying groceries, others laughing as they crossed Maple Circle. The town seemed so ordinary from this vantage, and that twisted something inside her. If only everything were truly that simple.

"All right," Gale said, leaning forward. "We're away from suspicious ears. Spill. You said something about a weird librarian, right?"

Emma hesitated. She pictured Catherine's intense stare in the library's dim reading room. But she didn't want to spiral into half-crazed talk of illusions and spells. Even with Gale, she felt reluctant to bear the full truth. "I —I've just noticed that there's more to her than meets the eye," Emma began carefully. "She sort of... appears behind shelves without warning. And jokes aside, her presence unnerves me."

Gale sipped her shake, arching a brow. "Is that a nice way of saying she creeps you out?"

"Pretty much," Emma admitted. "I don't want to judge her unfairly, but there's definitely an odd vibe."

"Huh," Gale said. Her expression stayed thoughtful, though a lopsided grin tugged at her lips. "I hear plenty of rumors about her. People call her a recluse, but rumor says she's got quite an interest in local folklore. Maybe she's the doomsday type who hoards old documents in the basement. Or maybe she's plotting the end of the world. Who knows in Crestwood?"

Emma coughed on her milkshake. "That's a bit extreme."

"Stranger things have happened," Gale said, leaning back against the vinyl cushion. "You've heard the old superstitions swirling around this place, right? Witches, curses, haunted woods, and a thousand stories nobody can confirm."

Emma's chest tightened. She wiped a stray dribble of chocolate from her straw. "I've heard the rumors," she said quietly. She pictured Sadie chanting over that injured deer. And, of course, Ian's silhouette in the moonlit clearing. The swirl of it all made her head spin.

Seeming to sense Emma's mood shift, Gale eased off her teasing tone. "Hey, we can talk about something else," she said gently, swirling her straw. "Maybe we share some safer gossip, like who's hooking up with who at that dingy arcade?"

Emma shook her head. "No, it's okay." Her heart pounded. "Actually, about those superstitions... I've seen some weird stuff in the last few weeks. Like, I'm not sure it's just rumor."

The admission slipped out before she prepared her words. Gale's eyes sparked with interest at once.

"Weird how?" Gale asked, propping her elbows on the table. "Spooky lights in the orchard?"

Emma chewed her lips, suddenly aware of how big this moment felt. Telling Gale the truth would open a door she might not be able to close. Still, she couldn't keep it all bottled in. "Well, about the gorgeous guy in the woods," she said, voice dropping lower. "He was doing something that looked like... magic. I know how that sounds but trust me. It felt real."

Gale's grin slid into a sly smirk. Her gaze flicked across the diner, but the only other patrons appeared too absorbed in their newspapers or fries to eavesdrop. "You mean actual magic? Like illusions or incantations?"

Emma nodded. Her cheeks warmed. "I panicked at first, but it felt... I don't know. It felt mesmerizing. He seemed equally surprised I stumbled onto him. We didn't talk much." She faltered, recalling the sense that he held secrets he could hardly contain.

Gale lifted an eyebrow. "So, you've definitely met Catherine and Ian, I see."

The mention of their names made Emma swallow around the knot in her throat. "Yes. What do you know?"

"Are you kidding?" Gale sipped her shake again, eyeing Emma's reaction closely. "Catherine is known for giving new arrivals the creeps at the library, though half the teens in town barely read. And Ian... well, he's that quiet, mysterious type. People say he's got some old family stuff going on. Some think he's broody, others think he's total eye candy. And from the look on your face, you probably fall somewhere in between."

Emma felt her shoulders tense, but a wave of amusement battled her embarrassment. "He is... I guess you could call him that," she finally managed. "But it's not about that. I'm just... concerned."

Gale leaned forward, lowering her voice conspiratorially. "Please. Spare me the disclaimers. You do realize you're basically the new girl in a place known for witchy tales, and you're crossing paths with a brooding local who might or might not be the guy from everyone's rumor mill. That's prime gossip real estate. If you wanted a shot of normal, you picked the wrong place, Em."

Emma stifled an uncomfortable laugh. "Yeah, that's the problem. I'm not sure I want normal. Or maybe I do, but I'm stuck in the middle of something else."

Gale offered a warm stare, letting a moment of understanding stretch between them. Then she broke the tension with a bright grin. "Either way, I'm so here for it. If you're going to be the mysterious new girl with a magnetic aura that draws in half the town's weirdos and hotties, I want a front-row seat."

"What if that's not what I want?" Emma asked, her voice betraying uncertainty. She took a slow sip of milkshake, the sweetness momentarily soothing.

Gale shrugged, toying with her straw wrapper. "You don't need to settle on anything. Just be honest with yourself. Explore the possibilities. Sure, maybe Crestwood has curses and illusions, or maybe it's all silly talk. The point is you don't have to figure it out alone." She tapped a playful finger on the table. "I know you're not telling me every-thing, but you have that haunted look—like you're carrying the weight of something big. Don't ever think I'm not in your corner."

Emma's eyes prickled. Gratitude rose in a warm wave, tangling with the guilt that she still kept so many things unsaid. "Thank you," she whispered, forcing a small laugh to hide the sudden emotion in her throat. "I guess I'll keep being the accidental magnet for the bizarre."

"Please do," Gale replied, taking another gulp of her shake. "I like living vicariously through you. Next, you'll tell me you performed a séance in the orchard or discov-ered a secret grimoire hidden under your floorboards."

Emma coughed, her heart banging against her ribs at that too-close guess. But Gale didn't seem to notice Emma's sudden discomfort, because she burst into fresh laughter, leaning back as the seat creaked.

They chatted more about harmless gossip after that—who in Crestwood might be hooking up behind the arcade, which teacher was rumored to be leaving for a new job, and who had the best homemade fudge near the pier. Emma felt her nerves uncoil, soothed by Gale's unflagging sense of humor.

"Earth to Emma," Gale said finally, tapping her finger on the table. "You spaced out again. That's the third time in five minutes. Are you possessed, or just smitten with your magic man?"

Emma rolled her eyes. "Neither."

Gale shot her a conspiratorial smirk. "Uh-huh. If you say so. Mystery suits you, but maybe it's time to let loose a little. You can be normal and still figure out your weirdness. We all have weirdness going on. I hoard pastel hairpins like a dragon with shiny coins, for example."

"That's not exactly the same as messing around with questionable magic," Emma pointed out, laughing softly.

"Well, give me time," Gale quipped. "In any case, I'm glad you vented about Catherine and that gorgeous guy. Maybe next time you'll actually give me the juicy details."

"You're terrible," Emma muttered, though her face felt lighter than it had in days. Sliding out of the booth, she dug for her wallet to pay. Gale swatted her hand away and insisted on splitting the bill, claiming her comedic commentary had a price.

Outside, the wind pinched their cheeks with an autumn edge, though the sun still shone. They lingered near the diner entrance, reluctant to part ways. Emma thought about Sadie, about the cottage and the orchard, and about how easy it felt to stand here with Gale, locked in a friendly chat. She almost felt normal—almost. A pang of sadness flickered. She retrieved the small bag containing her new starfish socks and turned to Gale.

"Thanks," Emma said softly. "For the milkshake, the jokes... all of it."

Gale's grin lost its teasing edge, turning gentler. "Anytime," she answered. "Look, I know your life is complicated, but I'm always down for a distraction. Maybe next time we'll try that new pizzeria or hit the beach cove. The ocean's still warm enough to dip our toes in."

"That sounds... nice," Emma said, though she didn't feel entirely convinced she could ever reclaim easy moments. She forced herself to hold on to the fleeting sense of normalcy, anyway, letting it anchor her for at least a few minutes more.

"Good. Text me later," Gale said, tossing Emma a casual salute. Her eyes sparkled as she added, "And maybe try not to get lost in any cursed orchard paths tonight."

Emma managed a genuine smile, short but heartfelt. She said goodbye and watched Gale's hoodie disappear around the corner. For a long moment, she stood under the glimmer of midday sun, hugging her tote bag. The gulls continued to circle overhead. A group of teens dashed past, shrieking with laughter as they carried fast-food bags. All around her, life ticked along with everyday routines—people strolling, shops displaying souvenirs, distant waves rolling in.

Yet Emma felt a hollow ache that her secrets separated her from that carefree bustle. She could giggle over socks and milkshakes, but a part of her remained tethered to something darker. On top of that, the faint swirl of sensation she felt whenever she thought about Ian haunted her. An invisible line divided her past life from this new path full of fragile spells and unknown dangers.

Softly exhaling, she clutched the crazy socks Gale had picked out. She pictured Gale's playful grin, the unwavering sincerity in her voice making jokes even as she showed fierce loyalty. Emma smiled, though her lips felt tight with unspoken worries. She had changed so much in these past days. Trying to fit back into an easy routine felt as impossible as ignoring the orchard's quiet call at sunset. Deep down, she suspected there was no going back.

And despite that knowledge, a touch of hope glowed in her chest.

She turned and walked down the street toward Sadie's cottage, hands curled around the bag in a quiet determination to hold onto small pieces of normalcy, even if they felt borrowed.

FIFTEEN

Emma pushed open the door to Sadie's study, wishing she didn't feel such an intense pang of guilt when she heard the hinges creak. It was well past midnight, and the cottage had settled into a soft lull under a moonless sky. Somewhere down the hall, Sadie's bedroom remained quiet. The only accompaniment to Emma's thoughts was the rhythmic rasp of pine needles against the rooftop. She listened to that sound for a moment, allowing it to steady the rush of questions swirling inside her head.

She nudged the study door fully open, letting the narrow corridor's light spill into the cramped room. A meager glow from the single lamp on Sadie's old desk guided her deeper inside. The faint scratch of her shoes on the worn wood planks felt too loud. Her pulse quickened as she took in the scattered journals, half-open boxes of parchment, and battered notebooks stacked precariously on every surface. She could almost sense the history contained in those pages. She felt a strange pull, a quiet beckoning from the swirl of old secrets.

Emma rotated in place, gaze skimming the dusty shelves lining the walls. A few near-empty jars of dried herbs slept beside thick tomes with cracked leather spines. She recognized the distinctive outline of Sadie's diaries: slender books with the date scrawled in the corner or along the binding. She had caught glimpses of Sadie scribbling in those diaries, yet had only glanced at one page, never daring to read. Tonight felt different. Something new burned in her chest, fueled by unanswered questions about illusions, hidden rituals, and the orchard. She wanted answers more than she wanted to spare Sadie's privacy.

Earlier that evening, Emma had gathered enough nerve to ask Sadie about the orchard's runic carvings, but Sadie's response was evasive. She had merely mentioned that certain families passed down protective traditions. She had followed that with a quiet warning to leave deeper research for another day. Emma had bristled at the gentle dismissal, though she recognized the worry in Sadie's expression. Still, she had let the conversation drop to avoid an argument. Now she stood in Sadie's domain, alone, determined to piece together the story that Sadie either could not or would not share.

She approached the desk, slipping into the creaky wooden chair. A faint breeze from the open window ruffled the pages of a thick notebook resting on top of a stack. Its edges were yellowed, corners dog-eared. She glimpsed a few scribbled lines about a local legend referencing something called the Turner orchard. Her eyes darted to the title scrawled on the front cover: Crestwood's Ancient Hexes. Her breath caught at the word hex. She had heard Sadie use it once, describing how cruel mind-bending spells could wreak havoc on unsuspecting victims. Emma wondered if the orchard's runes had something to do with repelling hexes, or if Sadie's caution hinted that the orchard itself held a far darker legacy.

She slipped her fingers under the notebook's parchment cover and began turning pages. The handwriting, spidery and sometimes scribbled in the margins, was difficult to follow. Diagrams of runic shapes dotted entire pages; swirling lines that resembled the carvings she had seen on the orchard's trunks. Each time Emma recognized a familiar curve or symbol, her pulse raced. A note in the margin mentioned the possibility that some runes were used to guard against unnatural storms. She whispered the words out loud, testing their shape on her tongue. Perhaps that explained why unexpected bursts of wind sometimes prowled the orchard at night, responding to no weather pattern she could understand. Or maybe she was chasing coincidences.

She paused when she reached a section titled *Turner vs. Williams*. The heading made her chest tighten. She flicked her gaze to the shadows trembling on the wall, half-expecting Sadie to materialize and scold her for prying. When no one appeared, she swallowed, then focused on the block of text beneath the heading:

For centuries, the Turners and the Williams families shaped the fate of Crestwood. Legend holds that a catastrophic betrayal occurred, igniting a personal feud between Lucian Turner and Alaric Williams. The resulting curse...

The sentence cut off where a fleck of mold or water damage had eaten away the paper. Emma chewed her bottom lip and carefully turned the page. The next section was smeared beyond recognition, the ink faded into gray smudges. Frustration spiked in her chest. She had never heard Sadie mention the Williams family name before. It had never come up in conversation with Gale, either. Yet the text implied that this familial conflict was crucial to understanding the orchard's enchantments. She considered setting the notebook aside to search for something more legible, but curiosity anchored her to the spot.

She rummaged through a few more loose parchments piled behind the notebook on the desk. Some appeared to be thrillingly old, edges cracking at her touch. She forced herself to handle them gently. Lines of runic script marched across the top page, interspersed with hasty English translations that referenced a time when witches in Crestwood banded together to ward off a monstrous storm conjured by unknown forces. Emma's thoughts drifted to the day of her parents' tragic accident, the memory of that ferocious storm that claimed them. She rubbed her eyes, trying to push away the echo of dread before it derailed her.

Her hand quivered when her gaze settled on a phrase near the bottom of the page: The Turner Hex. Beneath it, someone had scrawled a short note that read, *rumored final binding placed by Lucian Turner in desperation to contain...* The rest was unreadable, ink smeared into oblivion. Emma found her heart pounding. A hex named after her family suggested something catastrophic had happened. She scanned the next few pages with a renewed sense of urgency, hoping to find the gap filled by another record or diary entry.

She managed to locate a cluster of loose sheets tucked in a folder labeled *Family Bloodlines*. One line jumped out: *The local families once believed it had a protective intelligence, an energy that wards off prying eyes.* Emma thought back to standing among the orchard's trees, feeling the silence that almost breathed. She had assumed it was only nature. She realized it might be something bigger, something living.

Her eyes continued to flick across disjointed passages until they settled on a snippet referencing a name that made her inhale sharply: *Lucian Turner.* The note implied that Lucian's powers were revered for a time, though eventually they led to unrest. Next to his name, in a different ink color, someone had scrawled *Alaric Williams.* A short bracket connected the two names, with an arrow pointing to the word betrayal. Emma could only guess that these men once united for a cause before their alliance fractured. The mention of a curse between the lines made her stomach twist.

She thought of Ian, remembering how he introduced himself as Ian Williams on the night she first encountered him in the Enchanted Woods. The memory floated up: his eyes reflecting soft moonlight as he practiced a quiet incantation, the hush of magic thrumming around him. She had sensed something guarded in him, a tension that felt both alluring and dangerous. Ever since, she had wrestled with complicated attraction and curiosity about who he truly was. Now, with her finger pressed to the word *Williams* on the page, she felt a jolt of realization. He belonged to that family line.

Emma's mind churned with possibilities. Did Ian know about this long-ago feud? Was his quiet wariness at the orchard's edge tied to the mention of Alaric's betrayal, to the Turner Hex that might still haunt them all? The idea that their families were entwined by a curse made her heart beat faster, as if the orchard runes had imprinted themselves on her chest. She tried to calm her breath, but unease dried her throat. Could Sadie's protective attitude be linked to the knowledge that Emma's blossoming friendship with Ian was more complicated than she realized?

Pushing the old folder aside, she grabbed another battered journal from a lower shelf. Its leather cover bore Sadie's name, though the swirl of the cursive *E* suggested a younger Sadie had penned it. Emma lifted the cover, scanning hurried notes about powerful illusions in Crestwood's orchard. The final entry was half-finished, describing an attempt to replicate Lucian's wards. Sadie had written: *the orchard's power was not just silence. It was a living aura meant to conceal a deep magic from uninitiated eyes.* Emma felt goose bumps rise along her arms.

She remembered the day she had seen Sadie heal the

deer near the roadway, how Sadie had appeared suddenly without a call for help. At the time, Emma assumed it was a testament to her grandmother's unique power. Now, Emma suspected it was only a glimpse of the broader tapestry. If the orchard itself carried a living energy, then perhaps Sadie was only one part of a lineage that shaped Crestwood for generations. Emma's breath hitched at the thought. How many illusions and wonders had the orchard witnessed over the centuries, hidden from an unsuspecting population?

A chill skittered across the back of Emma's neck when she noticed a loose note pinned to the journal's inside cover. In Sadie's neat handwriting, it read, *Must not repeat tragedy with the Williams bloodline. Keep watch.* Emma dropped the note as though it burned her. The single line glowed in her mind, hinting that Sadie had known about the Williams family's role all along. Judging by the cautious phrasing, Sadie was worried about history repeating itself.

Emma realized she had grown cramped from the time spent hunched over the desk. She flexed her stiff fingers, only then noticing dark smudges on her knuckles after the ink had rubbed off the pages and onto her hands. She set the journals aside and gazed at the lamp's flickering light. She should have felt triumphant about unveiling pieces of this puzzle, yet her emotions tangled into dread-laced curiosity. The orchard, Lucian Turner, Alaric Williams, and the possibility of a lingering curse. None of it felt like dusty lore. Instead, it felt urgent, as though each incomplete page whispered a warning that it was far from resolved.

She sensed how late it was only when her eyes began to sting. Her body cried out for rest. The hallway outside remained silent, Sadie's door still closed. Emma had no idea how she would face her grandmother in the morning, or how she would hide the questions that now blazed inside her. She wondered if Sadie would finally tell her the truth if pressed, or if a half-truth would come again. Something in Emma's gut warned that she might have to seek the remaining answers on her own.

She rose from the chair, placing the old notebooks in the same precarious piles she had found them. A wave of guilt returned. Despite her frustration at Sadie's secrecy, she preferred not to ransack the place. With one last glance at the page that mentioned the Turner Hex, she closed the notebook. She reminded herself that knowledge, as frightening as it might be, was still preferable to walking blind. Then she flicked off the lamp.

Walking out of the study, she was keenly aware that every step echoed her internal turmoil. The overhead bulb in the corridor cast an elongated shadow across the floor. She paused by the window at the end of the hall, peering into the darkness outside. The orchard lay hidden in night's embrace, but she could nearly imagine the faint shapes of apple trees standing watch, runes carved into their bark. She pressed her palm to the window, feeling an odd sense of camaraderie with those silent guardians.

She retreated to her bedroom, shutting the door softly behind her. Muffled by the walls, the pines' rasp on the roof sounded more distant now, like a lullaby of secrets. Placing her backpack on the small wooden desk by her bed, she realized her hands were still trembling from the weight of new discoveries. She turned on the bedside lamp and observed the ink staining her fingers. It reminded her that she had stepped deeper into a story that spanned centuries.

She knelt beside her bed, rummaging for tissues to wipe off the worst of the stains, but the ink clung stubbornly to her skin. She gave an exasperated laugh that faded as quickly as it came. Her mind kept looping over the phrase *Turner Hex*, the cryptic references to Lucian and Alaric, the incomplete scrawls about betrayal. The orchard's hush pulsed vividly in her memory, reminding her that something powerful, possibly ancient, resided only a short walk away.

She wondered about Ian. He seemed so self-possessed, even while grappling with unnerving illusions that Emma had glimpsed once. Did he know how deeply his family's past was entwined with that orchard? A hundred questions stormed through her mind, demanding immediate answers. She pictured him in the clearing, seeming torn between curiosity and caution the night they met. Another wave of urgency washed over her. She knew that she would seek him out soon, no matter how awkward the conversation. Crestwood's fate, and her own, might hinge on understanding the truth behind that ancient feud.

Slipping under the covers, Emma flicked off the light. Darkness washed through the room, but her thoughts continued to race. She touched her amulet, recalling how Sadie's gentle voice had once told her it was only a family keepsake. Now the amulet felt like a key to secrets Sadie never fully explained. Emma closed her eyes, though rest felt distant.

Emma let the quiet of the cottage settle over her. She inhaled, catching a faint trace of the sea in the night air. The rasp of pines gently lulled her, though her mind still buzzed with unease. She would ask Sadie for more answers or maybe confide in Gale. Nothing about this hex or the orchard's runes felt safe anymore. At the same time, she felt a spark of determination. If the orchard truly housed curses or illusions, she would unravel it. She refused to remain on the sidelines.

Slowly, she stretched her fingers, studying the dark stains of ink from the diaries that refused to budge from her knuckles. She closed her eyes, admitting that exhaustion was creeping in. Despite her restless thoughts, her body demanded peace, if only for a few hours.

Slowly, sleep gathered at the edges of her consciousness, narrowing her worries to a single conviction: tomorrow, she would continue this search, whether or not Sadie approved.

CHAPTER

SIXTEEN

Emma pushed the library door open with a shaky exhale. The scent of vellum and aging paper surrounded her, clinging to the quiet air as though centuries of secrets hovered between the shelves. She cradled three thick books in her arms, their spines still warm from the sunny walk over. Each title focused on local myths or obscure historical events in Crestwood. To anyone else, they might look like nothing more than academic curiosities, but Emma knew that every page carried a fragment of the story she was desperate to uncover.

She slipped farther inside, determined to maintain a calm front. She had promised herself she would not invite suspicion by appearing frantic, so she adjusted the stack of books and prepared to drop them off at the circulation desk. At least that made for a reasonable excuse. She quickly scanned the room for any sign of Catherine, finding no immediate silhouette behind the desk. The only movements were faint flickers of her own reflection in the window glass.

Emma allowed her mind to replay Sadie's voice: Knowledge is power but be wary of prying eyes. Since the unsettling revelations in Sadie's diaries, Emma had been nibbling at every shred of historical evidence she could find. She had read about families rumored to practice illusions. She had picked through old genealogies linking the Turners to half the town. She had discovered scraps about the Williams line and had deduced that Ian was more than just a quiet local. Now, one person seemed to stand in her way of seeing the rest of Crestwood's archives. Catherine, the librarian.

Emma eased toward the large checkout counter. Her chest tightened when she heard some footsteps behind a side door. That had to be Catherine. She forced a polite smile, cultivating a casual air. If Catherine suspected Emma's real motives, it could make the librarian even more guarded.

"Returning books so soon?" Catherine's voice emerged like a soft whisper. She walked out from behind the tall rows of steel filing cabinets, her posture as unassuming as ever. Small glasses perched on her nose. The hem of her cardigan brushed her knees. She looked more like a timid teacher than someone rumored to dabble in forbidden magic.

Emma gently placed the three books on the desk. She tried to steady her tone as she answered. "Yes, I finished them quicker than I expected, so I thought I would come by before closing."

Catherine's lips curved into a mild smile, one that creepily, never reached her eyes. "My, you read quickly. And such an eclectic selection. Crestwood folklore, local histories involving orchard traditions, accounts of witch hunts in the region." She let the last words hang in the air, as though testing Emma's reaction.

Emma fought a churn of anxiety. She wanted to remain calm, but Catherine's pointed tone made that difficult. "I find the old stories interesting," she said. She made an effort to shrug casually. "Some of them are so dramatic. Secret feuds, curses... it's quite the read."

Catherine adjusted her glasses, eyes flicking over Emma's face. "You are aware that some of those feuds are not as... fictional as they seem in print," she said, her voice dropping to a near whisper. "Sometimes knowledge can lead one to dark places. Best not to linger there."

Emma's pulse fluttered. The way Catherine said *best not to linger* felt like more than simple caution. A subtle threat tremored in those syllables. She quietly inhaled and slid her fingers against the desk to keep them from trembling. "I suppose. People do love to exaggerate. I liked the historical context, though. I wanted to see if you had other local records. Maybe some genealogies or diaries stored in the archives."

Catherine tilted her head. "Diaries, dear? That is quite a step beyond light reading."

Emma tried to ignore the spike of worry rattling her chest. "I have a project in mind. I want to track how families came to settle in Crestwood. It might help me understand the orchard's significance to local culture."

For a long moment, Catherine said nothing. Emma shifted, self-conscious under the librarian's intense stare. Emma became acutely aware of the echo of her own breath. At last, Catherine turned and placed the returned books on a nearby cart. She moved with a slow care that left Emma uneasy.

"I see," Catherine finally murmured, still not turning around. "The orchard is quite special." She rested her hand on one volume with cracked leather edges. "You know, old traditions often define who is permitted to learn certain truths. Some powers are best left alone, especially by those who don't realize the consequences."

Emma clenched her jaw. She tried not to bristle at the cryptic warning, but her annoyance flared, mingling uneasily with the flicker of fear. Catherine's words were not random. They carried a caution, perhaps even a threat, and it felt directed precisely at Emma. The librarian must have noticed her slight tension, because she turned with her mild, unwavering gaze.

"You have quite the curiosity," Catherine said, keeping her voice low in the quiet library. Outside, the sun had shifted, painting the windows with a golden glow that stretched shadows along the floor. "Remember, pursuing certain histories can become more entangling than you expect."

Emma swallowed. "I appreciate the concern, Miss Catherine, but I can take care of myself. I only came to find a few more references. The orchard... well, it fascinates me." She tried to keep her tone light, as if she was a local student curious about her own hometown's folklore.

Catherine's smile sharpened. "I imagine it does." Her voice lowered. "Sometimes, curiosity leads to knowledge that can't be unlearned. There comes a time when you must decide what path you walk. Are you prepared to bear the weight of it?"

Emma's nerves hammered. She set her jaw, aware that any slip might betray her deeper intentions. "I am willing to read a few diaries to see if there is more about the orchard's significance. That is all," she said. She tried to keep her voice steady, but her palms felt stiff against the desk. She didn't want Catherine to sense the tremor in her heart.

Catherine nodded, though her eyes remained fixed on Emma in a way that made Emma's skin crawl. Then, in a gentle motion, she opened a drawer behind the counter and withdrew a small ring of keys. "The archives are closed to the public today," she said slowly, placing the keys on the desk, just beyond Emma's reach. "If you want diaries, I suppose we can speak in a day or two. After all, not everyone is allowed unrestricted access. There are protocols."

Emma exhaled, trying to keep her disappointment hidden. She had hoped to slip into the sub-level archives today, to rummage for more family records or vantage points on the orchard's runes. It was clear Catherine wanted to control the flow of information. Possibly, Catherine wanted to observe her more closely before letting her read anything else.

She started to speak but closed her mouth. This conversation was teetering into territory that made her heart pound. She knew it was safer to retreat, at least for now. Her rational mind urged her to get out of the library while she still had a semblance of calm.

"All right," Emma finally said, forcing a small nod. "I guess I will come back later. Thank you for your time."

She shifted to go, stepping sideways, but Catherine darted from behind the counter in an unexpectedly lithe movement. Emma paused, confused. The librarian drew close with a smooth, practiced grace, her cardigan brushing her knees. The hush of the library amplified Emma's racing heartbeat.

"Wait," Catherine murmured. "Is there nothing else you wish to ask? You came all this way just to return books and inquire about diaries. Anything else on your mind?"

Emma's throat felt tight. "No, that is all," she said, stepping back. "I should be going. I promised someone I would not be late."

Catherine edged another step forward, her posture deceptively casual. "You know, Emma," she said, lowering her voice, "some powers awaken at the slightest provocation. Many witches regret stirring them up. It is wise not to let your imagination lead you down dark corridors."

Emma's pulse pounded at the word *witches*. She resisted the urge to deny it or ask how Catherine knew. Instead, she managed a brittle laugh. "There are plenty of rumors around here," she replied, hoping her flippant tone concealed her unraveling composure.

"Yes, rumors," Catherine echoed. "Though some contain more truth than you may like."

For half a second, Catherine's gaze swept over Emma's shoulder, as though searching for someone else in the recesses of the library. The tinted afternoon light made the librarian's eyes glint with an unsettling sheen. Emma tried to move around her, but Catherine matched her step, too close and too calm.

Suddenly, a prickling of dread tiptoed up Emma's spine. She felt a faint touch, near the top of her shoulder, like the brush of delicate fingers lifting a strand of her hair. Her breath caught. She tensed, jerking sideways. Yet when she looked, Catherine's hands appeared at her sides, folded neatly. Emma's heart drummed with panic. Had Catherine just touched her, or was it some trick of the illusions people whispered about?

Emma bolted back a second step, cheeks flushing with alarm. The librarian watched her with an unreadable expression. "I really... need to go," Emma managed, voice taut. She clutched her shoulder, certain that Catherine had just stroked her hair, yet she saw no proof in the woman's posture.

Before Catherine could answer, Emma sidestepped, cutting a quick path toward the heavy double doors that led outside. A sudden wave of relief washed over her as her fingertips found the metal handles. She pried one door open, the faint squeak of the hinges echoing through the hush. She cast a final glance over her shoulder. Catherine stood in the center of the library's floor, not advancing but watching, with that same small smile on her lips.

Her parted mouth formed a murmur Emma barely

heard. "Take care that you know what you seek," Catherine said quietly, her tone laced with something akin to pity, or perhaps a warning. Another shaft of sunlight fell across her figure, turning her shadow into a stretched silhouette on the polished floor.

Emma refused to respond. Fear buzzed in her veins, but also a burning jolt of annoyance flared. How dare Catherine speak in riddles and then act as though these threats were for Emma's own good? Emma wanted answers. She wanted to unravel the orchard's secrets, explore the diaries in the basement, and figure out how her parents, Sadie, and the orchard all connected. Instead, this bizarre confrontation left her more unsettled than before.

She stepped outside at last, pushing the library door shut behind her. Crisp afternoon air rushed across her face, a startling contrast to the stale quiet she had just endured. She took two brisk steps away from the building, releasing a shaky breath and realizing her hands were clenched at her sides. The small effort to loosen her grip felt monumental.

Standing on the library steps, she replayed the fleeting moment when Catherine seemed to touch her hair. Her scalp prickled with claustrophobic dread. Emma glanced at the façade of the library one more time. She caught a glimpse of movement behind the tall, arched windows, though she could not be certain it was Catherine. Her pulse hammered faster. She had always felt uneasy there, but this encounter sharpened her caution into fear.

Catherine knew, or guessed, far too much. Even her mention of witches hung in the air like an accusation.

She forced herself to walk away, each footstep on the pavement echoing the jumbled chaos in her head. A fresh breeze carried the smell of harbor salt from the far edge of town. It should have been comforting, but she could not shrug off the feeling that she had just placed herself in the center of Catherine's watch list.

She wanted to call Gale, maybe set up a quick coffee to talk things through, but her nerves refused to settle. The last thing she needed was to pass her own anxiety to her friend. No, she would process this first, alone. She wanted to feel certain that her next moves would not give Catherine more insight into the orchard or her family. A pang of regret flashed when she realized she might have inadvertently confirmed her deeper interest by being so jumpy. If Catherine was suspicious, she now had proof that Emma would not drop her investigations easily.

She rubbed her arms, noticing goosebumps pricking her skin. A chill seemed to cling to her, one that had not come from the coastal breeze. She sensed Catherine's words still echoing: *best left alone, some powers are best left alone.* Emma wondered if the librarian was telling the truth, that she was meddling in forces older and darker than she imagined. Yet Sadie's diaries insisted that silence could be deadlier. If Emma didn't seek the truth, who would?

A seagull screeched overhead. Emma looked up, blinking away the fervent thoughts that threatened to overwhelm her. She wiped her palms against her jeans and, with a resolute breath, started down the sidewalk.

Emma exhaled hard. She could not deny it: Catherine was dangerous. She was more than a librarian with quiet obsessions. And Emma dreaded that this was not the last time their paths would cross in a dark and empty room.

SEVENTEEN

A cool twilight breeze fluttered through the orchard, causing the late-blooming wildflowers to tremble as the moon rose overhead. Emma stood beside Sadie; arms crossed against a sudden chill. Mixed scents of sea salt and damp earth clung to the silence, imbuing the clearing with a faint tang of magic that set Emma's nerves on edge. She had grown used to minor enchantments, small illusions in the garden or wards around the windows—but tonight felt different. Tonight, Sadie had ushered her outdoors for something more formal, urging her to wear sturdy shoes and to bring an open mind. Observing Sadie's calm authority, Emma suspected that whatever lesson transpired here would be unlike anything she had attempted.

Sadie's silver hair gleamed in the moonlight. She carried a candle stub in one hand and a small clay bowl in the other, both of which had appeared during dinner without explanation. The older woman placed them on a flat tree stump. When she turned toward Emma, her expression was gentle, yet purposeful. Sadie then tilted her chin toward the eastern edge of the clearing, where gnarled trunks pressed close in a half-circle. Emma sensed quiet expectation in every shadow.

"Breathe out your doubts," Sadie said, voice low. "This night belongs to your intent. Let go of hesitation and trust what you feel."

Emma nodded, though her heart pounded in her chest. She curled her fingers against the worn denim of her jeans. "I'm trying," she murmured, glancing up at the canopy of branches. The orchard had never felt so alive beneath the moon. Leaves shimmered in the pale light, stirring in patterns Emma's eyes could not fully track.

Sadie moved to stand before her. "We will call on ocean energies," she said. "You know the ocean's power better than most. Let that guide you. Tonight, I want you to recite the incantation I showed you earlier. Summon the watery essence and shape it with your will."

Emma took a small step back. Her pulse throbbed with both excitement and dread. She recalled Sadie's earlier instruction that very afternoon, when they spent hours practicing simpler spells: conjuring flickers of light across her palms, sensing the shape of a faint breeze in the orchard's clearing. She had managed those exercises with surprising ease, leaving Sadie openly impressed. Yet tonight's lesson was more advanced, promising an outcome neither of them had fully tested. Emma swallowed the dryness in her throat. "Alright," she said softly. "I'll do my best."

"Take your time," Sadie reminded her. "Settle your breathing. This is your magic to command."

Emma stepped to the center of the clearing, raising her eyes to the star-filled sky. The briny wind curled around her ankles, carrying the distant murmur of waves. Closing her eyes, she pictured those rolling waters as Sadie had taught her to do earlier in the day. She imagined a rolling tide, unstoppable and ancient, swirling in the depths. The orchard's hush seemed to soften around her, its branches swaying in patient encouragement.

When the first words of the chant slipped from her lips, her pulse skittered. She spoke with more confidence than she felt, letting the cadence carry her:

"O tide, O brine, O watery grace,
Gather in folds of moonlit space.
Flow through my spirit, calm this night,
Wash away fear with boundless might."

Her voice resonated in the stillness, every syllable seeming to quiver with latent power. The orchard grew quieter, as though the trees themselves had turned to listen. A rush of air gusted from behind, ruffling her hair and scattering fallen petals across her feet. For a breath, Emma thought she heard the surf pounding against distant cliffs, louder than usual for this time of night. Sensation flared along her fingertips; a tingling warmth akin to the electric spark one might feel before a bonfire roars to life.

Sadie's small smile encouraged her. "Keep going," she urged gently.

Emma repeated the incantation. Her words came out more firmly the second time, and something answered. She felt a strange drawing sensation in her chest, as though the tide itself beckoned from behind her ribs. A swirl of soft blue light flickered at the edges of her vision. Surprised, she opened her eyes and realized that minute motes of watery glow had gathered around her hands, shimmering in the night air.

She inhaled sharply. The lights resembled miniature droplets of moonlit water, translucent and drifting in graceful spirals. They pulsed with a faint bluish hue. Emma stood transfixed for a moment, scarcely believing she had called them into being. Her pulse hammered faster, delight wrestling with anxiety. She sensed the orchard's acceptance rolling beneath her feet, the runic energy beneath the soil thrumming in unison with her own excitement.

"That's it," Sadie said. Her voice was soft, yet it carried a note of triumph. "Invite the ocean's energy. Guide it gently."

Emma extended her palms, curiosity outweighing her unease. The motes danced around her fingers. Each spark glimmered with an otherworldly glow, bright enough to outline the shape of her hand. She twisted her wrist, testing how the lights responded to her movements. They drifted in smooth arcs. Flashes of reflected light glanced off the nearby leaves, painting them with motes of subdued silver.

Her mind reeled. Only weeks ago, she had been too afraid to admit that magic ran in her family. Now, she was conjuring watery illusions in a moonlit orchard. She felt the memory of her parents tugging at her chest, their voices lost to that final storm. The grief flared, brief and sharp, until the swirl of magic around her hands pushed it aside. An odd clarity took hold instead.

Emma repeated the chant in her mind, directing the watery motes to gather around her wrists. She heard Sadie's footsteps approaching from behind, though the older woman didn't interrupt. The swirling lights formed a gentle current around Emma, as though she stood in a shallow tidepool, letting the ocean brush around her ankles. The orchard's hush deepened until they could both hear the distant sound of waves, real or imagined, rolling steadily.

She lifted her gaze and spotted a lean shape at the orchard's edge. At first, she assumed it might be a tree trunk caught in the moonlight, but then she saw the glint of eyes. The fox stood there; its fur almost glowing under the starshine. It watched her in silent fascination, ears perked forward. Emma's breath caught. She had seen that fox many times before, but its presence tonight felt more significant, as though it had come specifically to witness her attempt.

The flickers of watery light danced around her elbows, spinning faster. Emma noticed she was trembling. The sense of wonder mingled with a pang of fear. Each success in magic seemed to pull her deeper into a realm where illusions had real weight and witches shaped reality with nothing more than whispered poems. Her parents' old life of normalcy slipped further out of reach.

She exhaled slowly, repeating the last lines of the incantation under her breath: "Flow through my spirit, calm this night. Wash away fear with boundless might." The swirling lights shimmered in a breathtaking final flare, then vanished into the night as though exhaling their own sigh of completion. The clearing's darkness returned with renewed potency, broken only by starlight and the soft glow of the moon.

Lowering her hands, Emma let out a slow breath. A wave of exhaustion followed the power she had just wielded. Despite her fatigue, excitement curled under her ribs. She had never felt so alive.

Sadie approached, setting a steady hand against Emma's shoulder. "That was beautiful," she said, voice thick with pride. "You learn fast. The ocean's energy responds well to your touch."

Emma tried to speak, but her throat felt tight. She managed a shaky laugh. "It's a lot to take in," she admitted. "Every time I manage something new, I realize how much there is I don't know."

Sadie stepped to her side, gazing toward the orchard's boundary where the fox had stood. The creature was gone now, disappearing into the shadows as quietly as it had arrived. "Magic is endless," she said with a small shrug. "You will find your own balance in time. For now, trust in these small successes, and don't let fear hold you back."

Emma glanced down at her empty palms, half-expecting to see stray droplets of light still dancing. "When I felt the power rising, it was like a wave was building inside me," she murmured. "It felt... bigger than me. For a moment, I thought I would lose control."

"I know that feeling," Sadie said, her expression shadowed by memories. "In the beginning, every new spell feels like tipping into deep water. The more you practice, the better you will learn to navigate the pull."

They shared a reflective silence. Fragrant night air lingered around them, carrying the sweet musk of orchard blossoms. A few pale moths fluttered above the stunted candle on the stump, drawn by the faint glow. Emma's heartbeat slowed as the wave of adrenaline subsided.

After a prolonged beat, Sadie took a measured breath. "This is your path, Emma. You have to decide how far you want to walk it. It is not only about spells," she added gently. "It is about acceptance—about realizing that what you carry inside you can bring healing and hope if used with integrity. I believe you are ready for more than the simple illusions we have done so far."

Emma chewed on her lower lip, recalling how easily she had conjured those watery motes, and how quickly they vanished into the orchard's darkness. "I want to learn," she said at last, though her voice trembled with earnest resolve. "I want to be able to protect this place. I want to understand the orchard's strange aura and why it reacts the way it does. Maybe if I do that, I can find some clarity for myself too."

Sadie slid a warm hand along Emma's arm and

squeezed gently. "Then we continue. We will proceed carefully. Nothing about magic is easy, but you are not alone."

Emma's chest eased. She watched the candle's weak flame quiver in the gentle breeze. In the back of her mind, she pictured Ian's quiet intensity, the flicker in his eyes whenever he struggled against illusions. She felt a stir of complicated emotions. The more she discovered her magic, the more she realized she might help him someday—if she ever gained enough confidence to do so.

Emma shoved the thought aside for now, focusing on the reassurance of Sadie's presence. "What's next?" she asked, forcing herself to smile despite the jitter of nerves inside her. "Do I try summoning a monsoon?"

Sadie shook her head, returning a half-grin. "One step at a time. Tonight, we rest. Tomorrow, we might practice forging a protective ward or delve deeper into reading orchard runes. But don't push yourself in a single night."

Casting one last glance at the spot where the fox had stood, Emma let out a breath she had not realized she was holding. The orchard's hush carried a gentle acceptance that sank into her bones. She wondered if the fox would appear again the next time she attempted something new. Though she would never admit it aloud, a part of her found comfort in the notion that some guardian spirit might be watching over them. The orchard brimmed with secrets, and part of her yearned to unravel them all.

She turned to Sadie, suddenly aware of how tired she felt. The summoning had drained more from her than her shoulders realized. Yet a small flicker of pride glowed in her chest. She had achieved more than she ever thought possible. The thought of returning to her old life—one without enchantments or orchard whispers—felt distant. She was not sure if she mourned that loss of normalcy or craved this new magic that pulsed in her veins.

Sadie set the clay bowl in Emma's hands, quietly instructing her to empty it by the foot of the nearest tree as a gesture of thanks. Emma poured out the contents—salt and water—onto the soil, noticing how the liquid soaked in almost instantly. An owl hooted from somewhere high in the canopy.

When she was done, she and Sadie turned back toward the cottage, leaving the clearing behind. Emma's thoughts whirled in the hush, brimming with lingering traces of ocean magic and the possibility that she was at the threshold of something far greater than she had ever dared to imagine. The makeshift amphitheater of trees stood in solemn witness to the future blossoming under the night's silver glow.

She paused by the edge of the clearing, glancing once more over her shoulder. The orchard's silence pressed close, but it felt welcoming rather than ominous. She recalled the swirl of watery motes around her hands, the faint sensation of controlling a tide older than Crestwood itself. For the first time, she truly believed that with enough practice, she might harness the powers that had so recently frightened her. A thrill coursed through her, blending with a healthy dose of apprehension.

As Emma stepped over a crooked root and followed Sadie along the moonlit path, her thoughts returned to the shimmering motes of light. They had reflected not only the ocean's energy, but her own yearning to grow. Practicing witchcraft might indeed be the key to understanding the forces that had reshaped her life. That knowledge made her pulse race with possibility, even as the night breeze lifted the hair at her nape and carried her whispered vow into the orchard's vigilant hush.

EIGHTEEN

Morning light crept into the orchard with the gentle touch of a secret. Emma rose from the bed, rolling her shoulders to ward off the faint stiffness left by a restless sleep. Her heart pounded softly when she remembered the incantation she had used with Sadie just hours before.

She dressed quickly, pulling on faded jeans and a light sweater. Cool air seeped under the front door of the cottage, wrapping around her ankles, but she hardly noticed its chill. She felt a new pulse in her chest, an undercurrent of energy that seemed to breath in tandem with her own. She touched the small silver amulet near her collarbone, thinking of her grandmother's warnings about practicing magic unsupervised. Despite that, curiosity burnished every thought, urging her to see how the orchard looked in the fresh daylight.

She stepped outside, inhaling the scent of damp grass and distant sea salt. The orchard spread before her like a slumbering labyrinth of bark and leaf. The apple trees stood in neat rows, their branches just beginning to show the subtle signs of a another season. Patches of moss clung to stones and protruding roots, forming a rich green carpet underfoot. Her footsteps made no echo, as if the orchard itself absorbed any noise.

She smiled tentatively and followed the narrow path that meandered among the trunks. With each slow step, she became aware of soft rustlings on her left and right. She paused. A squirrel perched on a slanted branch, tilting its head at her. A pair of chipmunks emerged from a cleft in an old stump, whiskers twitching. The small creatures watched her with bright curiosity, tails quivering in the hush. She swallowed, her heartbeat fluttering in a way that felt both exhilarating and strange. These animals behaved almost as if they recognized her.

Emma knelt to examine a patch of moss, pretending she didn't notice the animals creeping closer. She brushed the tips of the vibrant green clumps and watched them spring back under her touch. The chipmunks ventured a few steps forward, and a squirrel hopped closer from its branch, nose lifted to sniff the air around her. For a long moment, Emma held her breath. The orchard had always exuded a quiet magic, but today it seemed sharpened, as though every living thing sensed her presence.

She whispered softly, "Hello," and her voice barely carried beyond her lips. The chipmunks flinched but didn't run. Instead, one turned to the other, both twitching their small ears. Emma exhaled in cautious relief, a new warmth collecting in her chest. It might have been her imagination, or perhaps the orchard truly hummed with energy that welcomed these creatures at her side.

A part of her mind flickered with alarm. Sadie had once told her that the orchard's magic could amplify a witch's aura, making it easier for animals to sense spells or heightened energy. If these chipmunks and squirrels were drawn by something within Emma, she had to be careful that the townsfolk didn't notice. She glanced over her shoulder, half expecting Catherine or an over-inquisitive neighbor to appear. The path remained quiet, tangled with vines and shadows. No watchers. Still, the worry settled in her gut.

She rose to her feet and continued deeper into the orchard. The early sunlight filtered through the leaves, striping the mossy ground with streaks of gold. Here and there, she caught glimpses of other small animals. A raccoon poked its head up from behind a half-rotten log. A plump rabbit darted through the undergrowth, only to stop a few paces away and watch her with wide dark eyes. Emma's breath caught, both enchanted and uneasy. She pushed aside a low-hanging branch, carefully stepping into a patch of dappled shade.

A doe stood a short distance ahead, partially concealed by thick clusters of wildflowers. Emma froze, uncertain if the deer might be startled and bolt. Instead, the doe lifted its head, nostrils flaring. Sunlight glimmered on its tawny coat, and Emma felt a pang of wonder. She stayed completely still, letting the orchard's hush soften each beat of her heart. The doe's gaze swept across her, intense yet not afraid.

Her pulse fluttered. Was this truly happening? She closed her eyes for a second, remembering the incantation from last night: a summoning of the ocean's elemental flow, a spell that left her palms tingling with watery motes of light. That magic had felt vast, as though an invisible tide moved through her. Perhaps it left a residue of power that these animals could sense, or maybe her aura had begun to carry her grandmother's signature. She recalled Sadie's gentle caution: keep a calm mind and let your intentions ground you. But the orchard's power felt overwhelming now, brimming with secrets she only partly understood.

She heard a rustle of leaves and opened her eyes. The doe had taken a few steps closer. It watched her patiently, as though verifying whether Emma posed any harm. Emma's hands trembled at her sides. In a surge of eagerness, she decided to attempt a whisper of magic. She clenched one hand, focusing on a fragment of the incantation she had practiced under the moon. Her voice trembled with quiet hope.

"O tide," she began, pausing when she remembered not to recite the full invocation. She didn't want a massive rush of ocean energy flooding the orchard. Instead, she selected a single line, weaving it into a softer request. "Flow gently here," she whispered, letting the rest of the words remain unspoken.

Her free hand tingled as if brushed by an unseen current. She lifted her palm. A pale shimmer danced over her fingertips; a flicker so brief she might have imagined it. But when she looked closely, she saw faint traces of light moving across her skin, like the last glow of embers. A small gasp slipped from her lips. She could not help the swell of pride that ignited in her chest. The orchard felt alive around her, and she felt alive within it.

Then guilt crashed over her. She lowered her hand and pressed it to the trunk of a nearby tree, fingers digging into the furrowed bark. Her parents had never told her about witches or curses or orchard magic. They had chosen a more ordinary life, steering clear of Crestwood's hidden dangers. Practicing magic might have made them uneasy, if they were here now. She remembered her father's unwavering love for the ocean's mysteries, but he had always adhered to the rules of scientific exploration. Her mother had been more whimsical yet still tethered to practical realities. Would they have approved of Emma conjuring sparks in her palms?

She swallowed the ache in her throat. Losing them still tore her apart sometimes, especially when new experiences reminded her, they were gone. Yet she could not ignore the slow burn of magic in her veins, nor the orchard's acceptance. She touched the amulet again, whispering a vow to handle her powers responsibly. Her parents had known Sadie's secrets all along, and they had their own, as well. Maybe they decided their daughter deserved a life free from magical entanglements. Now that Emma had seen spells come to life under her own hands, she doubted she could return to the naive shell that existed before arriving in Crestwood.

She meandered a few more steps through the clearing. The doe watched her quietly, then turned and slipped deeper into the trees. Emma released a shaky breath, disturbed only by the rustling of small animals trailing behind. She didn't look back at them, half-embarrassed by how much their curiosity excited her. If so many creatures noticed, then a sharp-eyed local might notice too.

At the edge of the orchard, she found a small stone bench overrun with moss. She sat down, letting her gaze wander across the rows of ancient trunks. She traced one fingertip over the bench's stone surface, remembering how Gale had teased her about "mysterious orchard vibes." Maybe it was time she confided more in Gale. But the thought twisted her stomach in knots. Gale was bold and supportive, yet the weight of the orchard's actual magic felt like too big a secret to drop on a friend.

She glanced around. The animals had gathered at a respectful distance, nibbling at wildflowers or sniffing mushrooms hidden among fallen leaves. A sense of awe welled in her.

The orchard carried on with its own gentle rhythms, oblivious to her turmoil. In that small moment, she felt the orchard breathing alongside her, offering calm acceptance that eased her guilt. She closed her eyes and absorbed that solace like a balm.

A branch snapped nearby, and Emma's eyes flew open. For a heartbeat, she feared Catherine had found her here. But the figure that emerged was no menacing silhouette. A teenage girl with bright leggings and a messy ponytail picked her way through the brush, cheeks flushed as though she had been jogging. Emma's heart lurched. She recognized this girl from the local café—one of Gale's acquaintances. The girl paused, eyebrows lifting in surprise at the sight of Emma perched on the mossy bench. Two chipmunks darted away with squeaks of alarm.

"Oh, hi," the girl said awkwardly, scanning Emma's face and then the orchard around her. "I didn't think anyone else came out here in the morning."

Emma forced a polite smile. She felt tension coil in her stomach. "Just exploring," she answered. "I love the quiet."

The girl nodded slowly, eyes drifting to the squirrels that peered behind Emma. "Well, the orchard is... pretty, right?" She gave a halfhearted laugh. "I'm... just passing through. The old path leads that way, right?"

Emma stood, trying to appear casual. She pointed toward a trodden track that curled behind the orchard toward the main road. "If you follow that, you'll loop back into town."

"Thanks." The girl hesitated, eyes flitting between Emma's face and the small gathering of animals. "So... see you around, I guess," she murmured, as though uncertain what to make of the scene.

Emma gave no further explanation, just a tight nod. She watched the girl hurry past, stepping around a rotting log and disappearing behind a cluster of hawthorn shrubs. She worried if the girl had noticed the animals' odd behavior.

Emma pressed a hand to her forehead, grounding

herself. She stepped from the bench and continued her walk toward a narrow footbridge spanning a gentle creek. The orchard's boundary was not far, and she wanted to see if the morning light had changed the water's color. She remembered a fleeting urge to practice that tiny fragment of incantation again, to watch the small sparks swirl around her fingers. Once she reached the bridge, she paused and glanced over the wooden railing. Murky water gurgled below, swirling around rocks coated in green algae. She drummed her fingertips against the rail, considering whether to risk another wisp of magic.

Half an hour later, Emma slipped through the orchard's outer fence and circled back toward the cottage. A trio of sparrows fluttered in the branches above, chirping as if bidding farewell. The wind carried a hint of sea brine, coaxing her to hurry. She tucked a stray hair behind her ear, allowing a final glance at the orchard's mossy paths. Sunlight had grown bolder, painting each trunk with amber streaks. Animals continued to poke their heads from various hiding places, sniffing the air that trailed her wake.

Emma smiled in spite of her swirling concerns. For now, she would keep the orchard's wonders to herself, revealing only what felt safe to share with her grandmother. Gale might suspect something soon, but Emma was not ready for that conversation. Her new magic, however, gave her a sense of purpose.

Before she reached the cottage, she paused, letting the breeze ruffle her sweater. She held up her hand again and whispered the same partial line, summoning that subtle glow. This time, the sparks only lasted a second, drifting from her fingertips like flecks of starlight. Then they vanished into the morning air. A gentle pulse of pride filled her chest, and she inhaled.

Yes, she would tread carefully. She would let the orchard guide her, balancing caution with the stirring excitement that came from carrying a piece of Sadie's magic in her veins. That path was woven with illusions, runes, and the watchful eyes of every creature she encountered. It would be dangerous to stray too far, or to trust the wrong person. But each small success reminded her that she was not helpless.

Emma continued along the final stretch of grass toward the cottage door. Crossed branches overhead crisscrossed the sky, forming a gentle canopy that parted just enough to reveal the morning sun. She caught sight of the fox weaving between the tree trunks, its fur flashing orange against green shadows. It paused, glancing in her direction as though offering silent approval, then vanished. Her breath caught on a small tremor of wonder.

She placed her hand on the cottage door, pausing to steady her pulse. If she was honest, a part of her rejoiced in this newfound bond with the orchard.

She stepped inside, heart still thrumming. The cottage interior felt warm, scented with the faint smell of the herbs Sadie had stored in ceramic jars. Emma shut the door gently, hoping to pass by her grandmother's room without rousing any questions. For a few minutes, she just wanted to reflect on the orchard alone. She hung her sweater on a hook by the entryway and exhaled.

She recalled the flicker of power in her hands, the closeness of animals, and the sense of belonging. A small smile touched her lips, mingling pride with the guilt that her parents might have disapproved. For now, the best she could do was keep Sadie's warnings in mind, remain cautious, and quietly revel in the power that drew wildlife closer than ever, as though she was unlocking a side of Crestwood invisible to anyone uninitiated in its magic.

CHAPTER
NINETEEN

Emma felt the morning chill creep through her socks as she stepped onto the cottage's back stoop. She was only halfway through her first cup of tea when something in the garden caught her eye. Odd shapes covering the dew-laced grass often turned out to be fallen twigs from the orchard or stray seaweed flung by mischievous winds. Yet this twig didn't quite blend with the rest of the debris. Shading her eyes from the early light, she walked closer, noticing a dark, tar-like smear on the wood. A shiver raced across her shoulders.

She crouched, heart thumping. What looked like dried black resin clumped around fine strands of hair—a braided knot that sent her pulse into a panicked stutter. The hair braided into the twig appeared startlingly familiar: almost the same shade of brown as her own. She reached out, then froze, unwilling to touch it without understanding what it meant. Morning shadows stretched across the cottage's side, casting everything in an unsettled hush.

Sadie emerged from inside, a light sweater draped over her shoulders. "Emma?" she asked gently. "You look pale. Did something happen?"

Emma lifted her hand to point. Her voice came out hoarse. "That twig—there's something on it. And I think… that's my hair."

Sadie's eyes swept the garden. She set her mug on the windowsill, crossing the grass in long, determined strides. The lines around her mouth tightened the moment she saw the twig, braided strands, and inky substance. She didn't speak at first; the only sign of her alarm was the sharp hitch in her breathing. Quiet tension crackled in the air.

Emma swallowed. "Sadie, what is it?"

Instead of answering directly, Sadie bent down and hovered her hand over the twig. She exhaled a controlled breath. "Someone constructed a token," she said, voice taut. "A marker used in hex-work." The words pulsed with warning, and Emma felt her gut twist. "We need to burn it. Right now."

Emma's mind reeled with possibilities. She had read enough in the older diaries to guess that binding someone's hair to an object could give another witch—or warlock—unwanted access to the victim's personal energy. She felt a creeping sense of violation fill her chest. "Do you sense anything else?" she asked. "Any lingering signature from whoever left this here?"

Sadie frowned. "I can't confirm it without revealing

more than I should. But whoever created this had enough skill to single out your hair and bind it with that tar-like substance." She carefully lifted the twig using two fallen leaves, as though the twig might scorch her skin on contact. "We'll destroy it in a contained fire," she went on, glancing at the orchard's boundary. "Then we'll see if I can glean additional traces."

Emma watched Sadie's face, searching for comfort and finding only pale worry. "Could it be Catherine?" As soon as Emma spoke the name, her stomach lurched at the memory of the librarian's intense gaze and invasive chatter.

Sadie didn't answer immediately. Instead, she nodded toward the fire pit at the edge of the garden, where a few stones formed a small ring for safe burning. They moved like one, keeping a careful distance from the twig. Sadie placed the cursed object in the center of the charred ashes left from old garden debris. She touched two fingertips to her lips, whispering an incantation Emma only partly recognized. The words sank into the morning air, full of gentle urgency.

A spark of flame flared around the twig, flickering green at the edges before settling into a burn. Emma set her jaw, reminded of nights spent learning small spells in the orchard. Those lessons sought to channel the orchard's natural magic, but this felt different—like they were combatting something that wanted to seize her own energy and twist it for ill.

While the fire crackled, Sadie retrieved a pouch of herbs from her sweater pocket. Dried lavender and rosemary tumbled into the flames, sending up a swirl of scented smoke. The smoke pinwheeled above the fire pit, tinted strangely by the tar's residue. Emma caught the cloying stench and coughed, stepping back, but she refused to look away. If she let fear drive her away now, it would only weaken her resolve. Sadie's voice rose in a quiet chant:

"Foul token bound by ill intent,
Release the strand from malcontent.
By orchard's hush and dawn's first ray,
I cast this hex's power away."

She repeated it softly, each syllable emanating a subtle warmth that pushed against Emma's skin. The crackle of flames danced in Emma's ears, accompanied by her own thumping heartbeat. At last, the blackened twig crumbled to ash, flecks lifting into the sky before dissolving. The pungent smoke dissipated. Emma felt a chill snake through her limbs. She couldn't unsee the image of that braided hair—her hair—smeared with an oily substance, presumably intended to sabotage her magic or siphon her strength.

Sadie knelt near the pit and pressed her palm over the ashes, whispering one final word of dispersal. The faint glow around her hand flicked once, and then the ashes scattered, vanishing into the morning breeze. Emma's shoulders sagged. An ache gathered at the back of her neck.

They walked together to the small outdoor bench.

Sadie took Emma's hands in hers, expression tight. "I'm so sorry you had to see that. Hex tokens are an invasion of self, especially when personal items get stolen. You have every right to feel unsettled."

Emma squeezed Sadie's fingers. "Do you think it was Catherine? I mean... who else would do this?" Her voice wavered. She found herself looking toward the orchard's edge, half-expecting to see a figure lurking there.

Sadie inhaled, then sighed. "We can't say for certain. Catherine's illusions and fixations do raise suspicion, but I wouldn't accuse her without proof. Still, this is advanced hex craft—someone likely intended to sap your energy. The town's climate has many secrets, Emma. Dark curses or petty vendettas can lead to tokens like this." She hesitated, eyes searching Emma's face. "You've grown more proficient at magic lately. Perhaps that alone makes you a target."

Emma's throat tightened. She thought of the townsfolk's sidelong glances—of how gossip sometimes flared if they suspected witchery. If Emma's presence in Crestwood stoked old fears, then leaving a hex token was the ugliest wake-up call. She pressed her lips together. "Could... could it harm me even if we burned it?"

"It shouldn't," Sadie said firmly. "We caught it in time. It's destroyed, and I layered protective spells around the flame. You may feel a bit unnerved. But physically, you should be safe." She paused, letting the wind tug at the edges of her sweater. "Still, be vigilant. Don't wander alone at night and keep your personal items in secure places. We can't let whoever did this steal more from you."

She and Sadie spent the next hour reinforcing wards around the cottage. Sadie sprinkled lines of salt along windowsills, then placed small crystals etched with runic symbols inside key corners of each room. Emma followed suit, reciting the short phrases that lent the wards additional strength. She couldn't help scanning every shadow as though it might hold a lurking intruder. The unifying hush in the cottage felt different today: no longer a cozy stillness, but a tense quiet bracing for intrusion.

By midday, Emma found herself pacing the front room, hands restless at her sides. She considered calling Gale just for the comfort of conversation, but Sadie's deepening fatigue worried her. Sadie had used multiple protective spells in one morning, each requiring strict concentration. Emma decided to let her grandmother rest in her bedroom, hoping an herbal tea and quiet would help her recover.

Eventually, fed up with her own racing thoughts, Emma ventured outside again. She circled the cottage slowly, scanning every inch of the garden for more signs of tampering—footprints, maybe, or snapped branches. She discovered only a few scuffed patches in the soil near the side gate, though it was hard to tell if they were old. That sense of having been watched persisted. She glanced at the orchard's border, scanning it for a flash of movement or an eerie silhouette. When she saw nothing, a tremor of frustration made her shoulders tense.

Rounding the house, she noticed the fox sitting at the orchard line. Its ears flicked, and its bright eyes fixed on her. Paranoia skittered along her nerves. She lifted her hand in a half-wave, uncertain why she did so, and the fox tilted its head before padding deeper into the trees. Emma almost laughed at herself for expecting the fox to do something more dramatic. She found an odd comfort in that brief encounter; at least one living creature out there still approached her without malice.

Later that afternoon, Sadie emerged from her room looking exhausted but determined. "We'll do a second cleansing at dusk," she said, handing Emma a rudimentary warding amulet carved from driftwood. "Wear this. It's not a permanent solution, but it will block minor attempts at magical interference. Keep it on you at all times."

Emma looped the amulet around her neck, pushing aside her usual silver piece so both pendants rested above her collarbone. The driftwood was cool and faintly damp. "All of this feels like a warning—or maybe a threat."

Sadie nodded gravely. "Sometimes, a hex token is meant to scare you rather than cause severe harm. Fear itself can open cracks in your defenses. The best response is resilience. Let your caution be sharpened, not paralyzed."

Emma breathed in slowly. She tried to picture the watery motes she once conjured with Sadie's guidance, the orbs of glowing magic that had danced across her palms. Those moments convinced her that she could harness her energy for good. But the image of the cursed twig with her hair coiled around it refused to leave her mind.

At sunset, they prepared the second cleansing, sprinkling a circle of crushed sage around the cottage's front stoop. Emma lit a beeswax candle and followed Sadie's guiding words, reciting the orchard-based incantation that invoked protective strength:

"Beneath orchard sky, I claim my ground,
Let twilight hush seal wards all around.
By trusting heart and bond of kin,
Cast malice out, let calm begin."

They repeated it thrice, the candle wavering against the encroaching dusk. A quiet seemed to settle, not the comforting power Emma associated with the orchard's acceptance, but an uneasy calm that spoke of tension held at bay. Sadie's gaze flicked to Emma's face. Emma offered a brittle smile.

Once night fully arrived, Emma retreated to her bedroom, checking each window for any sign of disturbance. She drew the curtains tight. Then, remembering the hex token in the garden, she tested the lock on her door. A sudden wave of shame coursed through her. She rarely needed to lock her bedroom inside the cottage, yet she couldn't ignore the sense that someone wanted to manipulate or harm her.

Twice she nearly drifted off into a shallow doze, only to jolt awake at the faint click of a branch against the window. She tiptoed to the window, heart hammering, but saw only the moonlit orchard and a swirl of distant clouds. She whispered a small reassurance, perhaps hoping Sadie's wards truly shielded them.

Minutes stretched into hours. She finally admitted defeat on sleep. Pacing across her room, she tugged on a heavier sweater and slipped into the hallway. A battered lamp glowed near the kitchen, and she spotted Sadie sitting at the table, sipping a steaming cup of tea. Their eyes met, each reflecting the same restless worry. Neither spoke. Emma accepted a mug from Sadie—delicate peppermint laced with a calming mixture of chamomile. The taste soothed her throat.

After the tea, Emma returned to bed. She forced herself to lie still, if only to rest her body. She pressed her cheek to the pillow and stared at the window's outline.

Somewhere around midnight, she propped herself on one elbow and glanced out at the hallway. She decided to check the locks one final time. Creeping to the front door, she tested the knob—secure. She willed her fear to settle, exhaling softly. Returning to her room, she pulled a spare blanket around her shoulders and sat on the edge of the bed, gaze drifting to the window again. She could no longer pretend ignorance or rely on half-meant reassurances. Someone had targeted her. Pressing her palm to the driftwood amulet, she inhaled, grounding herself in the knowledge that she was not alone. Sadie's presence and protective spells gave her a buffer, and her own fledgling power might be stronger than she realized. Tonight, that had to be enough.

TWENTY

Emma woke that morning and pulled on a soft sweater and jeans, slipping into the hallway on quiet footsteps. The cottage's wooden floors creaked under her weight, and she paused by Sadie's door, half-expecting her grandmother to call out in greeting. Though Sadie no longer slept as soundly, she seemed to be enjoying a slow start this morning. Emma continued toward the kitchen, letting the mingled scents of chamomile and thyme soothe the jitters in her stomach.

It wasn't long before a chipped teapot steamed gently on the stove. Emma reached for it, filling her mug with the floral brew Sadie had made the night before. She breathed deep, hoping the warmth might quell the faint tremble in her hands. Outside the window, the orchard slept beneath a thin haze of morning mist. The apples on the nearest tree glimmered with dew, and a short distance beyond them lay the path that had led her to so many private discoveries.

She brought the mug to her lips, taking small sips as she moved to the cottage's front door. Her plan for the morning was hazy: she might try practicing a tame incantation Sadie had shown her, or perhaps revisit some notes from the diaries stacked in her room. She wanted to feel more confident about controlling her powers.

When she reached the living room, she slid open the drapes to let in a stream of pale sunshine. She paused at the window, gazing down the short lawn to the low gate that guarded their property. With her mug in both hands, Emma made a half-turn—only to gasp as a figure appeared at the gate. Startled, she nearly dropped her tea. Instead, she put the mug on the windowsill.

he squinted at the shape, heart pounding. Her vision cleared, and a jolt of recognition spiked through her. Ian stood there, wind ruffling his dark hair as he rested one hand uncertainly on the gate. He wore a simple black jacket and looked both determined and hesitant, as if something tugged him forward against his own will.

She felt an inexplicable pull toward him, and her cheeks heated at the realization that he must have come unannounced for a reason. Could he sense the same kind of magnetic tether she had felt in the orchard?

She hurried to the front door, heart thrumming with both excitement and caution. She opened it partway and peeked out. Ian stood completely still; his gaze fixed on her with an intensity she found impossible to ignore.

"Hey," she managed, stepping onto the small stoop. "I... I didn't know you were coming."

He inclined his head, almost formally, though his eyes

betrayed uncertainty. "I'm sorry," he said. "I should have called first, but I didn't really plan to show up. I was walking and just felt like..." He paused, swallowing hard. "Something drew me here."

Her pulse quickened. She recalled how weeks before she had been compelled to explore the orchard at a particular moonlit hour and had met Ian. She realized the power might flow both ways, uniting them through some mysterious link neither fully understood. The thought made her skin tingle.

Before she could respond, Sadie's voice drifted from behind, calm yet edged with a protective note. "Emma, dear, who is it?"

Sadie stepped out of the living room, wearing a gray cardigan wrapped snugly over her shoulders. Her perceptive gaze flicked from Emma to Ian, and though her expression remained polite, it became clear she was measuring every detail. Emma opened the door wide so Ian could properly greet her grandmother.

"Sadie," Ian said with a nod, shifting his feet. "I... I'm not intruding, am I?"

Sadie watched him closely. "No intrusion," she answered. Her tone stayed civil, but Emma read the undercurrent of caution in Sadie's voice. "Will you come in?"

Ian hesitated, glancing down at the threshold as if he expected wards to spark. He took a breath and stepped onto the stoop. Emma found herself holding her breath too, waiting to see if any protective spell would react. Nothing flickered, and Ian exhaled in relief.

Emma tried to regain her composure by picking up her mug from the windowsill. "Come have some tea with me in the garden. It's, um... quieter there."

Sadie's gray brows lifted, but she motioned politely toward the side door, which opened onto a modest patch of lawn bordered by shrubs. "I'll fetch another mug," she offered.

Ian glanced around, his gaze brushing over the hawthorn tree and the trellis beyond, where a sparrow flicked its wings. She watched his expression carefully, hoping he felt at ease, hoping he didn't sense the nervous energy thrumming beneath her skin.

They walked around the cottage to a small seating area where a wooden bench and two mismatched chairs stood beneath the shade of an old hawthorn tree. The grass still held crystalline droplets from the mist in the air, and Emma spotted a single sparrow perched on a nearby trellis. It fluttered its wings nervously when they approached, then took flight.

As she settled onto the bench, she noticed the tiny imperfections of the space—how one chair wobbled slightly, how the grass still clung to the mist of the morning. Would he think the garden was too overgrown? Would he find the cottage too strange?

She swallowed against the rush of uncertainty. It was home. She just hoped it would feel that way to him too.

Sadie came out with teacups and a teapot balanced on a shallow tray. She placed it on the table and Ian accepted the cup she offered with a murmured word of thanks. Emma gripped her mug more firmly now as she settled onto the bench. She kept her eyes on Ian, noting how the lines of his shoulders looked tense, as if he still doubted he belonged here.

She moved to shift the tray into the middle of the table, but as she stood, Ian's knuckles brushed her arm as he reached for the sugar. A faint, fleeting touch, but enough to send warmth curling up her spine.

He pulled back immediately. "Sorry," he murmured.

"It's fine," she said quickly, maybe too quickly. Her fingers trembled slightly as she adjusted the teapot, hyper-aware of the space—small, charged—that still hung between them.

Ian's fingers skimmed the edge of his teacup, his grip careful, like he was anchoring himself with something solid. The early morning light caught on his dark hair, and for a moment, Emma was hyper-aware of just how close they were sitting. The thought sent her pulse into an uneven stutter.

Emma had always thought Ian was good-looking but sitting this close to him now? Yeah, she was definitely dwelling on how gorgeous he was. Everything about him seemed impossible to ignore—the way the sunlight caught in his dark hair, the sharp angles of his jaw, the perfectly proportioned nose. Even the slightest movement drew her attention, like the way his fingers flexed around the cup or how he casually brushed his hair out of his face.

It wasn't just that he was objectively hot. It was the way he looked at her, like she actually mattered, like he was paying attention in a way most people didn't. That kind of focus made her stomach flip, made her aware of every small shift between them. There was this quiet intensity about him, something controlled but restless. She curled her fingers into the hem of her sweater, trying to act normally, but her heart was already racing ahead of her.

Sadie watched them, as she sipped her tea. "You mentioned feeling drawn, Ian," she said, her voice measured. "Do you mean that literally?"

Ian swallowed. "Yeah, it was... strange. I've never quite felt the orchard's presence in town before, but this morning, it felt impossible to ignore. Like something whispered that I should come."

Sadie studied him in silence for a moment, then nodded. "Magic can manifest in subtle ways," she said. "It often responds to emotions we might not fully understand."

He shifted the teacup from one hand to the other, something like vulnerability stirring behind his eyes. Emma watched him openly now, remembering the swirl of conflicting impulses she felt whenever he stood too close. He never quite fit the mold of a calm warlock. There was always a flicker of anxious intensity about him.

"I feel like I'm intruding on your space," Ian said quietly, addressing Sadie. "But at the same time, I couldn't sit still until I came here."

Sadie sat herself in the chair across from them. "I'm not offended by curiosity," she replied. "Still, I have responsibilities to guard certain wards." She paused, lifting her chin with gentle firmness. "You encountered them when you arrived, I believe."

Ian blinked as if realizing what she meant. "Yes," he said, looking at Emma. "I felt more active protective wards from the runes. It felt like something parted to let me through." He offered Emma a small, uncertain smile. "That might be your doing?"

Emma felt heat burn across her cheeks. "I've... tried to help maintain the wards," she admitted, voice faltering. "Maybe the orchard recognized you aren't a threat." Or perhaps, she added silently, the orchard recognized the connection sparking between them. She had no idea how to phrase that possibility out loud.

Sadie tapped her fingertips on her teacup's rim. "Actively shaping wards is a sophisticated skill, Emma." Her eyes flicked to Ian knowingly. "You told me you were practicing, but I didn't realize you were confident enough to let them shift around visitors."

Emma tensed, unsure if her grandmother was impressed or disapproving. She expected a mild reprimand for meddling with wards beyond her skill. Instead, Sadie's voice hung in a neutral space, neither quite praise nor censure.

Ian's expression softened. "Ah, you've discovered your own magic, have you?" he said, turning to Emma. "You have a presence that's... more tangible than the night we met in the woods. I could feel it." His voice quieted. "It's impressive." He sounded genuinely respectful, a thread of awe lacing each word.

Emma's belly fluttered, and she almost forgot to be embarrassed, touched by the earnest note in his tone. She had tried not to crave validation but hearing him say it made warmth spread under her ribs. She swallowed and lowered her gaze, studying the swirl of tea in her cup.

Sadie's sharp gaze passed over them both, and she exhaled gently. "Well," she said, "I admit I'm relieved you came peacefully. Wards aside, we're all going through uncertain times. Caution is a habit I can't shed."

Ian nodded, carefully setting his teacup on the tray. "I understand," he said quietly. "I don't want to break your trust. I just… needed to see if the feeling pulling me here was real." He let out an unsteady breath. "Guess it is."

Emma noticed the subtle clench of his hands. He looked as if he was afraid she might reject him or dismiss his strange magnetism as a foolish fancy. She could not dismiss the notion that something in their auras, or in the orchard's living magic, had tethered them.

She rose, intending to gather the tray, but the moment she stood, Ian's knuckles brushed her arm lightly. Even that small contact sent a shiver through her skin. Her breath caught, and she nearly fumbled the teapot.

"Sorry," he mumbled, pulling back. "I didn't mean—"

She forced a laugh, though her heart hammered. "It's okay," she said, cheeks flaming. "I'm just clumsy in the mornings."

She sensed Sadie's presence behind her, silent yet keen. Despite her grandmother's guarded stance, Sadie allowed the conversation to continue. Emma set the tray on a small side table while trying to keep her pulse from jumping whenever Ian's hand was anywhere near hers.

After a moment's hesitation, Sadie stood too, her expression turning kindly but firm. "Perhaps I should give you two a moment," she said, casting Emma a pointed glance. "I need to check something in the cottage."

Emma pressed down the bloom of nerves in her chest. "All right," she said, trying to mask how grateful she felt for a chance to speak with Ian alone.

The quiet of the garden settled around them, punctuated by the faint rustle of the hawthorn's leaves overhead. A breeze wove through, carrying the slight tang of sea salt from the distant cliffs. Emma breathed in, searching for composure.

Ian took one step closer. "A part of me was afraid the wards would slam shut," he confessed. "I can't quite explain it, but the orchard has always felt... different around me. Like it watches."

Emma lifted her gaze to his. She noticed a raw honesty shining in his dark eyes. She remembered each encounter they had shared beneath moonlight or orchard boughs, the subtle glances that hinted at deeper truths. "Sometimes I think the orchard does watch," she said softly. "It has a mind of its own."

He nodded, then his mouth twitched. "You don't seem surprised that I followed a pull here. In a way, it's comforting. Means I'm not the only one feeling these strange things."

Her lips curved into a faint smile. "You're definitely not alone." She hesitated, then continued more quietly. "I'm glad you're here."

His eyes flickered with relief. For a beat, neither of them spoke.

At last, Ian gestured toward the orchard. "Would it be rude if I asked you to walk with me?"

Emma raised her eyebrows. "You mean right now?"

He gave a slight shrug. "Not necessarily all the way in. Maybe just near the edge," he amended. "But only if it's allowed. I don't want to... break any rules."

Emma's heart gave a small flutter at the thought of him lingering near the orchard with her. "Sadie might prefer we stay in plain sight," she said, lowering her voice. "She's protective."

His expression shadowed momentarily, as if he expected that. "I understand," he said. "I don't want her to worry. Or you." Then he rubbed the back of his neck, gaze darting to the hawthorn. "I'm sorry if this is complicated. Your grandmother, you... you probably have enough to deal with."

Emma stepped closer, just one pace, but it brought her near enough that she could see a faint golden fleck in his dark irises, an echo of magical energy. "It is complicated," she admitted, letting her fingers curl around the edge of her sweater. "But not in a bad way."

He exhaled. "Thank you for not turning me away."

She cleared her throat. "My grandmother is teaching me some basic spells," she said, hoping to steer the conversation somewhere less emotionally fraught. "Small wards, a couple illusions." Her stomach twisted at the memory of the orchard's animals reacting to her aura. "I'm trying to control it in a safe way."

Ian's gaze lit with interest. "Sadie is teaching about illusions too?"

Emma nodded, feeling strangely shy. "We... practiced, though not much." She recalled how her early attempts had flickered in the orchard's hush. "I guess you know more about illusions than I do—given your background."

He smiled ruefully. "Some illusions happen whether I want them or not," he said. "That's why I admire your ability to shape wards. Mine always feel as though they're teetering on the edge of unraveling."

She absorbed that quietly. I "I guess we could... compare notes sometime," she offered softly.

"Compare notes," he echoed, breathing out a gentle laugh. "I'd like that and more."

His amusement rippled through her, sparking an answering smile. Their eyes met, and her heart pounded faster. She sensed a question hanging unspoken between them, some unnamable longing that had brought him here without warning.

A rustling at the cottage door made them both glance over. Sadie stepped onto the stoop with a polite tilt of her head, as if to let them know she was returning. She folded her hands in front of her sweater and walked closer, posture composed. "How are you two getting on?" she asked.

Emma mustered a smile. "We're fine."

Ian cleared his throat. "Thank you for not barring me from the property," he said to Sadie, his voice earnest. "I promise I won't linger if you want me gone."

Sadie's eyes narrowed slightly, as though balancing her desire to be cautious with her granddaughter's obvious comfort. "Well," she began, "I'll be honest. I have concerns, but I also trust Emma's instincts." She glanced at Emma. "You're learning, dear, and you're allowed to invite those you trust."

Emma's cheeks warmed under Sadie's quiet scrutiny, but she nodded. "I do trust him, Grandma."

Ian dipped his head in gratitude. "I promise I'll respect your boundaries."

"See that you do," Sadie said. Her tone bore a gentle edge, but she offered him a real, if small, smile. "It might help to share a bit of your perspective with my granddaughter too. Sometimes it enlightens one's own magic to see how another person wrestles with theirs. You both have a lot to learn."

Emma's pulse skipped. She heard the subtle suggestion in Sadie's words and realized it granted them room to talk magic, illusions, or anything else that hovered unspoken. "We'll be careful," she managed, swallowing past the tightness in her throat.

Sadie gave a small nod, then she cast a look toward the orchard. "I'll leave you to your conversation for a bit longer. But do stay close to the cottage."

With that final edict, she retreated again, footsteps light on the grass. Emma turned back to Ian, who looked equal parts relieved and braced for more questioning.

"This is probably the most welcome I've felt in a while," he confided in a soft murmur. "Thank you."

Emma shrugged, trying not to show how his words made her chest spark with warmth. He was more vulnerable than he let on, and she found that vulnerability unexpectedly endearing.

She eased onto the bench, and he settled beside her, leaving a careful gap between their shoulders. Every time a breeze ruffled her hair, she caught the faint scent of the orchard. A thought flitted through her mind: maybe the orchard had orchestrated all of this, pulling him here so they could break past the usual wariness.

"I didn't realize I might be the reason you felt compelled," she admitted. "But maybe...? If that's how magic works when people's powers resonate..."

Ian's low laugh vibrated in the hush. "It's a possibility. I don't know. I just know I couldn't sleep until I stood at your gate and saw you again. I haven't been able to really rest since I first met you in the woods." He lapsed into a long glance that made her heart flutter.

She forced her attention onto her cooling tea, sipping once. A flush crept across her cheeks. "I'm sorry you've been restless. Then again," she teased faintly, "I wouldn't mind if you told me more about illusions sometime."

He smiled, though a flicker of uncertainty lingered in his eyes.

"I will," he said quietly. "It helps to talk about it... with someone who understands."

Emma's stomach gave a pleasant flip. She marveled at how everything about him felt heightened—the steady rhythm of his breathing, the way his gaze flicked over her face, the gentle space between each word. That intangible magnetism bound them in a private bubble of tension and unspoken trust.

From the corner of her eye, she saw his hand lift slightly, then drift back as if he almost reached for hers but lost courage. Her chest constricted, a wave of tenderness hitting her. She beamed at him, letting her arm rest near his on the bench. They didn't touch, but the closeness itself felt charged.

"Sadie said it might enlighten us both," she said, trying to sustain the conversation. "Maybe that means we can practice small spells. If you show me illusions and I show you wards… we might learn a few important tricks."

He nodded, biting his lower lip. "I'd like that," he repeated. "Truly."

Those words glowed between them like a shared vow. Emma sensed that Sadie watched from a distance, but she found she didn't care. Excitement sparked along her skin, pushing back her anxiety about the orchard and the dreadful hex that recently haunted her.

She turned her head to find Ian studying her. His cheeks held the barest hint of color, and his eyes seemed to search for reassurance that he was not imagining the warmth passing between them.

Her heart thumped loud enough for her to hear it. "I… appreciate the compliment," she said at last, recalling his praise for her magic. "It means a lot, coming from someone who knows illusions and power firsthand."

His voice came out soft. "I was worried you might think my arrival was an intrusion. But it's good to know…" He trailed off, exhaling in relief. "I'm just glad you're okay with it."

Ian hesitated, his fingers tightening around his teacup before he set it down like it suddenly felt too heavy. He took a breath, then let it out in a slow exhale, his shoulders dropping like he was trying to shake something off. But whatever it was, it stayed. When he finally spoke, his voice was quieter, rougher, like it was costing him something just to say the words.

"There's something I haven't told you." His gaze flicked to the ground, then back to hers. "The reason I stayed away from you for so long." His jaw tensed for a second before he forced himself to keep going. "I didn't want to drag you into this—into me—because... I'm cursed, Emma." He let out a sharp breath, like getting it out didn't actually make it any easier. "It's not just some weird magic thing or an old spell I can shake off. It's in me. It digs in at night, turns my dreams into things I can't outrun." He shook his head, jaw tight. "I don't know if I'll ever be free of it, and I—" He cut himself off, rubbing the back of his neck. "I didn't want you getting too close. Because I don't know if it'll ever touch the people around me."

Emma's chest tightened, not with fear, but with something deeper, something heavy that settled in her ribs at the way he said it, like he fully expected her to back away. But she didn't. She wouldn't. Instead, she just met his eyes and let the words come, steady and sure. "Ian." She waited until he looked at her, no more glancing away. "You don't have to push me away for my sake." She gave him a small, careful smile. "I can handle being your friend."

And she meant it. She really did. But as the words left her lips, something in her twisted, because friend didn't quite cover it. It wasn't enough, not really. Not when every part of her was aware of him sitting so close, of the space between them feeling smaller than before. But he already looked wary, unsure if he should even be here, and she wasn't about to make this harder for him. So, for now, friend would have to do.

"I'm glad you're here," she said. "And I'm glad you're safe here."

Ian placed one hand on the bench between them, so near that his knuckles brushed Emma's sleeve. Her pulse jumped.

She sensed a thousand questions in his eyes. He didn't voice them. Yet when he finally spoke, the sincerity in his tone held more weight than any illusion. "Your magic... it's special. I hope you know that."

Emma's cheeks flared with heat. "I'm learning, but thank you," she whispered. The simple words somehow carried an entire world of emotions.

Their arms touched briefly when she shifted, a soft brush of fabric, enough to send an electric pulse through her. She saw an echo of that same jolt in his expression. He glanced at her with warm admiration, then exhaled softly.

Ian's fingers curled slightly where they rested on the bench, so close that Emma barely had to move for their hands to touch. Her pulse stuttered. He wasn't reaching for her exactly, but he wasn't pulling away either. The space between them felt thin, like the air itself was holding its breath.

Slowly, as if he wasn't sure he was allowed, Ian lifted his hand, brushing a loose strand of hair behind her ear. His fingertips were light, barely there, but the touch sent a shiver down her spine. Her breath caught, her heart hammering against her ribs. He was looking at her differently, not just with quiet admiration, but with something softer, something unguarded.

Emma wasn't sure who moved first. Maybe it was him. Maybe it was her. Maybe it was both of them caught in the same pull, the same fragile, uncertain moment. But suddenly, he was closer, and his lips barely grazed hers—just the lightest, hesitant press, warm and fleeting, like the first drop of rain before a storm.

Her first kiss.

It was over almost as soon as it began, but Emma knew, without a doubt, that something had changed. Ian pulled back just enough to look at her, searching her face, waiting for any sign that he had misread everything. She could still feel the ghost of his touch, the lingering warmth of where his hand had brushed against her skin.

"I—" Ian started, but the words faltered.

Emma didn't trust her voice either. Her thoughts were a tangle of what just happened? And did that really just happen? But underneath the nervous thrill, one thing was clear—she didn't regret it. Not even a little.

So, she did the only thing she could. She smiled, small but sure, her fingers barely grazing the sleeve of his jacket. "It's okay," she whispered, and the words held more weight than they should.

Ian let out a breath, his shoulders loosening just slightly. Then, with the same quiet hesitation, his fingers brushed hers once more before retreating. The moment had passed, but Emma knew—something between them had shifted, and there was no pretending otherwise.

She heard Sadie's muffled movements near the cottage window. Tension laced every breath, but Emma let the spark of hope carry her. She looked at Ian, heart pounding.

He smiled, and she sensed pure relief in that simple gesture, as though he had finally found the place he was supposed to be. Her cheeks glowed with mirrored contentment. Her mind whirled with thoughts of illusions, wards, and the uncertain roads ahead. Yet she found she could only focus on the closeness of his hand, the warmth in his eyes, and the promise in his voice every time he spoke her name.

In that delicate aftermath, she drew in a steady breath. Sadie would soon return, and they would likely go back to careful conversation and polite invitations. For now, Emma let herself savor the softness in Ian's presence and the undercurrent of awe in his words. Each small brush of contact reminded her that the orchard's magnetism was not just a story. It was real, binding them in ways neither had planned.

And when he whispered gently that her budding skills were impressive, she believed him. The compliment buzzed in her veins like a silent vow. He respected her power, and he was also unsettled by it. That tension thrummed beneath each polite exchange; an unspoken current that drew them ever closer.

CHAPTER

TWENTY-ONE

Emma breathed in a lungful of crisp midday air and tried to slow her racing thoughts. She stood with Gale at the edge of Crestwood's main street, eyeing the narrow cobblestone road that wound through the heart of town. She had come here seeking a lull in all the magical chaos, a respite from the constant vigilance demanded by wards and hexes. Yet even with the sun shining overhead, a sense of unease pressed against her. Shadows clung to doorways, and the stone underfoot felt colder than usual.

She and Gale set off, side by side, weaving past a handful of wooden stands where locals displayed battered antiques, old books, or foraged herbs. A tangle of whispers greeted Emma's ears. Old women in shawls paused in mid-conversation as the two girls walked by. Their lips moved quickly when they noticed Emma glancing over, as though they feared missing the chance to spread rumors. Emma picked up snippets of words—witch, orchard, curse

—and she pressed her mouth into a thin line, forcing herself not to retreat.

Gale, dressed in a bright hoodie splashed with paint-like patterns, glanced at Emma. She offered a brief, reassuring grin before wrinkling her nose at the onlookers. "They could at least wait until we're out of earshot," she muttered, voice kept low. "But I guess some folks prefer a front-row seat to drama."

"Hey, Em?" Gale's voice broke through Emma's reverie. "We can skip town if you'd rather. Catch a bus somewhere, pretend to be normal for a day."

The suggestion carried a teasing note, but Emma knew Gale's concern ran deeper. The silver amulet around Emma's neck felt heavier than ever. She unconsciously lifted a hand to it, brushing her fingertips along the familiar shape. "No," she answered quietly. "I need to walk these streets without flinching. If I hide, it only makes the rumors worse, right?"

Gale nodded. "Atta girl. In that case, I vote we get something fun to drink. The café is a few blocks down." She gestured with her chin, and her pastel-streaked hair bobbed.

They started forward again, turning onto a busier lane. Shops lined both sides of the road, their small windows displaying local crafts and jars of preserves. Despite the scenic charm, an undercurrent of tension threaded through nearly every passerby. Emma caught a glimpse of two older men huddled by a lamppost. They paused in their conversation to give her a hesitant once-over. She forced herself to keep her chin high, ignoring the heat creeping into her cheeks.

She sensed Gale's gaze flicking over her. "You all right?" Gale asked, voice gentle.

"I'm hanging in," Emma replied. "As best I can."

When they neared the café, Emma spotted a small group gathered near the door. The glass-paneled entrance stood propped open, letting air circulate through the snug interior. Familiar faces hovered at the threshold—locals around Emma's age, mostly students who looked starstruck. Their focus, Emma realized with a lurch, was drawn to a figure standing among them: Ian.

His dark hair, always a little unruly, caught hints of bronze when the light hit just right, the strands shifting with every restless movement. His face was all sharp angles—high cheekbones, a strong jaw that tensed when he was thinking too hard, a straight nose that suited the quiet intensity in his expression. But it was his eyes that stood out the most. Deep and dark, like shadows rippling over still water, they carried the weight of things left unsaid, things he probably wished he could forget.

Emma's pulse jumped. Ian stood in casual jeans and a dark shirt that fit him just right across the shoulders. Despite the easy smile on his lips, tension coiled in the set of his jaw. The small group, three or four admirers at most, hung on his every word as though under a spell. One girl with curly hair held a notebook pressed to her chest, eyes shining with awe as she watched him.

He was certainly charming. There was something in the way he tilted his head when he listened, the quiet amusement in his gaze when he caught someone staring, the way his voice dropped just enough to make it feel like he was sharing a secret meant only for you. It wasn't an act, and maybe that's what made it all the more potent.

Gale sidled closer to Emma. "Is that him?"

Emma swallowed. "Yes." It felt like an unnecessary answer, since Gale obviously recognized him. A quiet swirl of magic seemed to spark around Ian, amplifying his presence. Emma couldn't tell if he was consciously doing it or if his inherited warlock aura naturally drew people in. She remembered the feeling of that energy directed at her during their first encounter in the woods—an intensity that made her skin prickle and her heart pound.

Right now, though, his expression didn't match the scene. His grin looked forced, and the line between his brows betrayed discomfort. Emma edged behind a nearby stall, silently wishing the group would disperse so she could avoid an awkward confrontation. She murmured to Gale, "He looks uncomfortable."

"Captain Obvious," Gale quipped, but she didn't follow it with her usual smirk. Her voice softened. "You want to slip away before he notices?"

Emma didn't answer. A flicker of guilt twisted through her stomach. She'd left her grandmother's cottage in hopes of escaping the heavy atmosphere, but the sight of Ian—even amid these giggling admirers—brought it all crashing back. Ian was tangled in the same swirl of secrets and curses that she was, and part of her wanted to cross the street, wave politely, and ask if he was all right. The rest of her, however, warned that stepping forward might draw more stares, more rumors. Word traveled quickly around Crestwood, especially concerning anything that involved Emma Turner or the Williams warlock.

She hovered in indecision for only a breath. Then Ian locked eyes with her. The straight line of his shoulders tightened. The cluster of admirers kept chatting, but he seemed to forget them. Emma's cheeks warmed under that steady gaze. She recognized the question in his eyes: Were they going to speak? Or pretend they hadn't noticed each other?

Gale caught the exchange and sank into stillness, offering Emma silent support. Emma felt her heart hammer. She wanted to say something, but no words came as Ian took half a step toward her—then halted, likely realizing the entire group would follow if he walked away from them. The moment stretched taut.

Emma stood helpless, palms clammy. She certainly wasn't going to greet him in front of so many onlookers.

The corner of Ian's mouth twitched, something like regret shimmering in his brown eyes. He offered a small nod, as if to acknowledge her presence, before he turned back to the group around him. Emma exhaled a breath she didn't realize she'd been holding. Her chest ached from the tension of that tiny exchange. She caught sight of a few onlookers, including someone perched on a nearby bench, observing them carefully. Indeed, the old rumor-mill of Crestwood thrived on moments like this.

Gale gently touched Emma's elbow. "We can go somewhere else if you want," she suggested softly. "This café doesn't have to be the plan."

Emma cleared her throat, worried her voice might waver. "Let's just head inside," she said, forcing a firmness she didn't entirely feel. "We shouldn't let a group of curious bystanders scare us off."

Gale gave an approving hum. Together, they skirted the crowd at the café's entrance. The tight circle surrounding Ian had parted enough to let Emma see him one more time. He gave her a swift, apologetic glance. She knew that look meant he wanted to talk, but he was stuck juggling the ardent interest of people who seemed fascinated by the mystery of a warlock in their midst. She wished she could rescue him from that cornered conversation, but she had no idea how.

Stepping inside the café brought a welcome wave of warmth and the comforting smell of roasted coffee beans. The mellow lighting contrasted with the hush outside. Only two customers sat at the handful of tables in the cozy space. Gale led them to the counter, where a vintage menu board advertised cappuccinos, mochas, and pastries.

"Coffee or tea?" Gale asked, trying for a light tone.

"Tea," Emma decided. "Something with chamomile, maybe."

Despite the tension thrumming in her mind, Emma placed her order and offered a small, tight-lipped smile to the barista. She dropped a few coins on the counter. Gale went for an iced coffee, claiming she needed the jolt to stay awake through the rest of the day's drama. They settled by a circular table near the window, from which Emma could see the café's entrance through the glass.

Ian's group was still out there, though the crowd had thinned to only two admirers.

Gale sipped her coffee, tapping her foot nervously on the floor. She seemed to be searching for something to chat about that might distract Emma. "I think we owe ourselves a real spree sometime," she said suddenly. "Maybe a day trip to the next town, buy random clothes and pretend we're normal teenagers. We could even watch a loud action movie or something."

Emma traced the rim of her tea cup with a fingertip. The steam coiled upward, smelling of chamomile and honey. "That sounds nice," she admitted quietly. "It's been ages since I felt normal, though. I think I've forgotten how." She caught Gale's sympathetic look and had to look away.

"Sorry," Gale said softly. "I didn't mean to make you feel worse."

"You didn't," Emma replied. "It's just... being in town, seeing how everyone stares, it reminds me that nothing here is simple. My grandmother's house, everything in that orchard—" She paused, carefully choosing her words. Even saying orchard invoked so many tangled feelings. "I guess I'm not used to gossip being directed at me instead of Sadie." She gave a shaky laugh. "Now I see it was always about her—and me, eventually."

Gale nodded, expression thoughtful. "Sadie never seemed to bother with rumors. Maybe she was beyond them, you know? She put up wards and minded her cottage, letting people think whatever they liked."

Emma recognized a pang of longing for her grandmother's unshakable composure. She missed the soft rustle of Sadie's sweater, the quiet hum of spells weaving through the cottage walls. "I wish some of that rubbed off on me," she murmured.

They sipped in silence for a couple of minutes, letting the café's ambient chatter fill the background. A few older customers browsed a chalkboard listing daily specials, but no one stepped near Emma and Gale, as though fearful of crossing some invisible barrier. Emma tensed, fairly certain they were being avoided on purpose. Even so, it was a relief not to be crowded by more curious strangers.

Eventually, Gale put down her cup. "Look, if you want to step out for a second, we can. Or you can wait. Maybe Ian will come in if he escapes those folks."

Emma inhaled. Did she want to see him? Yes... and no. She wasn't sure how to reconcile the swirl of emotions. Her chest still fluttered from the memory of his eyes locking onto hers. Part of her wanted to run across the street and discuss everything: the orchard's wards, her sense of being watched.

A burst of laughter sounded from outside. Emma glimpsed the figures near Ian. One of them touched his arm, leaning in with excited body language. Emma's stomach twisted at the sight of Ian's polite, pressed-lip smile. She sensed how forced it was, but the onlookers interpreted it as a sign he welcomed the attention. Gale's gaze flicked from the window to Emma's face, reading her expression.

"You know," Gale said abruptly, "there's plenty of

things I could tease you about right now. Like jealousy or longing or that moony look in your eyes—"

"Gale," Emma groaned, pressing her hands to her cheeks, which now felt hotter than the tea.

"Calm down. I said I could. But I won't," Gale finished, a faint grin flickering. "I'm not that clueless."

Heat flared behind Emma's face, but she appreciated Gale's restraint. "Thank you," she muttered. She sighed, glancing out again. "He's obviously not loving this. But he's too polite to push them away."

They finished their drinks. With no reason to linger, Emma and Gale carried their empty cups to a small bin by the door. Emma paused, hearing the soft clatter of crockery against the metal. She peeked once more through the open entryway. Ian was down to just one person talking to him. The air around him looked uncomfortably stiff, as if he was trapped. Distantly, Emma considered stepping out to rescue him by calling him over, but she imagined the gossip that would spark.

She heard Gale sigh. "Let's go," Gale said, hooking her arm through Emma's. "We're not obligated to save him from his admirers. He's a big boy, right?"

Emma mustered a nod, though part of her remained uneasy. The memory of his eyes searching hers stung. "I guess so," she whispered. Her chest felt tight, as though she were turning her back on something important. But she saw no easy solution to the tension.

They emerged into daylight. A fresh gust of wind danced across Emma's hair, scattering the stress-heat trapped on her skin. She tugged her sweater closer, letting

Gale lead her away from the café. Together, they headed deeper into the narrow street, not quite hurrying but not strolling slowly, either.

Half a block later, Emma sneaked a glance over her shoulder. Sure enough, Ian was still there, but the last person had drifted off. He stood alone for a moment, scanning the street. Their eyes met across the short distance. Her pulse skipped, and she realized with a pang that he was looking for her. A flicker of decisive energy rippled through her. She might actually go back. But a car drove past, briefly blocking her view. By the time it moved, she saw him ducking inside the café. She tried to calm the swirl of emotions in her gut.

Gale squeezed Emma's arm lightly, sensing her conflict. "Maybe next time," she murmured. Her eyes shone with genuine understanding. "This is all so complicated, Em."

"Everything in Crestwood is complicated," Emma replied with a shaky laugh. They stepped aside as a man carrying grocery bags brushed past. A faint hush followed him, like the townsfolk were waiting to overhear something—anything—that could feed their curiosity about the orchard or the rumored warlock-loves-witch drama. Emma clenched her jaw, refusing to meet their eyes.

She and Gale kept walking, turning onto a quieter side street.

Gale glanced at her sideways. "You're thinking about him again, aren't you?"

Emma groaned. "Do I have a sign on my forehead or something?"

"No, but you get this look," Gale said, smirking. "All dreamy and conflicted, like you're starring in some tragic love story."

Emma rolled her eyes. "It's not that dramatic."

"Mm-hmm." Gale gave her a knowing glance. "So, what's the crisis this time?"

Emma sighed, kicking at a loose pebble on the path. "Even if Ian and I figure out whatever this is, I feel like the rest of Crestwood is just waiting to tear us apart."

Gale shrugged. "People are nosy. They'll always talk."

"Yeah, but what if it's more than that?" Emma frowned. "What if they never let it go? What if it makes things worse for him?"

Gale nudged her with an elbow. "You can't control what other people think. You just have to decide if he's worth the headache."

Emma huffed out a laugh. "Great. Love that for me."

They turned down a quieter alley, the chatter of town fading behind them. Emma slowed her steps, glancing over at Gale. "I'm sorry I keep dragging you into all this," she said, a little sheepish. "I know it's probably exhausting, listening to me spiral."

Gale waved a hand. "Eh, I've heard worse." Then she smirked. "Besides, I'm invested now. I need to see how this whole brooding warlock romance plays out."

Gale's grin returned. "Please. My life was too boring before you showed up, what with your talk of orchard magic. I can't complain." She refrained from delivering a playful elbow to Emma's side, probably knowing Emma was too tense to appreciate it right now. Instead, she jerked her head toward the main street behind them. "You want to do anything else in town?"

Emma considered. The day was still bright, the sun inching across the sky. Yet she no longer felt like browsing shops or snagging pastries. She felt drained. "Not really," she admitted. "Maybe we walk around for a bit longer, then head home."

Gale nodded. "Okay. Lead the way."

They turned another corner, the path narrowing until they had to walk single file. Emma remained at the front, scanning the old buildings with their chipped paint and crooked shutters. She remembered how, when she was younger, her parents would laugh about small-town superstitions. They used to stop in Crestwood for supplies before heading to visit Sadie on the outskirts. Back then, she never really noticed the watchful eyes.

At a small intersection, they paused. Emma glimpsed a cluster of Shasta daisies planted by a fence, their white petals swaying in the light breeze. A faint, unexpected wave of hope stirred within her. Maybe the orchard wasn't the only patch of color in her life. She still had friends—Gale and possibly others in the future. And Ian wasn't purely a storm waiting to happen. He could be a source of strength, too, if they allowed each other the room to breathe.

She pictured him again, pressed into that corner by people who wanted to glean some warlock secret from his every smile. A tremor passed through her heart at the thought of how lonely he must feel, living in a swirl of illusions and rumors. She had no idea that her own presence would grant him immediate peace, but she wanted to try. If only the gossip swirling around them both wasn't so thick. If only she could find the words to break through.

Gale cleared her throat, drawing Emma's attention back to the day. "Where to?"

Emma inhaled, resolving to keep walking a bit longer. "Let's just roam around, I guess," she said with a small shrug. "I'm not quite ready to go back to the cottage."

Emma noticed a handful of teenagers she recognized from the arcade talking animatedly near a cluster of bicycles. They fell silent the moment she walked past, eyes flicking nervously to Gale, then back to Emma. She gritted her teeth, pressing forward, determined not to let hurt spike through her. But she felt it all the same, a hot coil of shame and frustration.

She could almost taste the gossip traveling in her wake: family of witches, their orchard is strange, that grandmother of hers practices incantations at dawn. A fearful part of town wanted to blame Sadie and Emma for every unsettling phenomenon. Another part saw them as curiosities to be examined. Emma felt tears prick at the corners of her eyes.

They walked for several minutes in companionable silence. Then Gale gave a soft exhale. "I won't pretend to have solutions," she murmured. "But I'm here, okay? If you want me to be your witty sidekick while you figure out your... feelings about Ian, or that orchard, or anything else? I'm up for it."

Emma pressed her lips together, nodding in gratitude. The simple promise of companionship eased the sting of a hundred suspicious stares. "Thank you," she said. "I mean it."

As Emma and Gale walked farther from the café, a cool gust of wind rushed past, raising goosebumps along her arms. It wasn't just the chill—it was the way the air carried something else. A whisper.

Not a sound exactly, but a feeling, a thread of something brushing against the edges of her mind. It was soft, almost too faint to catch, but the moment she focused on it, she swore she heard a voice. *Be careful with him.*

Emma's heart stuttered. She glanced at Gale, who was scrolling through her phone like nothing had happened. Which meant... it was just her. The whisper—whatever it was—had been meant for her.

Her pulse pounded in her ears as she shook off the sensation. It was probably nothing. Probably just her own subconscious, warning her not to get her hopes up about Ian. Yeah. That had to be it.

But then, as they turned a corner onto a quieter street, Emma's stomach dropped.

Ian stood by the park fence just ahead, not alone.

A girl Emma didn't recognize stood close to him, way too close, her body angled toward him like she belonged there. Her dark curls tumbled over her shoulders as she reached for his arm, her fingers brushing the sleeve of his jacket in a way that made Emma's chest tighten.

And then Ian... let her.

He didn't pull away. He didn't step back. He just stood there, watching the girl with that same guarded intensity that always made Emma feel like he was seeing straight through her. Except this time, it wasn't directed at her.

Something sharp twisted in her stomach.

Gale must have felt her freeze, because she followed Emma's gaze and let out a low whistle. "Oof. That's... interesting."

Emma didn't answer. She couldn't. The whisper from before echoed in her mind, winding through her thoughts like ivy. *Be careful with him.*

And for the first time since meeting Ian, she wondered if maybe—just maybe—she should listen.

TWENTY-TWO

Emma felt the faint evening chill curl around her as she stood at the library's threshold, one hand pressed to the heavy door. A wavering light glowed through the tall windows. She had come here on a mission, determined to track down local records that might shed more light on Crestwood's oldest curses. Anxiety gnawed at her edges. Each time she ventured into this building, she thought of Catherine standing behind the desk, a mild smile shielding darker intentions. She inhaled once, steeling herself, and pushed inside.

The door's old hinges squeaked, echoing in the hushed foyer. The overhead lamps cast weak pools of light across scuffed floors. Emma slid past the main desk, half expecting a glimpse of Catherine's dark, lacquered hair or keen eyes peering over a stack of books, but no one materialized under the glow of the reading lamps.

She exhaled softly, relieved yet uneasy. Without Catherine's usual presence out front, the entire space felt emptier, as though the library itself held its breath. Her pulse fluttered with every step. The overhead air vents rattled, and a far-off lamp flickered, sending jagged shadows dancing across the aisles. The dryness in her throat felt worse than she had anticipated, especially after hours spent telling herself she could handle this search alone.

Pressing deeper into the library, she passed through a corridor connecting to a cramped side room filled with battered reference volumes. A small fluorescent bulb buzzed overhead, and the corridor's gloom closed around her. She peered at the spines of the books, searching for titles that might provide the next clue toward unraveling Crestwood's hidden history. Her fingertips skimmed over the worn covers, eyes narrowing at cryptic text. She saw glimpses of phrases like "ancestral anomalies" and "regional hex lineages," but the earliest copies were missing or half-burned. The frustration mounting in her chest felt like static.

Emma's heart gave a startled kick when she rounded a short row of shelves and spotted a familiar figure hunched over a wooden table in the corner. Ian. He sat with his back to her, dark hair ruffling at his collar whenever he flipped through the thick book. The soft glow of the lamp above him cast sharp contrasts across his face, high-lighting the strong angles of his jaw, the slight furrow in his brow as he concentrated. His long fingers traced the worn edges of the pages, moving with careful precision, as if whatever he was reading mattered more than anything else in the world.

For a second, she hesitated, torn between rushing forward to greet him and shrinking back into the shadows so he wouldn't feel cornered. Had she misunderstood everything?

The memory clashed with the way he had acted around her before—his hesitations, his quiet intensity, the way he always seemed to see her in a way no one else did. He had been so careful in public, keeping his distance, as if he was afraid of fueling the town's suspicions.

And now, here he was, alone in a dim library corridor, chasing the same forbidden knowledge she sought. The thought sent a ripple through her, the invisible thread between them pulling tight again, despite everything.

Her breath caught in her throat. She took a cautious step forward, letting her shoe scuff the floor so he wouldn't be startled. Part of her wanted to demand answers. Another part of her wasn't sure she wanted to hear them. He stiffened, turning his head just enough to glimpse her silhouette. The tension in his shoulders eased when he realized who stood there, and he nodded in tentative greeting. She ventured closer, her pulse skipping erratically. Her gaze slid to the book as he closed it. She could make out a swirling pattern on the cover and a single faint word for the title: *Witchling*.

She swallowed hard, the image of Ian with that girl flashing through her mind. The way she had leaned into him, the way he hadn't pulled away. That small, almost private space between them that Emma had never seen him share with anyone else. It had been casual, but not distant. Familiar.

Emma didn't know what to do with that.

Part of her wanted to demand answers, to ask who the girl was, what she meant to him, why Emma felt like she had misread everything. But she wasn't going to do that. She wasn't going to be that girl, the one who made things weird just because she had thought they had something special. If there was an explanation, Ian would give it. And if he didn't...

Well. That would tell her something too.

She took a cautious step forward. "Fancy meeting you here," she said, pitching her voice low. Nervousness shaped her tone into something shakier than she intended.

Ian gave a wan half-smile. "I could say the same to you." He closed the book, resting one hand on it. "I didn't think you would drop by this late."

"I needed more information on curses and... methods to break them." Her words felt clumsy, but there was no point tiptoeing around the obvious. "I don't want to rely on rumors anymore. I need facts."

Something in his eyes flickered. "Yes," he agreed softly. "Facts matter when illusions can threaten reality."

Emma's heartbeat pounded louder than the faint hum overhead. Iconic illusions that threatened reality, those words felt too apt, describing the swirl of rumors suffocating Crestwood. She nodded.

He gestured for her to join him at the table, carefully lifting a ragged tome from the chair next to him to clear space. She wished her hands would stop trembling as she settled into the seat, knees almost brushing his. The wooden chair creaked under her weight. His presence made her acutely aware of every breath she took, especially in the silence of these dim shelves.

"Find anything useful?" she asked, gaze drifting to the open pages in front of him. She needed something to focus on other than the mess in her head.

Ian exhaled. "A little. Mostly old accounts of witches fighting 'dark forces' and warlocks losing their minds when illusions took over." His fingers tapped restlessly against the table. "Nothing on how they actually started. Just a lot of cryptic warnings about family feuds and betrayals."

Emma forced herself to nod like she was totally fine, like his words weren't hitting a little too close to home. "Sadie mentioned something about curses acting like living things," she said, keeping her voice steady. "Like they grow stronger with every generation." She paused, debating whether to say the next part. "I want to help. I just don't know how."

His eyes flicked to hers, and for a moment, something flickered there—something deeper, maybe even relief. "I have nightmares," he admitted, voice quieter now. "I tell myself they don't mean anything, but they feel real. Like someone's feeding them to me." He swallowed hard. "Like someone is getting inside my head. Someone like that creepy librarian, Catherine."

Emma's stomach twisted. She had thought as much but hearing it from him made it worse.

"I think she can manipulate illusions beyond what's

normal," she admitted, keeping her voice low. "I just don't have the proof yet."

Ian nodded, flipping through another book. "I've been reading about illusions that drain people, like... living nightmares." His jaw tightened. "Some records say they come from broken family vows."

Emma traced a finger over the old script, trying to ignore the way her pulse jumped every time she thought about what she'd seen earlier. "Maybe the truth's buried in all of it," she murmured. "Somewhere between old feuds and magic no one fully understands."

They kept reading, comparing notes, whispering. Emma should have focused on the books. Instead, her mind kept drifting. The way Ian's shoulders tensed when he was thinking. The flicker of gold near his pupils in the lamplight. At some point, she reached forward to point at a passage, and the back of her hand brushed against his. The touch barely lasted a second, but it sent a spark through her anyway.

Ian froze. So did she. Their eyes met, the air between them shifting, like the entire library had gone too quiet. Emma's heart hammered. And suddenly, it wasn't just about the books or the magic or the hexes haunting Crestwood. It was about this, whatever this was, simmering between them for weeks.

Ian didn't pull away. But he didn't say anything, either. He still hadn't mentioned the girl she saw him with. Maybe it was nothing. Maybe she was overthinking. But her chest felt tight, the doubt settled deeper.

Ian shifted, clearing his throat. "You, okay?" he asked, a little hesitant.

Emma forced a small smile. "Yeah. Fine."

He didn't look convinced.

Her throat constricted. She recalled tidbits Sadie had revealed. "My grandmother has made some references to the Turner bloodline, and the possibility that the Williams lineage—your lineage—had once shared a fragile alliance with the Turners". She wet her lips.

The mention of the family history sent a skitter of dread along Emma's spine. "But I don't have all the details. Not yet."

Ian nodded, setting aside the thick tome in his lap. He reached for another volume on the table, flipping past brittle pages that crackled. "Well, that's interesting but I haven't been looking into the family history. Rather, I've spent hours reading about illusions that some call *living nightmares*. Others say they manifest from a broken vow between families."

Emma fixed her eyes on the runic script etched across the book's illustration. Curved lines resembled orchard vines. She thought of the orchard's power again, how it both sheltered her and seemed to pulse with its own awareness. The orchard's magic had felt Ian's presence once, too, in ways neither of them could fully explain.

They compared a few more notes in tense whispers, hoping to piece together anything resembling a solution. At some point, Emma set her palm on the table as she leaned forward to point at a passage describing protective wards.

When she did, the back of her hand brushed against Ian's fingers, and the slight contact jolted her. For the second time, a tiny arc of warmth raced up her arm, making her draw in a breath far too sharp for such a small movement.

He stilled as if the contact surprised him, too, and for a moment neither pulled away. Their eyes met; the closeness intensified. Emma's pulse pounded in her ears. She saw the same swirling tension in his face, the same question: why did such a simple touch spark this wild sense of recognition?

Firm footsteps echoed somewhere beyond the nearest shelf. Both of them froze. Emma's heart lurched, panic surging. The overhead lamp flickered, and a soft blur of light flitted across the row of books behind Ian. She didn't need to see Catherine's figure to know who was approaching. Her stomach leaped into her throat as the footsteps drew closer. The distinct click of heels on the old wooden floor made every hair on Emma's neck stand on end.

Ian's gaze darted to Emma's, and in silence, they agreed on what to do. He snatched up the volumes from the table, hugging them to his chest, and Emma did the same with a ragged ledger that lay open. They scrambled from their chairs without a sound, creeping into the deeper recesses of the aisle. The footsteps slowed, pausing near the table they had just abandoned.

Emma's mouth went dry. She and Ian pressed themselves against the old shelves, half hidden by the darkness. A single overhead light flickered above them, sending their shadows dancing across the dusty floor. Her pulse hammered in her ears, overshadowing all other sounds.

She squeezed the ledger so tightly her knuckles turned white.

Smothered by tension, she tried to breathe quietly. The faint scent of old parchment and the stale dryness of the books hung thick. A wave of regret stung her—she had let her guard slip. Even if Catherine didn't spot them right now, how long until the librarian realized Emma had come seeking forbidden references? Her imagination ran wild with visions of illusions swirling down the quiet aisles, searching for them. She swallowed.

The footsteps resumed, echoing closer to the corner. Emma clamped her mouth shut, leaning nearer to Ian, who stood so close that her shoulder brushed his arm. Despite the risk, her heart thrummed with the odd comfort of not facing this moment alone. An anxious heat rose in her cheeks. She caught the subtle tension in Ian's posture.

Emma prayed that Catherine would turn away or decide the place was simply deserted. For a single agonizing moment, everything hung in a silent lull, broken only by Emma's nearly inaudible breath. Then the footsteps retreated, moving in measured paces toward the front desk.

They waited, silent, until the clacking of heels faded behind the stacks. Emma forced herself to count three more breaths before she glanced at Ian. He remained tense, all the cords in his neck standing out, but when she exhaled, he did, too. Relief mingled with leftover fear.

Emma swallowed, stepping an inch away from him, trying to quell the heat burning across her cheeks. He cleared his throat softly. "We shouldn't linger," he whispered, voice half-strained with adrenaline.

She gave a shaky nod. "Agreed." Then she dared to lift the ledger. "But I need to copy a few lines from this. If it has anything about illusions or curses, it might help. I can't leave empty-handed."

He bowed his head, pressing his lips together as though weighing the risk. A flicker of resolve crossed his face, and he glanced over his shoulder. "Let's move to the far side. There is a small alcove behind the reference table." He looked worried, but the set of his jaw said he would not let her do this alone.

She followed him through narrow aisles, stepping around battered piles of unfiled books. The library felt like a maze of half-forgotten knowledge, each corner threatening to reveal Catherine's watchful presence. Emma tensed at every squeak of the floorboards. At last, they reached a cramped nook where a single overhead bulb flickered. A battered wooden stool and a built-in desk provided just enough space to set down their texts.

Emma perched on the stool and flipped open the ledger, carefully flattening the yellowed pages. Her eyes scanned the spidery old handwriting, searching for references to illusions or hex lines. Ian hovered behind her, leaning in to study the page over her shoulder. She could feel the gentle heat of his breath; an unsettling closeness that somehow made her feel safer. She forced her eyes to stay on the text.

"This paragraph," she whispered, pointing to a line describing an "ancestral rift" that hinged on unfulfilled promises between two families. The margins noted something about nightmares intensifying whenever the orchard's wards faltered. Her stomach clenched. She traced the runes in the margin. They resembled the symbols Sadie used near the orchard's boundary.

Ian's voice was soft near her ear. "We keep seeing the same pattern. A dispute between families, illusions feeding on fear, and some orchard reference about wards." He hesitated. His next words fell lower, threading the quiet air. "If there is a way to sever the illusions at their source, we might find it in something your grandmother or my family once knew. Some alliance that was never properly finished."

Emma gathered her courage enough to reply. "Then we should keep looking for practical spells or accounts of successful protections. Maybe an incantation that disrupts illusions at their root." She turned a page, heart jolting at the sight of a half-faded incantation scrawled across the bottom. The script was nearly unreadable.

Ian reached to steady the ledger, and his hand brushed her sleeve. She blinked, wondering how they had come to share so many charged moments in such a short time. Every glance, every brush of fingers, felt like it carried more significance than she could understand. But if unraveling all these mysteries meant forging uneasy bonds, then maybe that was the path forward. She quietly jotted down the partial incantation onto a scrap piece of paper she found tucked beneath the ledger's cover.

When they finished copying what they could, Emma closed the ledger with care, tension rippling through her shoulders. She felt Ian's gaze lingering on her. The vulnerability in his eyes echoed her own. She remembered how lonely she had felt that morning, dread twisting every time she thought of entering this library. Now, with him at her side, she still feared Catherine, but she no longer felt quite so alone.

At last, she lifted her gaze, meeting his eyes in the dimly lit alcove. "We can compare more notes later," she whispered, the faintest tremor in her throat. "Someplace safer."

He nodded. "Yes," he agreed. "We should."

That fragile agreement passed between them. Without speaking, they agreed it was time to leave. She rose slowly, tiptoeing down the corridor with him a breath behind her. They wove around the nearest shelf and retraced their steps toward the building's exit, hearts fluttering every time a board creaked underfoot. The overhead lights still flickered at irregular intervals, deepening each shadow.

When they reached the main doors, Emma carefully eased one open. The cool night air rushed in, filling her lungs with crisp relief. No sign of Catherine lingering at the front desk, but Emma refused to let her guard down. She stepped onto the library's front stoop, exhaling a ragged breath. Ian followed her outside, letting the door close behind them with a muted click.

Neither spoke for an excruciating moment. Emma's cheeks burned from a mix of nerves and exhilaration. He shifted the books in his arms, as though he was unsure what to do next. Their eyes met, tension still quivering between them. She hesitated, wanting to reassure him that they would find an answer to these illusions, that they were not doomed to chase cryptic notes forever. But the right words refused to form.

He broke the silence with a low murmur. "Thank you for not running away tonight. I know you saw Linda kiss me in the street the other day. I want you to know that I was humoring her. I hardly know her, and she means nothing."

A faint smile curved her lips. She'd thought about running away. She still wasn't sure she shouldn't. "Oh, that was you I saw?"

He smiled and looked deeply into her eyes and then gave her the faintest of kisses on the mouth.

"I know you saw me, and I know that it hurt you to see me like that. I have these powers where I just know things. The truth is that I'm only interested in girls named Emma," he laughed as he kissed her hand lightly.

Emma smiled, "So, if I changed my name, I'd be out of luck, or in luck, depending on your perspective?"

"You'd definitely be out of luck so don't think of it. I love the name Emma," he whispered in her ear while giving her a long hug.

Ian finally put his arm through hers as they turned into the moonlit street that stretched away from the library. She clutched the slip of paper in her pocket. Its scribbled incantation might be a steppingstone, or it might prove worthless, but at least they had one more clue to follow. The thought tempered her anxiety. Their footsteps echoed on the stone as they moved away from the library's flickering lights. All the while, Emma's heart still pounded with the memory of warm fingers brushing hers, those gentle kisses on her mouth and hand, a spark of recognition that felt more unsettling—and more thrilling—than any illusion she had ever faced.

"Take care, lovely Emma, until we meet again, "Ian said, blowing her a kiss as he let go of her arm and turned. She watched him walking away with a smile on her face. They exchanged one last, searching glance. Her cheeks stayed flushed long after he disappeared into the shadows. Even as the wind carried a distant hush through the empty street, Emma felt her heart hammer with new resolve. She pressed forward, clutching her notes, certain that tonight's discoveries were just the beginning of unearthing the truths buried in Crestwood's tangled past.

TWENTY-THREE

Emma closed the cottage door behind her and leaned against it, heart still fluttering from the encounter with Ian at the library. The midnight cool clung to her clothes, a reminder of how close she had come to stumbling into more trouble than she could handle. Shadows danced in her peripheral vision, as if the lingering traces of illusions had followed her home. She exhaled slowly, trying to shake away the frantic memories of creeping footsteps and flickering lamps in the library aisles. Despite her nerves, an undeniable current of excitement sparked through her. Ian had been in that darkened corner, wanting to help, wanting answers—just like her. They had whispered in half-spoken confessions, forging a moment of trust so fragile it might shatter under scrutiny.

She took a careful step forward, letting the soft glow of lamplight guide her into the living room. The faint crackle of the fireplace beckoned her, and she saw her grandmother sitting in her favorite armchair, posture rigid but alert. A crocheted blanket draped Sadie's lap, and a few well-worn journals filled the little table at her side.

Sadie raised her gaze, eyes reflecting quiet concern. "You're back later than I expected," she said gently, though Emma caught the edge in her tone—worry mingled with weary acceptance. "I trust you're all right?"

Emma swallowed. She nodded and moved to place her satchel on a nearby stool. "I am. Just... a lot on my mind." She hesitated. The library felt like a secret more complicated than she could summarize in one breath. She settled for a quiet admission: "I saw signs that Catherine might be skulking around again. And—someone else was there, too."

A spark of understanding flickered in Sadie's expression, as though she had already suspected who Emma meant. "Ian Williams, wasn't it?"

Emma's cheeks grew warm. She had not told Sadie every detail of their meeting, but her grandmother's instincts never missed much. "Yes," she confessed. "He was researching illusions. We ended up—well, we talked and compared notes." She fiddled with a loose thread on her sweater, uneasy admitting how much her mind kept circling back to him.

Sadie gave a contemplative nod and patted the armchair across from her, beckoning Emma to sit. The fire popped, casting shifting shapes across the worn hardwood underfoot. Emma complied and let the warmth of the hearth wash over her tension.

Sadie's voice slipped into the hush. "Your pulse is racing, Emma. I can nearly feel it from here." She sighed, thick with fond exasperation. "That boy has you unsettled, I imagine."

Heat rose in Emma's cheeks again. "Unsettled," she allowed, twisting her fingers in her lap. She finally lifted her eyes to meet Sadie's. "I know we can't fully trust him. We might share a common goal—learning how illusions twist curses—but I'm not sure if he's safe. I don't even know if I'm safe from him." The words poured out in a rush: vulnerable, half-formed, revealing how deeply Ian had gotten under her skin.

Sadie nodded, curling her hands around her own wrists, as though grounding herself. "Warlocks don't always walk a single path. Some use illusions for creation, healing, or harmless wonders. Others fall into darker corners." She studied Emma's face. "Do you believe Ian has chosen one side more than the other?"

Emma tried to recall the haunted look in his eyes when he'd described nightmares that bled into his waking sight. She thought of how his voice hitched when he admitted he needed help breaking a cycle older than either of them. A flicker of empathy rose in her chest. "I'm honestly not sure. His presence is... complicated." She paused, fiddling with her sleeve. "It rattles me. But I also can't shake the feeling that somehow, he's more frightened by his own curse than I could ever be of him."

Sadie pressed her lips together. A thoughtful quiet settled, broken only by the wind outside pressing against the cottage walls and the faint crackle of the fire. "Then that feeling is something we ought to respect. Perhaps you and Ian are both wrestling with burdens bigger than preliminary assumptions."

For a moment, Emma allowed the comfort of Sadie's words to sink in. She felt the truth of it, Ian was burdened by illusions that locked him into restless nights. And she was bound by inheritance, discovering magical gifts that fizzled wild whenever her emotions ran high. "He came close tonight," Emma whispered. "We nearly got caught by Catherine's footsteps in the library. It was... tense, but also, I felt weirdly relieved that we weren't facing her alone." She glanced at Sadie. "I just don't know if following that relief is wise or reckless."

Sadie pursed her lips, worry evident in her careful frown. Still, she nodded. "That's precisely why we should reinforce your own wards and gather your focus. Your power came quickly, Emma, and it's bound to respond to strong emotions—like the mixture of fear and connection you feel toward Ian." She pulled two journals onto her lap.

Sadie said softly. "We're due for a protective recitation. The guiding lights." She paused, eyes roaming Emma's face.

"Yes, I feel like I need more protection," Emma managed, mind drifting to the orchard nights when Sadie had shown her how to conjure orbs of gentle glow. Those orbs functioned as wards, pushing back malevolent energies. Emma had mastered them, surprised at how easily she learned how to control them.

Sadie's firm, caring voice pulled Emma from her reverie. "Come on. We'll do it slowly. Once you're steady, everything else may feel clearer."

With shoulders squared, Emma lowered herself to the rug. The cottage's magic enveloped them like a protective cloak. Outside, gusts of wind scraped the pines, making the entire house groan in protest. Growing up on the coast, Emma was use to storms, yet she heard an edge in tonight's wind—a promise that something was swirling just beyond the orchard's boundary.

Sadie laid one of her journals beside them, open to a page of delicate script. She raised an arm so Emma could see. Then, in a measured, resonant tone, she began:

"In corners dim and secrets kept,
Let brimming light protect what's wept.
By orchard root and hearth aflame,
Guard every fragile thought by name."

The words felt gentle, yet they vibrated with underlying strength. Emma took a slow breath and joined in on the next verse, letting the syllables align with the steady rhythm of her heartbeat:

"Shadows coil where hearts lie bare,
We banish dread with watchful care.
A light in gloom, a hope in dark,
We kindle sparks where fear might mark."

Her voice trembled on the final syllable, but Sadie gave her an encouraging nod. The fire sputtered, throwing flecks of orange across the walls. Emma sensed a shift in the air, as though the budding wards recognized her voice.

She closed her eyes, inhaling the smells of burning pine and aged parchment.

Sadie struck a match and lit a slender candle beside them, continuing in a calmer whisper:

"By Turner lines, by spirit's grace,
Let guiding glow fill time and space.
Affix our will in swirl of night,
Protect these halls with watchful light."

Emma felt the incantation weaving around them. At the edges of her vision, luminescence flickered. Like delicate fireflies, they hovered near Sadie's outstretched hands. The swirling glow brightened, lingering in the corners of the living room. Emma repeated the refrain with her grandmother, voice steadier now:

"In corners dim and secrets kept,
Let brimming light protect what's wept."

When they finished, everything settled. The motes of light whirled above Emma's head before drifting around the room, pushing away the stale worry that had clung to her from the library. Emma's heartbeat slowed, though her thoughts still circled Ian. The incantation left her calmer, more present in the moment.

Sadie exhaled, letting her shoulders relax. "There." She sounded tired but satisfied. "That should cushion us from any stray influences for a while. The orchard wards will reinforce these guiding lights."

Emma swept her gaze around, noting how the living room looked brighter, as if the everyday shadows no longer lurked in corners. She let out a breathy laugh. "My head already feels less crowded. Thank you." She paused, remembering the swirl of confusion earlier. "But the relief is temporary if I keep letting my emotions tangle with Ian's... presence. I might slip. I'm not sure if that's more dangerous for me or for him."

Sadie closed the journal, resting a gentle hand on Emma's arm. "It's good that you're questioning your feelings. That doubt can be a clarifying force, provided you don't let it paralyze you. Still..." She leveled Emma with a look. "Ian's path is not something you alone can control. Whether he truly means to help you or stands at the brink of a darker road, you can't decide that for him."

The flames crackled, sending a burst of sparks up the chimney, and Emma glanced toward the window. The wind outside rattled the panes, a restless reminder that the orchard was never fully quiet. She rubbed the slight ache in her temples. "I feel like I'm dancing through illusions on one side and my own uncertain magic on the other."

Sadie's hand remained steady, a comforting weight on Emma's forearm. "I won't pretend to have every answer. But it's vital you hold onto caution, especially around a warlock with a complicated past." She hesitated, gaze darkening with a memory Emma could not read. "I have read somewhere about his family being cursed by one of our ancestors many generations ago so there's something about old feuds or unhealed rifts, perhaps. You may be drawn to him—maybe it's curiosity, maybe something deeper—but never forget you're still learning to protect yourself."

Emma gave a small nod, words catching in her throat. She pictured Ian alone in that library corner, struggling to decipher spells that might keep illusions from devouring him. He had looked so guarded when their eyes met, as if he expected her to vanish if the truth of his curse became too overwhelming. The thought made her chest tighten with empathy. "I can't just turn my back," she said softly. "Maybe that's unwise, but if he's in danger... if the illusions are driving him closer to the edge—"

Sadie's voice was firm yet gentle. "No one says you have to abandon him. Just be mindful of what lines you draw. And also know that he's not responsible for that curse from long ago. It's his unfortunate legacy."

The tension in Emma's body ebbed. She recognized her grandmother's caution came from love. Sadie wasn't trying to push Emma away from Ian out of suspicion alone. She truly wanted Emma kept safe, especially after all the suspicious whispers that had circled them both for so long. "I understand," Emma murmured. "I'll be careful." She paused, letting the crackle of the fire fill a moment of silence. "I appreciate your guidance."

Sadie reached for a second candle. A soft swirl of leftover magic still floated around the flame, glimmering like stardust. "We have one more incantation to finish binding these wards," she said.

Together, they repeated the last lines of the protective

incantation, bridging them with an additional verse Sadie improvised:

"Let trust be wise and caution strong,
In drifting hearts, discern the wrong.
No ill intent shall cross this door,
We guard in peace, forevermore."

As Emma spoke the final words alongside her grandmother, she felt power resonate through her, an almost comforting ripple in her veins. Warmth spread across her arms, gliding over her skin in a ghostly caress. She glanced down and saw faint traces of pale light shimmering at her forearms, like ephemeral bracelets. They glowed briefly then vanished, leaving behind a gentle tingle. She exhaled and passed a hand over her eyes. "You were right," she said. "My head is clearer when we do these incantations."

Sadie smiled, though her eyes held that lingering worry reminiscent of an unspoken question: how far would Emma's resolve hold if illusions tested her again? But she only said, "Good. You must practice them regularly, especially now that your emotions are a magnet for stray energies."

A gust outside nearly shook the cottage, drawing a startled gasp from Emma. The wind howled through the pines, and she could imagine the orchard's branches rattling in the night. Despite the comforting glow inside, the world beyond the windows felt unsettled, a place where illusions and watchers might gather unseen. She slowly pushed to her feet and stepped to the window, peering into the darkness. Only the faint silhouette of twisting tree boughs was visible.

Sadie joined her, resting one hand lightly at the small of Emma's back. "Whatever you're feeling about Ian or the orchard, keep in mind that we can't see every path. All we can do is strengthen ourselves, watch for signs, and remain open to the possibility that trust, once offered, can also be tested."

Emma's reflection in the window flickered—she saw her hazel eyes, shadowed by fatigue, and the glow of candlelight behind her. Ian's face emerged in her memory, the way he had looked at that moment before they parted, his gaze almost pleading for her not to vanish. She didn't know how to shape that bond, or if it was even wise to try.

"I keep waiting for a sign," she admitted. "Something to tell me if it's safe to let him close."

Sadie's voice was even. "Sometimes the only sign is your own instinct. I can give you caution; I can help you harness your gifts—but I can't decide your heart's course."

Emma pressed her fingers to the windowsill. Outside, the wind carried an eerie moan, as if warning them that illusions still lurked. "You're right," she said. "I have to trust myself as much as I trust you."

As the last swirl of magic faded, an unexpected sense of calm descended on Emma. The wind still rattled the cottage, but it could not infiltrate the glow they had woven. She became acutely aware of her own breathing, the steady in-and-out pattern that told her everything in this moment was safe.

Sadie angled her head, thin lines of worry easing at the corners of her mouth. "Better?"

Emma offered a slight smile. Her voice was softer now, less burdened by the frantic swirl of worry. "Yes, better." She paused, letting the moment hold. "Whenever I think about him, though, I still get this flutter right here." She tapped her sternum, laughing quietly at how silly it sounded. "I can't tell if it's dread or—hope."

Sadie didn't scold her, nor did she show censure. Instead, she slid her hand over Emma's and gave it a reassuring squeeze. "Many powerful truths begin as a muddle of fear and longing." She let go and blew out both candles. "Just promise me you'll keep your eyes wide open. Watch for any signs that illusions might twist your feelings. Keep your wards strong. Let that spark of caution remain bright."

Emma bowed her head, mildly embarrassed to be so transparent about her conflicting emotions, but also grateful for the acceptance in Sadie's gaze. "I will," she whispered, pressing her palm to the faint warmth lingering on her forearm. The last swirl of magic reminded her that she was no helpless bystander. She had inherited skill and potential. And if she approached her connection with Ian with both curiosity and vigilance, maybe there was a path forward that didn't end in heartbreak.

A gust outside battered the windows again, and Sadie stood to poke at the fire, stirring it into a steadier blaze. The living room brightened, the final vestiges of swirling light drifting into the corners and dissolving. Emma rubbed her hands together, letting the renewed warmth seep into her skin.

She gazed at Sadie's hunched shoulders, noticing the way her grandmother's age showed in quiet moments like these. Worry pressed at Emma's chest when she thought of Sadie expending so much energy to keep the orchard safe, to keep illusions from seeping into the cottage. Perhaps that was all the more reason for Emma to manage her own entanglements carefully. She refused to be a liability. If her heart demanded that she care for Ian's struggles, she would do it responsibly, warding her thoughts so no manipulator —Catherine or otherwise—could exploit the link.

The protective atmosphere in the living room left Emma feeling both emboldened and strangely solemn. She quietly moved to kneel by the hearth, watching the flames lick the blackened logs. "You mentioned that this guiding incantation was once used to stave off minor illusions. Is it enough if to keep Catherine at bay?" The memory of stealthy footsteps in the library made her shiver.

Sadie shook her head, her expression turning serious. "It holds smaller threats at bay. But for illusions wrought from deep curses—or from a powerful witch—these lights only provide a buffer. I'll reinforce the orchard wards tomorrow." She straightened, drawing a crocheted blanket around her shoulders. "You, meanwhile, practice daily. Keep your energy attuned. If you sense Ian is truly earnest, you can share a fraction of what we do here—but remember, trust is a risk, not a guarantee."

Emma's throat tightened. The reference to trust as a risk heightened her sense that everything about her bond with Ian teetered on a precarious edge. Organization, caution, and practice. Those were the steps to ensure she didn't lose herself.

She stood slowly, her limbs heavy with a mixture of relief and exhaustion. The wards shimmered faintly whenever she breathed too deeply, reminding her how linked her magic had become to her emotions. She turned to Sadie, who was folding the journals on her lap. "Thank you," Emma said softly. "I promise I'll stay grounded. I have no intention of rushing into the unknown without a shred of caution."

Sadie's smile looked tired but proud. "Nevertheless, keep your flame of prudence alive. Sometimes the heart beckons us forward, but the mind and spirit must ensure we aren't diving into illusions." She walked Emma to the foot of the stairs. "Now get some rest. It's late, and your mind will be clearer after you sleep."

Emma nodded. She clasped Sadie's hand for a moment, letting the older woman's steady presence sink into her. Then she padded up the narrow staircase toward her bedroom. The old steps groaned underfoot. A swirl of the orchard's crisp air drifted through the window at the landing, carrying the faint tang of pine needles and distant sea salt. She paused to gaze into the darkness outside; she saw only a slice of moon and vague shapes of swaying pines. Tucking her hair behind her ear, she closed her eyes and recalled the way the guiding lights incantation had felt—like a promise that she was no longer stumbling blind.

Before slipping into her room, she heard Sadie's voice float up behind her, quiet but purposeful: "Remember, Em, not all warlocks walk the same path—yet none of us can see the road until we step onto it. You must decide how far you're willing to walk with him."

Emma replied with a murmur; her answer lost in the rustle of the night wind. She pushed open her door, lit a small lamp on the bedside table, and sank into the mattress. The protective hum from earlier still glimmered in her thoughts. Warm and calming, it reminded her that she had control over her own choices. She pressed her hand to her racing heart, thinking again of Ian's haunted stare. He might be a hazard. He might be a hope. Perhaps he was both, and that duality made her chest ache with something close to longing.

She recalled Sadie's final instructions to keep practicing, to keep the flame of caution burning. The swirl of new possibilities tugged her, yes, but she would not fall blindly into them. She set aside her lingering jitters and closed her eyes, letting the day's last threads of tension unravel. Tonight, the wards would watch over the cottage, and she would hold tight to her vow.

Lips parting in a quiet exhale, she sank deeper into her pillow, calm gradually replacing the fretful energy. The guiding lights had bestowed her with a rare sense of peace, and she intended to safeguard it. Even if she stood at the brink of an uncertain alliance, even if she was drawn to Ian in ways she could hardly articulate, she would not abandon prudence. She would stay vigilant, forging a new connection only if she could do so with clear eyes. The wind outside continued to moan, but within herself, she felt a steadier hush. She clutched that calm as though it were a lifeline, and as she drifted closer to sleep, she resolved not to let it slip away.

In her dream, Emma stood in the orchard, but something about it felt off. The air was thick, charged with this weird mix of warmth and unease. The moon hung low, silver light spilling through the branches, but the shadows stretched too far, twisting at the edges of her vision. Everything was quiet. Too quiet. Like the whole place was holding its breath.

Then he was there.

Ian stepped out from between the trees, moving like he belonged to the dark. His hair was a little messy, his eyes catching just enough light to look almost unreal. He didn't say anything, but she felt the pull between them, this thing she didn't have words for but couldn't shake.

Emma took a step forward, and suddenly he was right in front of her, closer than she expected. Close enough that she could see the way his breath hitched, the way his lips parted like he wanted to say something but didn't. His fingers brushed along the inside of her wrist, and the touch sent a slow, burning warmth through her.

"I shouldn't be here," he murmured, but he didn't step back.

She wasn't sure if he meant the orchard or being with her.

"You always are," she whispered back. "Even when you're not."

His mouth quirked into something that wasn't quite a smile, wasn't quite sadness. Then his hand lifted, fingertips grazing her cheek. She felt the warmth of him, solid and real, and something in her chest squeezed tight. He traced the line of her jaw with his thumb, slow and careful, and suddenly, the space between them disappeared.

Then he kissed her.

It was soft at first, hesitant, like he was afraid she might disappear. But when she didn't—when she leaned in instead—his fingers slid into her hair, his other hand settling on her waist, like he was trying to memorize every inch of her. Heat spread through her, the kind that made her toes curl, the kind that made her forget where she was.

She kissed him back, like she'd always known she would. Like she'd always meant to.

And then everything changed.

A chill crept in, sliding down her spine. The orchard shifted, no longer watching—warning.

Ian stilled. His breath, once warm, turned ice-cold against her lips. The shadows around them stretched wider, curling at the edges of his face, pulling at him. Emma's heart slammed against her ribs. She tried to step back, but his fingers were still tangled in her hair, holding on like he was afraid to let go.

"Ian—" her voice barely broke the quiet.

His eyes darkened, swallowing the light. The flicker of pain in them hit her like a punch, raw and open and breaking right in front of her.

"You have to wake up," he whispered. But his voice wasn't his anymore.

The orchard trembled beneath her feet. The roots cracked through the earth, twisting like they were alive. The moon overhead flickered, like a candle struggling to stay lit.

She tried to move, to shake off the fear crawling up her spine, but her body wouldn't listen. Ian's hands fell away, his whole form unraveling like smoke, slipping through her fingers no matter how hard she tried to hold on.

And then he was gone.

The silence shattered.

Emma shot up in bed, breath ragged, heart pounding so hard it hurt. The darkness of her room felt too still, too empty. She pressed a shaking hand to her chest, trying to slow the thunder inside her.

Her lips still tingled.

And in the pit of her stomach, something heavy and hollow settled in, like she'd lost something—someone—before she ever really had him.

THE STORY CONTINUES

The story continues in book two, *Family Curse,* coming soon to Amazon.

EXCERPT FROM FAMILY CURSE

CHAPTER ONE

Emma stared at her bedroom ceiling, tracing tiny spots of moonlight that slipped past the lace of her curtains. She had tried every method of calming her mind that Sadie once taught her—slow breathing, a mental catalog of the day's smallest blessings, even a whispered protective verse —but none of it quieted the restlessness rattling inside her. Every time Emma closed her eyes, she felt the orchard's silent pull, beckoning in ways she couldn't ignore.

A chill ran through her when she finally rose from bed and got dressed. She pressed a palm to the window, feeling the glass vibrate slightly in the night breeze. Beyond the cottage walls, the orchard glowed under a pale moon, branches swaying as though they called her name. She chewed her bottom lip, debating if she should risk stepping out by herself. Yet the restlessness in her bones was too strong to bear. She wasn't going to sleep tonight unless she confronted whatever tugged at her senses.

She slid open the window, letting the orchard's nocturnal air wash into her room. The freshness smelled of damp leaves and distant salt, a combination that made her heart skip. With quiet determination, Emma climbed onto the sill and swung her legs over the edge, pausing only to make sure her foot found steady purchase on the low ledge below. She glanced around for the fox that sometimes roamed around Sadie's property, but the yard was empty. Her breath wavered in her throat as she dropped softly to the ground, brushing grass and dirt off her hands.

No lantern was lit outside, but the moon was bright enough for Emma to navigate the winding path that separated the cottage from the orchard's entrance. Silver light spilled across the edges of drooping apple boughs, illuminating each twist in the trunk. She tugged her sweater closer, remembering Sadie's many warnings. The orchard might provide sanctuary for those who knew how to listen, but illusions could lurk here as well, especially if a powerful witch or warlock wanted to manipulate the shadows. Emma felt a distinct awareness beneath her feet, as though the orchard recognized her presence and rose to greet her.

She slipped into the grove, letting the row of trees guide her deeper toward the heart of the property. Weeds and wildflowers brushed against her ankles. Every now and then, a night bird called from somewhere above, but the orchard was mostly quiet. Her fingers lightly touched the trunk of a nearby tree, seeking comfort in the rough bark. A faint warmth broke through her anxiety, reminding her that she refused to cower from magic that could be harnessed for good. Sadie had said that if Emma trusted her instincts, the orchard would reciprocate.

She followed an unspoken sense of direction, turning past clusters of apple branches into a small clearing. There, half-hidden by the curved trunk of a venerable oak, she spotted a familiar figure. Ian leaned against the bark; one hand curled loose at his side. His dark hair caught thin streaks of moonlight. His jacket was slightly rumpled as though he hadn't planned on sleeping either. At first, Emma tensed, uncertain if he wanted her company in a place that felt so private. Then she remembered the conversations they had shared, the mutual worry that kept them both on edge. Part of her suspected he might be relieved she found him.

Emma's soft footstep on the thick grass made him glance up. Their eyes met, and the tension in his shoulders eased. He made no effort to hide a small, grateful tilt of his lips. She stepped closer, drawn by the quiet magnetism she felt every time they stood in the orchard's hush together.

"I didn't think anyone else would be awake," Emma said, keeping her voice low. The night pressed around them, muffling every sound. Even the distant rustle of leaves seemed muted, as though nature herself held her breath.

Ian exhaled a shaky laugh. "I could say the same. Though I can't remember the last time I slept without nightmares." He looked away, his gaze fixed on the moonlit clearing as if searching for answers he had yet to find. "Something told me I might find peace here."

Emma nodded, a lump forming in her throat. She had heard him mention nighttime restlessness before, hints that illusions haunted him more severely than he admitted. She recalled Sadie's cautions against ignoring the signs of an overburdened warlock. Yet Emma couldn't help feeling a fierce sense of empathy whenever she saw the flickers of exhaustion in his eyes.

She shuffled closer, arms folded for warmth. "The orchard soothes me, too," she confessed. "I keep hoping it will calm the worst of my doubts, but lately I can hardly tell if the orchard is offering guidance or simply letting me wander."

He studied her in bluish gloom. "Maybe you're the one guiding it. Sadie told me once that land containing old magic learns to reflect the witch who walks it."

A swift ache of memory burned in Emma's chest. She hadn't realized Sadie ever spoke with Ian at enough length to offer orchard secrets. Yet something about that made sense: Sadie was protective of Emma, but she also recognized anyone wounded by illusions deserved a chance at healing. Maybe Sadie had seen the same pain in Ian that Emma saw now.

She gave him a faint, uncertain smile. "Did my grandmother mention anything else?" The question came out timid, as though she wasn't entirely sure she wanted the answer.

He hesitated, the tense line of his jaw hinting at the weight of unspoken truths. "She warned me to tread carefully around illusions, yes, but she also said I shouldn't bury my need for connection out of fear." His tone thinned, as though embarrassed by the candid admission. "Part of me thinks she caught me once, rummaging in the orchard, hoping to glean a protective object from one of the oaks. I told her I was hungry for any small relief. She gave me one of her handcrafted wards, but it never seemed as strong as when she cast it."

Emma's mind returned to the wards Sadie used over the cottage. The protective runes had always glowed faintly whenever Emma or Sadie felt a spike of dark energy. If Ian had tried to replicate those wards alone, she understood how that might have fallen short. Sadie's magic was complex, shaped by generations of Turner lineage. Emma wondered if her own blossoming power could help him more than he realized. The thought was both comforting and terrifying. She patted the tree behind her, nervously sliding her fingers across curling bark.

"Sadie's wards are rooted in our bloodline," Emma said. "She tried to teach me some of her incantations, but I'm still learning. I worry I will do more harm than good if I try to help you. This is all so new." She realized how vulnerable her words sounded, but the orchard's aura made pretense feel pointless.

A soft glimmer of understanding crossed his face. "I know. If it helps, your presence alone dulls the edges of my nightmares. Whenever you appear, I feel... steadier." He swallowed, his gaze dropping to the ground. "That probably sounds desperate."

Emma's heart gave a sharp tug, some combination of

compassion and a spark of bittersweet longing. She remembered their brief, charged moments in the library corners and how her pulse had pounded with the sense that they were dancing near a cliff. "Then we can be desperate together," she finally managed, voice almost breaking. "I don't exactly have a perfect handle on illusions or curses. And the more I learn, the more I realize how reckless it is to charge ahead. Sometimes I question if I should trust magic at all... or trust my heart over reason."

"It feels like something bigger than either of us," he said quietly, letting the orchard's quiet swallow the space between them. The wind picked up, stirring his dark hair away from his forehead. He still looked exhausted, but in the moonlight, Emma caught a gentleness in his expression that made her throat tighten.

She remembered Sadie telling her not to run from powerful connections, even if those bonds seemed fraught with risk. Emma also remembered every rumor that warned her about warlocks with illusions in their blood. She stood at a precarious crossroad: either she reached out, or she walled herself off before the orchard's magic could entwine them further. Her heart hammered with the thought of stepping closer.

When she shifted her weight a fraction, her boot scuffed a patch of dirt. Ian lifted his head. For a moment, they simply stared at each other, the orchard's quiet giving shape to unspoken confessions. Emma's mind spun with questions she lacked the courage to ask. She wondered how many times he had come here alone, hoping to outrun illusions that twisted his sleep. She wondered if her own presence could truly offer him a brief reprieve.

In silence, she stepped forward. Night air pressed warm against her cheeks, or perhaps that was just the heat flooding her veins. They were not quite shoulder to shoulder, but close enough that she could catch the steady cadence of his breathing. His jacket smelled faintly of pine and something else, a lingering trace of salt from the nearby sea.

She swallowed. "Ian?"

In the shadows of the orchard, his eyes appeared more luminous than usual, flecks of gold hinting at the energy that so often wrestled inside him. "Yes?"

Emma felt her pulse rattle as she gathered the nerve to speak. "I don't want you to be alone with your nightmares, but I'm also afraid I can't protect everyone. I don't even know if I can protect myself from illusions that might be lurking in Crestwood."

His voice was gentle. "Maybe protecting me is not your burden alone. Maybe what we need is a chance to figure this out together." He paused, letting the breeze dust leaves across the clearing. "I realize that might come across as naive, given all the caution your grandmother has offered you. I just—" He pressed his lips into a firm line. "I can't spend every night fighting illusions single-handedly."

Emma's chest constricted. She thought of the library's dim corners, where they had whispered about half-researched spells and haunted memories. She remembered physically trembling at the slightest hint of Catherine's footsteps. Yet amid all that, she had felt safer with Ian than she ever expected.

She lowered her gaze to the ground, noticing a trail of fallen leaves scattered like silver coins in the moonlight. "I understand," she murmured. "I don't have many solutions, but I know I can't let fear drive me away from you. It is sickening, sometimes, how confusion and yearning get tangled up in my head." Her confession made her cheeks burn, but she forced herself to hold his gaze again. "Sadie once said that the orchard listens for the truth in our hearts. Maybe tonight it will listen to yours... or mine."

Ian took a quiet step forward, the grass under his feet seeming louder than any thunder could have been in that moment. A subtle tension radiated from him, not hostility but something coiled with emotion. Emma felt her heartbeat quicken, uncertain if she wanted to pull back or close the distance between them. She stayed put, letting her nerves unravel in the orchard's silent watch.

He held her gaze. "Your grandmother told you that you have a knack for focusing magic without fully realizing it. You bring clarity just by being near. I have never had that clarity before. It feels like a luxury to stand here, not drowning in illusions."

Emma wondered if he felt the same crackle that wove through her, as though the orchard's energy pulsed under their feet, bridging invisible lines between their uncertain hearts. She couldn't deny that something about Ian's presence gave her a sense of completeness, a notion that baffled her rational mind. They had barely known each other for more than a handful of encounters, yet a lifetime of secrets seemed to bind them.

She looked down, trying to quiet the trembling in her hands. The orchard glimmered under the moon, branches twisted overhead in a canopy that felt both protective and ominous. Tendrils of vine curled around the nearest trunk, and Emma sensed a heartbeat in the ground, if only in her imagination.

"You asked if you should trust magic or your heart," Ian said softly. "Maybe they are not separate. Maybe your heart is just telling you where your magic wants you to step."

Emma's lips curled into a delicate smile, the orchard listening in on their conversation like a silent third presence. The moment was so unexpectedly intimate that she had to coax herself to take a steady breath. She recalled how earlier that evening, she had wrestled with the question of whether this unsettled feeling in her chest was excitement or fear. Now, it didn't seem to matter. Both emotions filled her with equal measure.

She lifted her eyes and found his expression mirroring her own. A slight tension lingered in the quick movements of his hands, as if he was counting the reasons to hold back but lacked the will to do so. Moonlight carved the angles of his face, highlighting the worry that lingered just beneath his calm.

Without warning, a wind swept through the orchard, lifting stray leaves into a gentle dance around them. The hush that followed felt charged. Emma had the sudden urge to bridge the final gap between them, to touch him in a way that might reassure them both they were not alone in this labyrinth of illusions and curses.

She took one last breath for courage. Then she closed the space between them, heart pounding so loudly she was certain he could hear it. Her voice trembled as she spoke. "You once said my presence blunted your nightmares. Let me try."

His eyes darkened with emotion, and for an instant, Emma wondered if she had overstepped. But he didn't move away. Instead, he swallowed hard, lips parting with words that didn't fully form. Their proximity sent a warm hum along Emma's skin, the orchard's hush intensifying as though each branch, each leaf, waited for her to speak again.

She didn't speak. Instead, she lifted her hand, hesitant fingers hovering near his arm. Part of her mind clambered for an escape in case he recoiled. But he didn't. A flicker of hope lit his features, and that was all the encouragement she needed.

By the time Emma tentatively placed her hand on Ian's arm, they were closer than they had ever been—bonded by uncertainty, yearning, and the promise that all roads ahead would be as dangerous as they would be intoxicating.

OTHER FLORID ROMANCE BOOKS

To be notified of new releases and special promotions from Florid Romance, please join our email list:

https://floridromance.lmbpn.com/about/sign-up-for-our-newsletter/

For a complete list of books published by Florid Romance please visit our website:

https://floridromance.lmbpn.com/

BOOKS BY KELLI ROBYNS

The Enchanted Orchard
The Orchard (Book 1)
Family Curse (Book 2)

BOOKS BY MICHAEL ANDERLE

Sign up for the LMBPN email list to be notified of new releases and special deals!

https://lmbpn.com/email/

For a complete list of books by Michael Anderle, please visit:

www.lmbpn.com/ma-books/

CONNECT WITH MICHAEL ANDERLE

Connect with Michael Anderle

Website: http://lmbpn.com

Email List: https://michael.beehiiv.com/

https://www.facebook.com/LMBPNPublishing

https://twitter.com/MichaelAnderle

https://www.instagram.com/lmbpn_publishing/

https://www.bookbub.com/authors/michael-anderle

www.ingramcontent.com/pod-product-compliance
Lightning Source LLC
Chambersburg PA
CBHW032345310726
48973CB00007B/1861